# ONE SUMMERS DAY

## THE SUMMERS CHRONICLE
### BOOK FIVE

# PHILLIP ROSEWARNE

Published in Australia by Silverbird Publishing Pty Ltd,

First published in Australia 2025
This edition published 2025

Copyright © Phillip Rosewarne 2025

Cover design, typesetting: WorkingType (www.workingtype.com.au)



ISBN: 978-1-7644124-4-5

# ABOUT THE AUTHOR

**Phillip Rosewarne** has lived and worked in various places on the east coast of Australia, his first job being for a shipping company. After working in New Guinea, Phillip was a project clerk for the Australian Government in Canberra and the Northern Territory, where he worked in Darwin and Katherine, initially for the Commonwealth Department of Works, and then for three years as head storeman for Woolworths in the Darwin area, two years either side of Cyclone Tracy. Phillip then bought a cattle property in Queensland, which he operated for four years.

After returning to Canberra, he initially worked at Mount Stromlo Observatory as a groundsman. It was here that he obtained a Certificate of Horticulture from the Tafe College. He then spent the next twenty-five years at the Commonwealth Department of Primary Industries as it was then known. During this time, he worked in a science bureau within several primary industry sections and gained an Applied Science Degree from the University of Canberra.

Phillip always had a desire to write novels as opposed to scientific papers. He began writing after leaving school, and the passion to write never left him. It was only later in life that he had the opportunity to write fiction on a more permanent basis.

Phillip is currently retired and lives on the Northern Beaches of Sydney.

**OTHER BOOKS BY THE AUTHOR**
The Summers Chronicle
*Book 1: Beyond His Station (Sid Harta)*
*Book 2: Growing Wings (Sid Harta)*
*Book 3: Looking Back at a Stranger (Sid Harta)*
*Book 4: Beyond Life Without Purpose (Sid Harta)*

# CHAPTER ONE

John Summers sat back in his large comfortable leather chair in his spacious lounge. He was deep in contemplative thought. He wondered at the total mystery of life. He was recalling with some fondness the event that resulted in the company of two of the most remarkable human beings he had ever encountered. In his self-imposed isolation on his well-established but remote large rural property north-west of Cooma, he did not come across that many people other than the younger members of his ever-growing family. To have had the privilege and blessing of the interactions with these two outstanding individuals he regarded as quite an honour, and a masterful addition to his limited circle of close friends. He realised that he had had a long and very fruitful life, but he was fully aware that that life was nearing its end. He considered himself enormously blessed. John believed that things happened for a reason. Why he was so seemingly blessed, he was at a loss to account.

John had accumulated a vast array of valuable assets in his early days. This did not just occur by accident. It involved much planning and was achieved through the dint of hard work, and indeed much sacrifice, though he did not view the sacrifices with much regret. He marvelled at the timing of the meeting of his beloved and adorable angelic wife, the late Livinia, after he had experienced the utopia of his early living in splendid isolation and when the time was apparently auspicious for that added blessing. He was now a most contented man.

There had been some administrative re-arrangements regarding all his treasures as he had succumbed to the inevitable approach of his earthly demise. An occurrence, incidentally, that he was not approaching with any savour. He still harboured some cringe-worthy misgivings about the way he acquired his fortune. Time would tell the severity or otherwise of his judgement.

With this thought in mind, he was cast back to a most memorable incident that occurred many years ago now. It was for one of the Merritt's dowager great aunts' eightieth birthday celebrations to be held in her ancestral mansion on Sydney's North Shore. John rather unashamedly clearly recalled with some degree of amusement, after causing quite a scene in front of the whole gathering, his departing the stunned assembly with these sanctimonious words uttered to all and sundry about the feisty old dowager:

'There's nothing wrong with that old trollop that a good flogging wouldn't cure. As for dying, I can assure you, even God is in no hurry to have her.'

With that, he headed for the door with Livinia firmly attached by the hand, she in a complete state of despair. The issue for him was not the enormous ructions that this episode entailed, but the literal content of his smug departing observations. He hoped that the comment about God being in no hurry to have her back did not apply to his recall to eternity.

There was one other issue that troubled the now much more mellow John Summers. The acquisition of so much valuable property and the total freedom, autonomy and the feeling of self-worth that that instilled in him had allowed to surface in him this one aspect of his character that he was, until then, totally unaware that he possessed. It troubled him then and it still rankled with him now. That was the matter of his subjugated and then-unknown ability of possessing an explosive temper. It occasionally surfaced, often with little provocation. The memory of the old dowager incident reawakened in him the episodes that he most regretted doing.

He clearly recalled the first time it ever erupted, because he for ever after, sorely regretted treating the poor messenger so badly. John was working way up in the far reaches of his so beloved brand-new rural acquisition at the time when it happened. John had erected about a third of the back fence and put in most of the posts along the boundary. The incident involved the two farm hands of Dave Quiggin who, at that stage, owned the large property over the hills behind him.

They had obviously been sent up there to ascertain what was transpiring along their common boundary. The interaction was unpleasant enough for John, not because of the incident *per se*, but because of his reaction to it. He still cringed at the thought of his treatment of poor old Ray.

'What's your name mate?' John was looking him straight in the eyes, while at the same time spearing the heavy crowbar deeply into the shaly soil with one mighty plunge from his powerful right arm. This sudden movement made both the horses lift their heads and turn in his direction, causing the other man to gather their reins slightly. John's left hand remained unmoved, covering the top of the half-tamped post. He hoped this manoeuvre sent the appropriate signal to both of them.

'Ray.' he replied. John detected a slight change in demeanour; he did not seem quite so cocky now.

'Well Ray,' said John slowly and deliberately, lowering his voice to an even more authoritative pitch, 'you tell your boss that if I wanted him to pay his share, he'd get a demand from me accompanied by a solicitor's note.'

Ray decided that this bloke was not to be stirred up and might be a bit too much for him to handle at this point so he turned to go, muttering under his breath and shaking his head. As he got to his horse John said,

'And you tell your boss (John emphasising the word disparagingly) he knows where I live and not to send his boys to deal with me again.' He paused, and then imperiously continued, 'Is that clear?' Ray just nodded and reined his horse with a jerk to head back off in the direction from where they had come. John could hear them chatting as they receded into the distance.

John had been annoyed with himself that he had reacted so disdainfully to poor Ray. After all, it was not he that was at fault. This had been a new feeling for John and it had disturbed him slightly that he would react that way. He was unaware that he had this troubling trait in him. That first memory was still seared in his reminiscences.

The next time it occurred, John was even more explosive. It amused him now with the benefit of fond retrospection, but it could have ended very badly. It involved his newly-acquired unit block in the central area of Manly in a most auspicious position. This was in the days when he was desperately trying to unload his great stash of pounds sterling hidden in his bunker before the onset of decimal currency rendered them redundant. He leased the units out through an agency in Manly. John had insisted on the insertion of three clauses in the leasing contracts for the flats in the Manly building. One stipulated no pets, a not uncommon clause; another strengthened the 'noisy party' clause and the annoyance of fellow occupants of the building, and the third was one of his own design. It stipulated that, under no circumstances, was anyone to park a vehicle in the rear parking space of the building adjacent to the north-east wall. This space was reserved for him and he had a sign erected saying 'do not ever park here'. The reason for this was, whenever he came up to Manly in those early days, he usually arrived late at night after a torrid, long and difficult trip from Cooma and arrived without notice. He also often towed a trailer heavily laden with items for the flat, including antique furniture. He felt strongly about this clause and it was listed as serious enough to allow for the termination of the offender's lease. The agent doubted it would stand up if tested, but inserted it anyway.

John had owned the building for nearly two years when this clause would be tested out. He had done considerable renovating in the top flat that he had kept for his own use. In fact, he had made it a pet project of his to renovate and furnish the flat in expensive and difficult items that he acquired over careful years of buying. The acquiring of antique furniture was one of the laughable attempts by John to diminish the huge stash of cash he had hidden in his underground bunker on the farm. He had loaded up the trailer with a particularly valuable piece of antique furniture, a heavy mahogany sideboard destined for the dining area of the flat. He had had to man-handle it carefully onto a wooden pallet and loaded it gingerly with his forklift onto the trailer. He would not have the advantage of the use of the forklift at the other end but would confront that problem when he arrived.

He was already on edge about moving this item. When he had not had a good trip up with things going wrong on the road, what with roadworks delaying him considerably and a minor vehicle problem with a radiator hose, he was in a terrible mood by the time he finally arrived at the flat. The upshot was that he arrived at one thirty in the morning, a

Tuesday morning, a normal working day for the locals, and he was not in a condition to handle any more difficulties.

The first hint of trouble was the loud music coming from the building as John pulled up in the street to check that the yard was clear for him to drive into, after all he was towing a trailer and had limited manoeuvrability. That was annoying enough and, he thought, very inconsiderate to the other residents. But worse was to confront him, as there in his 'do not ever park here' space was a bright yellow souped-up car, the type the 'New Australians' liked to drive. He was already crabby, but this, for some reason, incensed him.

The loud music was coming from the flat under his and the windows were open, enhancing the effect of the noise. He could hear the giggling and loud talk above the music. He also thought he detected a dog barking. He glared about the semi-lit yard and then stormed back out to the Rover in the street. He noisily unhitched the heavy trailer, leaving it on its jockey wheel. Slamming the Rover door, he drove into the yard and pulled up close to the Cortina. He then went around to the side toolbox on the roof rack and retrieved a heavy metal snigging chain, its clunking and clanging echoing around the yard. One end he then hitched to the chassis of the Land Rover. The Cortina had a silver-covered tow bar protruding from its rear and to that he dropped on the large eye of the snigging chain. There was a clunk as he dropped the Rover into low range and unceremoniously began to drag the shuddering Cortina backwards along the edge of the building. At the corner of the building, it received a long scratch and a minor dent along its driver's side as John noisily revved the Land Rover and continued to drag out the car. In the street he unhitched the Cortina along the gutter and proceeded to re-hitch the trailer and then bring it into the yard and park in the now free parking space. He was seething with rage and realized he might do something rash but was going to fix this problem now. Some of his rage was due to the fact that he felt the agency was not managing his affairs properly if this sort of thing was going on. That could wait till the morning. Right now, he would fix this problem himself. He went again to the rear internal guttering channel of the Rover and retrieved the old short stock whip that old Jack had made for him as a young man way back in the Merritt's farm days. He had carried it for years. He summoned Kelly, his faithful old dog, he still fondly thought of her, now of course sadly long dead, and together they ran upstairs to the offending flat.

John banged heavily on the door with the whip handle; no reply. He banged again even harder, all the time his temper getting worse and that irritating foreign music driving him madder. Finally, the door was tentatively opened by a slight Greek-looking young woman who peered quizzically at John and was about to speak when he pushed open the door and strode menacingly into the room. He glared around and then demanded that that racket be turned off. Everything then happened in quick succession. There came over the room a slight hush as everybody stopped talking but the music kept playing. John strode over to the record player and ripped it from the wall and hoicked it through the open window way out into the middle of the yard. It landed after a few seconds with a clinking jingle of shattering glass and plastic parts that could be heard in the now silent night. He was mindful of his precious cargo below.

He then turned to be confronted by an Alsatian growling at him threateningly and ready to pounce. Kelly was growling and a couple of the blokes were noisily approaching him. He raised the whip and struck the Alsatian a painful clip to its ear upon which it shrieked in pain and fright and cringed yelping away to the front door. There was now a deathly silence in the room, except for a slight growl emanating from Kelly. John, his blood boiling and looking seriously threatening, stared at them with a severe scowl and demanded,

'Who owns this flat?' Meantime, one of the men had gone over to the window to check on his car which was supposed to be below. On seeing it missing he began to remonstrate and demand its whereabouts. John ignored him and again demanded who owned the flat. No answer. He pointed the whip handle at the nearest person, a girl and shouted,

'You!'

'No, sir.'

'Get out!'

'You?' pointing to a young man and his cowering girlfriend.

'No.'

'Well get out.' he again demanded. People began to slink out the door and down the stairs with the howling dog now in the street. That left the man who had demanded to know where his car had gone and two others.

'I ask again. Who rents this flat?' and with that he gave the whip a searing crack that sounded like a rifle. Kelly was running excitedly around the room barking and growling and John was threateningly standing near the door now still waiting for an answer.

'You rent this place?' he asked the car owner.

'No, me mate does but he's away.'

'Well get out then. And don't come back. EVER! Now, one of you must rent this place?'

'Well, we're sort of minding it for him.'

'I will be back in here tomorrow morning early and if any of your stuff is still here it's going the way of the player. That clear?' With that he stormed out and went up to his own flat and, with hands shaking violently, he opened his door and strode in. He was so disturbed and wound up that he could not calm down. He decided to work some of his anger off by unloading the vehicle and trailer as best he could; most items except the heavy sideboard. It took him a few hours to walk up and down the stairs many times unloading the vehicle. Eventually he was calm enough to try to get a little sleep but it would soon be morning and he had plenty to do in the day light – especially dealing with the agency.

John slept fitfully for only a short time and was awakened by the sounds of people moving about the building. He got up and looked about at the mess in his usually tidy flat and heard people talking on the stairs. He was pretty wound-up last night and hoped he had not gone too far. Better check on happenings in the flat below. He could still hear voices on the stairs but thought he had better get things under way outside. He sheepishly opened his door and there was immediately a silence in the stairwell. John tucked his shirt in and ran his hand over his hair. He was unshaven and looked pretty rough. He usually did not appear in public quite so dishevelled. He began descending the stairs and approached the offending flat. There had been a little activity this morning and most of the non-permanent items were gone. There were still a few things though and he thought about chucking them out the window. That reminded him of his still-covered sideboard standing in the yard hopefully undamaged in the trailer. He went further down and out into the yard to inspect his property.

The record player was still lying shattered in pieces where it had landed from last night. The Rover appeared to be all right as did the trailer. There were people in the yard talking as he came out of the door and they immediately stopped their conversation. On seeing John, one got into an old car and started the engine and another began walking back to the building. He was an effete and slender young man with a weird hairstyle that was strange to John. As he walked past John he said in a squeaky voice,

'Good morning, mister.'

'Morning.' said John and proceeded to inspect his gear.

'Had a long trip up then?' John was slightly taken aback. Even though he visited the flat regularly he never really knew the people who lived there and rarely spoke to any of them.

'Yes. It was a bit rough.'

'Well, you certainly sorted that lot out, my good man.' *This bloke spoke in a funny manner* John thought, but was pleasant enough.

'Does that happen often?'

'Occasionally, lately. Most disturbing you know.'

'Well, I plan to put a stop to that. Tell me, do you live here?'

'Yes.'

'Does the agent come here often to check on the place?'

'No, not a lot. Don't see anyone here much, you know.'

'Thanks, mate.' replied John.

John was going over last night in his mind. He was again surprised at his violent actions and the way he so quickly boiled. He must have a nasty streak that he had not known about before these incidents. Anyway, next step was to confront the agent and find out why this was happening. The snigging chain was still lying strewn about on the bonnet of the Rover, just where he had left it last night. Kelly was still sleeping under the trailer; she had had a busy night too. All appeared okay so John began to clean up the remains of the player and then went back upstairs to clean up himself.

Confronting the agent was not going to be pleasant either for John. He had already blown a fuse in the flat last night, so he hoped he could control his emotions when dealing with the agent. He would go round there at nine when they opened, meanwhile he would busy himself tiding up all the mess he had brought up from home this visit. Periodically, he would also wander up and down to the flat below to check up on the clearing out that was supposed to be happening there.

At a quarter to nine, John, after cleaning himself up again, walked around to the agency on the Corso. It was a well-known local agency with a good reputation, that was why John chose them to manage his property. The office girl there that John vaguely knew from his dealings with the firm, opened the door at nine precisely. John walked into the office in a brusque manner and asked imperiously to speak to the manager. She enquired whether he had an appointment as the manager was rather busy. He could feel his blood boiling again. He advised her that he did not require an appointment and enquired was that his office in there as he pointed to a room at the side. She objectingly replied that it was but said again that he was rather busy right now. John advised her as he headed for the manager's office that he sure was going to be busy in a minute.

John marched into the manager's office and firmly closed the door. The manager, Mr Dawes, looked up and asked if he could help.

'Too right you can mate. I own the block of flats in Ashburner Street and you manage the rentals for me.'

'Yes, I know it. Mr Summers, isn't it?'

'That's right mate. Now I want to know what you've been doing around there to earn your dough.'

'What do you mean?' Mr Dawes could see that John was agitated.

John explained what was going on there on his arrival at one thirty in the morning and discovered that it was not the first time. He explained also that he expected a much better management style and more supervision where his property was concerned. He wanted the no parking policy policed and the tenants to obey the clauses that forbad pets and limited noise and nuisance. He advised Mr Dawes that he had evicted troublemakers last night and expected the agency to be around there within the hour to repair the damage to the flat and install a new tenant immediately or he would change agencies. Mr Dawes began to protest but John cut him short.

'No discussions.' he blurted. 'Just fix it now or I change. And I better not get charged for this either. I will be here for one week only so you better get on with it now.' Mr Dawes stood up to again protest but John turned and walked out the door.

'One hour.' he again blurted to Mr Dawes.

John went back to the flats and waited to see if there would be any activity. The rooms below his flat were now cleared out and, he had felt a little vindicated by his outburst after two other tenants had approached him supporting his actions. The agency finally arrived to inspect the property and to arrange repairs. He was able to grab a couple of the workmen to assist him in carrying up his precious heavy furniture, for a small consideration.

John spent a lot of time reliving those events and was fearful of his own unexpected eruption. This was a side of his character he was unaware existed until provoked by events. Firstly, there had been Ray at the back fence, then the explosive incident at the units, and then the kerfuffle at the dowager's eightieth.

Then there was one other incident that still rankled with

him, a more serious incident in that it involved a family member. That was the time, way out from the house when Thomas, his wayward and neglected fourteen year-old unplanned first grandchild, had first been sent to them to be his unwilling guardian from his last-chance juvenile court appearance. John had actually struck Thomas and sent him sprawling across the stockyard ground. He still cringed at the mere thought.

John could safely survey his responses now, with the benefit of decades of time passing, but, despite some of their amusing aspects, he wished he did not possess that weakness. He also realised that those actions would not be tolerated these days. My how times have changed, even in his short lifetime.

Back to the present. John began again to reminisce about his management desires. His very first foray into the investment property market had consisted of buying houses in the suburb where Livinia had lived before they were married. John still kept the rental agency for his five Freshwater properties in the hands of his original office, still located in the main street of the small, off-highway village of Harbord as he fondly recalled its original suburban name. He also had kept the unit block of apartments in Ashburner Street in Manly with that agency on the Corso. They lodged their returns to a local accountancy firm which now forwarded the details onto his new head office located in Comma. He had finally succumbed to the rigours of old age and had moved all the head office details from his Sydney city office building to a new address in Polo Flat, where he owned a small industrial estate. This had removed the necessity of his having to travel up to Sydney to conduct his property portfolio matters.

It was now some years since he had travelled up to the unit he owned in Manly. The desire had diminished greatly with advancing old age, but also with the demise of his beloved Livinia some years ago. There were plenty of family members that were prepared to utilise it however. As well, John really did prefer the enjoyments he obtained from his country life-style rather than any real attraction to city living. John had consolidated his accounting processes as well by now using the local Cooma accountancy firm that he initially only used for local matters. He still occasionally stayed in his Cooma unit on the top floor of the block that he owned in Commissioner Street.

John surveyed his massive property portfolio with quite some satisfaction. He had extracted from Ethan, his elder son and heir-apparent, that he would attempt to maintain all the assets as insurance against bad seasons on the land and as a source of secure off-farm income. He trusted him to fulfil that commitment. John realised that after his demise, that assurance would have scant meaning, but he also realised that, with his departure, all these earthly concerns would be of very little import to him.

He was fond of reminiscing over his most favoured and favourite aspect of his empire, his rural lands. He often warmly recollected the adventure that was his slow and exhilarating acquisition of what eventually became a substantial land-holding in the Monaro region. His favourite above all else was still his original purchase of the block of land that now housed not only his magnificent homestead, but also still held his most fondly remembered original 'shed' that was his first home and the centre of his life. He absolutely adored that time and the sense of total and complete fulfilment at that acquisition. He recalled often the sad old figure of the man that was his neighbour, and that he, in all honesty, battered down to a give-away price for the admittedly run-down and neglected block.

As the years rolled by, John became sincere friends with his neighbour, such that he was offered first refusal on the adjoining larger block of country next to his original block when Frank became too ill and infirm to work it properly. He purchased that at the price the neighbour requested, no questions asked. That in some way was restitution and amends for what John always perceived as slightly disingenuous to his old mate for the first harsh terms on which he acquired his original home.

Despite that first inaptness in his relationship with the original owner, they both became dear and fond friends over the years they shared together, to the point that the alone and lonely old neighbour, Frank Dougherty, bequeathed to John his last earthly possessions, including his entire land holding opposite his own block. So, John ended up with his original small block, the adjoining much larger one to the west and, after the demise of Frank, he got hold of the beautiful river flats opposite his own land.

When, years later, but before Frank died, he acquired the

block of land next door to Frank's old house block from the retiring Crosses, he ended up with prime river flats, two houses and extensive lucerne irrigation paddocks. This was where his peculiar son, Damien lived and supplied the properties with drought feed and saleable fodder and silage for sale.

The last of the land he acquired contiguous to himself was the large and extensive grazing land over his back boundary that he purchased from his neighbour, Dave Quiggin. It was an enormous and productive property with very good accommodation and equipment. This was the property where his elder son lived at present with his advanced sheep-breeding program.

The last rural procurement he made was the inordinately advanced technical breeding property, Auvergne. He purchased that place with the miraculous financial gains from the Terry Storeman saga, involving his Sydney city buildings. That windfall allowed him to purchase Auvergne solely with the intention of returning Thomas to the fold from distant outback Queensland. It was this investment that, via intricate and devious means, led to the inclusion in his life of the fearful Jessie MacIntyre. He says fearful because he still remembered vividly when he first met her. He definitely did not like her at all and mistrusted her entirely.

Jessie MacIntyre had come to his Auvergne property after meeting Thomas in suspect circumstances. John did not really know any of the facts, but gathered that they met somewhere in outback Queensland. She contributed enormously to his own wealth, asking almost nothing in return. He never did fully understand her motivations. In the end, despite his initial detestation of the woman, he grew to admire her tenacity and character, and her hard-earned fame. She certainly seemed to be the perfect person for the much-troubled Thomas.

John was very grateful to life for giving him the luxury of these final days to contemplate the meaning of, and to evaluate, his existence. He fondly reminisced often about the wonder of the woman who became his wife and contributed so much to his greater learning. He also wondered incessantly why his precious son was taken from him at the prime age of only ten. If it were not for Livinia, he would never have had the spiritual development that emanated from his knowing her. He could now gladly admit that the addition of the spiritual learning emanating from her deep understanding and firm belief in that aspect of life, gave to him a deeper appreciation of things and a more accepting approach to the blessings and tragedies associated with being alive.

John surveyed his children. How different they all were from each other, and indeed from himself. His first born, Audrey was a complete mystery to him. She was a lovely child, well-mannered and agreeable, but somewhere along the way she was taken from him, not literally, but figuratively. It appeared to both him and to Livinia, that that process must have started at late high school. Both he and Livinia were totally naïve when it came to drugs. They suspected she got into that scene in high school. Once she entered university in Sydney she was gone.

Whomever she became entangled with was certainly not the people he and Livinia would mix with. The sad results of her liaisons were threefold. Firstly, she was lost to them. Secondly, her choice of partners was catastrophic for her and for them, and thirdly, the legacy of that lost life was the arrival of the neglected Thomas. He still had no idea who his father was. In the end, John had to finally dismiss Audrey from the family private company, as her inability to hold to confidences and her totally inappropriate choice of partners could not blend in with the family ethos. A lot of the issues surrounding her attitude and involvement in the company culminated to finality with the removal from their sphere by the death of that despicable rouge, Geoffrey Bales, her totally unsuitable husband, in the end. Oh, how John hated that man. He did not know any of the details, but he also knew that Jessie MacIntyre loathed him with a vengeance, she having had a much deeper involvement with the scandalous character over a much longer time-frame.

Thomas was his first grandchild. He was conceived in total ambivalence from Audrey and was neglected from the start. John never lost the pain of not knowing his own parents, when he was orphaned as a baby, so to deliberately impose that on a child was, as far as he was concerned, a mortal sin. How Thomas turned out to be so sane and balanced, he never knew. Now Thomas ran the high-tech Auvergne Station along with that other marvel in his life, Jessie MacIntyre. He still thought of her as a MacIntyre, somehow that seemed to differentiate her from the humdrum of the average Summers.

His other child, Damien, was a complete enigma to him. John readily acknowledged that, when it came to Damien, he really had little idea how to cope with the obviously superior intellect of this wonderful offspring. Damien seemed to settle down very early once it was agreed that he could leave school at fifteen and began work on the lucerne property opposite Bridgehead, Frank Dougherty's old place. And he made a great success of that enterprise.

His last child was Hannah. She now lived in town, doing very well at her chosen field in the Council. She was now married to a nice young man who also worked for the Council. John bought her a house in town and she seemed to be happy with her lot. To his mind, she never really appeared to get over the loss of her twin brother, Brendan. Ah, poor Brendan, what would he have turned out to be. It was the biggest sadness in his long life to have lost that child. He never really recovered fully himself, nor understood the meaning of that incident.

All these children were members of the family company, except Audrey. They all received a substantial income from the enterprise. He spent some time contemplating how the spoils of his accumulation would be distributed after his demise, but he began to realise that that was not ever going to be a concern of his. He secured, and hoped it to be honoured, an assurance from Ethan, the chosen successor to himself that the entire enterprise would remain intact for the foreseeable future, but, again, that was not really any province of the aging John.

John contemplated his young self. John was fond of his grandmother and she loved him. She was an elderly and quite ill person when he knew her. He still held disturbed feelings about the way he departed her life and what he took from her safe when he left. The fact that this horde of moolah may have actually been his never really softened the sense of wrong-doing he imposed on her and especially the Merritt cousins he defrauded, no matter how much he felt that the way they mistreated him was deserving of such a recompense.

John, if nothing else, certainly made very good use of his ill-gotten gains, unquestioningly much better than the profligate and entitled Merritt children would have made, of that he was convinced. He managed to navigate his entire life without any revelation or even suspicion of his deed being uncovered, at least that was his considered opinion. Yet, he had been unsettled by the nearness of the circumstances arising with, not one but two personages that seemed to have access to information and conditions that he would rather they did not.

One of those people was his beloved, or rather really, respected and, in some ways, admired and slightly feared, granddaughter-in-law, Jessie MacIntyre. He always called her that, even though she was married to Thomas and bore the Summers' name. She was involved with people and conditions that were always sailing too close to the sources of information about his checkered past.

The other one was that enigmatic and rather mysterious personage, Graham Longley, who came into his circle late in affairs but seemed to have even more access to information than Jessie. He just wished that were not the case.

As he aged into restrained conditions of advancing

retrospection, he found himself thinking more about his lost parents. He sorely missed the normal condition of family relationships that was denied him, seemingly now not by accident, but by some act of deliberate intent. He hoped to be reunited with them, but that was a thought of which he had no proof, only anticipation. John had the fondest memories of his genesis on his original property that he eventually called Bridgehead. All the other additions were economically and strategically very beneficial, but his first endeavour was always his most favoured.

That thought kindled the strange interaction with an eccentric young man who came into John's life via an almost bizarre set of circumstances. He clearly remembered the period, as it was exactly the same time that he had just bought Auvergne Station in order to have Thomas return to the fold and be the manager of the new enterprise. He was sitting on his spacious veranda of the house that replaced the shed as their home, contentedly contemplating his treasured life when his darling wife Livinia announced that there was a car coming down the tree-lined avenue that was his entrance road. He distinctly recalled the moment because it disturbed his idyll, but also, he detested the unexpected. That was not the reason that he recalled that day so vividly though. It was what it led to that made that encounter so memorable.

It was an older model car of some indeterminant make that showed its age and was in quite some condition of disinterested care, shabby but serviceable. A young man exited the vehicle and wandered over to where John was sitting on his veranda. John did not know the young man at all, so, suffering some disquiet at the intrusion, did not make any attempt to encourage his entrance by getting up and out of his chair.

He was cleanly but casually dressed in reasonable city-type clothes, with heavy boots and sporting a fairly substantial beard, though well attended and groomed if nothing else. He was also fairly tall and muscular from possibly being used to hard work. He had a pleasant smiling face, what he could see of it under the mop of unkempt dishevelled hair and the generous beard that he had obviously been attending to for quite some time. The young man strode over to the veranda where he saw that John was sitting and in a strong confident voice, said,

'I'm looking for Mr Summers. I was told by one of your neighbours that you lived here.'

'What do you want, son?' asked a brusque John.

'I believe you may be the owner of the land along the river there about four miles further along the road.'

'What about it?'

'My name's Roger, and I was wondering if I could talk to you about it.'

John did not like the name Roger, it reminded him of Roger Holpin, of PFR fame and all the trouble that entailed with his city buildings, despite his huge profit from that encounter. That was the second mark against this unwelcome intruder.

'Which piece are you talking about?' asked a still brusque John.

'The piece along the river there.'

'Which side?' asked John. That seemed to confuse young Roger. He assumed we were all talking about the same block.

'Why the one on the right side going away from here. The one with the little river flowing through it.'

'I own both sides, son. They both have little rivers.' was all John said.

'Oh, I see. Well, it's the right-hand side going away from here, the piece that has the stony ridges and is a bit scrubby. Not the flats that have all the cultivation on 'em.'

'Okay. Well, what about it?'

'I have a proposition for you. If you could just hear me out, I'll explain it to you.'

'Okay, I'm all ears.' said a decidedly uninterested John.

Roger stood on the ground off the veranda, making his eye level about the same as the seated John. He was rather a cheerful sort of lad, about twenty-five or so, and began his tail. He explained that he was interested in growing Radiata pine trees for use as Christmas trees. He would like to plant about five acres of them over a rotation of about five or six years, planting a new five-acre plot each year for the five or six years so that he had a new lot ready every year. It would take somewhere between three to five years for them to reach the size he wanted. Then he would restart the process over again.

John had no interest whatsoever in any other form of projects on his properties, but the novelty of the suggestion piqued his interest ever so slightly. He asked,

'What are you going to do for five years while you wait for the first lot to be ready, supposing they become ready by then? Plus, what exactly is this pine tree you're talking about. Is it a pest?'

'Pinus radiata, the Monterey pine. No, it's not a pest. It has the most lovely timber. It is extensively grown all around the ACT for its timber harvesting. It also makes excellent Christmas trees when young. And I am currently working for some land-care and environmental groups, plus I have a contact in the forestry industry where I can get the stock.'

'What's your plan?'

'Well,' began a slightly more animated Roger, 'I have only seen the plot from the road, but it looks pretty suitable for Radiata trees. The ground looks shaley with some soil depth, not too rocky, and with a fairly gentle northerly slop. It seems protected from the westerlies and looks pretty sundrenched to me. Besides, you don't seem to be using it at present. It has a moderate growth of small bushes and some weeds, almost no trees and the creek might supply a little irrigation for me. I would like to lease it from you.'

'I'm not too sure about this.' said John.

'I'd be no trouble. I will do absolutely everything myself, with no input from you other than the good parcel of land.'

'What gear have you got?'

'I have a small tractor and ripping gear, plus a posthole digger. I'm not sure whether to rip along the slope or dig individual hole, it depends on things.'

John sat in deep silence. He was thinking about this offer. It was no skin off his nose if the young bloke wanted to do anything there, as long as there was no impact on his enterprises. He certainly had no use for that almost troublesome parcel of land, as it was not much use to Damien. John was softening to his proposal, as he rather liked the young fellow. Then he said,

'Let's go for a drive. No promises here mate.'

Roger smiled a large and friendly grin in acknowledgement.

John yelled out into the house, 'Livvy, I'm just going over to the Crosses place. Won't be long.'

John's property holdings here were fairly straight forward. He had his original block that he now called Bridgehead. It was about four thousand acres. He eventually purchased the adjoining eight thousand acres from old Frank Dougherty some years later. This was a triangular block that ended some miles down the road in a point where his back fence finally ran into the gravel road that went off into the far hills.

The block behind his first place, over his back fence, was originally owned by Dave Quiggin, but John bought that also some years ago. However, opposite John's place, over the road, he had inherited Franks last piece of land that he had willed to John on his death. It was about fifteen hundred acres, but had very good river flats that his son Damien now used to grow irrigated lucerne on all year round. Many years ago, the next block along the road next to Damien's was originally owned by an elderly couple by the name of Cross. John also bought that piece of land as it had even better flats than Franks. Damien also used that for irrigated lucerne.

Both these pieces of land had very good creek flats, except, right at the far end of the Cross block, the land surface changed as the river flowed into the rocky foot-hills and the road and river diverted out of the valley and onto the more rugged hilly country further west, culminating in quite high mountainous country in the ranges.

Right at the end of the Cross block was this land that was not much good for anything that John was on about. He basically fenced it off and left it, but with a substantial fenceline. He occasionally put some old wethers on it to keep the weeds and grass down, but that was not always very satisfactory. It did carry some notifiable weeds on it, such as love grass and serrated tussock, and the occasional blackberry and rose-hip briars, but nothing of note. If this young bloke could make use of it at no inconvenience or expense to himself, he might just be interested.

To access this piece of land, John had to enter the old Crosses' house entry and drive across the paddocks nearer the road where there was no irrigation cultivation and then go through a small cocky-gate in his good fence near to the road and then they were in the neglected paddock. They got out of the car and walked over to nearer the middle of the block to survey the scene. John did not actually know much about the adjoining tract of land to the west of this acreage. He knew that it was an enormous tract of land, fairly rugged, very hilly, steep in some places, and wild, neglected almost natural scrubby bushland. He had seen some poor-quality cattle on it, but never seen anybody there to attend to things. It had neglected fencing that was adequate for the job, but was otherwise, basically left to itself.

John had, on several occasions, particularly in the early days, driven a fair distance along this rough road until it basically petered out into a coarse fire track that wound its way over the rugged foothills all the way to the other valley to his south, eventually connecting up to the roads back to Cooma. He had seen what he assumed was an entry point into his neighbouring property, but it was rarely used and obviously poorly maintained. He could not see any form of residence on it either. He believed it was owned by a well-known local identity of some note, but, as their interests were divergent, he had no real curiosity in his story. As long as the block was not a threat to himself, he did not care what the owner did.

John and Roger spent some time scouting about this parcel of land. John was impressed with Roger's attention to detail, his perceptiveness to the vagaries of this neglected plot, his thorough investigation of the soil types, the vegetation makeup, the suitability of the creek, if John were in agreement to his ever needing its use, the topography, the aspect and the general layout with regards to the suitability to growing seedlings basically with little attention. Roger seemed satisfied with what he saw. The slope was gentle enough, and at a very good aspect to the north, and with the creek. Though it had some deep holes here, it was easily accessible, despite several large wombat tunnels in some areas.

While he was there, John had a good inspection of the boundary fence. It was not up to his usual standard, but it was adequate for its purpose. It was quite neglected and the wires were ancient and rust-prone, but still sturdy. The posts were also rather rickety, but mostly holding up. He was loathe to spend any time and money on what was otherwise an unnecessary project. He felt that any cattle in there would have scant interest in seedlings of pine trees, he thought that they would find them most unpalatable. Roger reconnoitred a suitable site along the roadside boundary to install a cocky-gate to avoid having to use Damien's own entrances. He promised to do all the necessary work for its installation.

The two men had a long discussion. The upshot was that John was sympathetic to the suggestion from Roger. He would talk to his solicitor and get back to him. Roger lived in Cooma and had recently completed a degree in environmental studies, so he was conversant with these types of industries.

For his part, John contacted his solicitor in Cooma and had a chat. He also contacted the agency of his old friend, Tom Grady. Tom was the estate agent in Cooma that had sold him his original block way back in 1958. John had maintained a constant contact with this firm, and his old mate Tom, and they kept their fingers on the pulse of local matters. He was very friendly with the people therein and John had maintained a friendship with them because of their common encounters in the early days. The reason he did this was in order to try to find out more about the mysterious neighbour who owned the very large tract of land next to this neglected paddock of John's.

In the meantime, John decided to do a little investigating himself. He had little or no real knowledge about this adjoining block. He had checked all the common fencing as far as it went along the Crosses old place, but nothing else. He relied on Damien to maintain that aspect over there. John went for a drive along the road as far as he thought that this property went. The road from there began to veer slightly to the south to avoid the growing hills and then climbed out of his valley into the foothills. It was an almost pristine block, with little evidence of any improvements. There was a metal gate to an entrance some distance from John's place. It was quite substantial and, he noted, was also securely locked, so he could not gain access that way. He wondered how far back over the hills this land went that belonged to whomever the owner was.

Frank's original old property that was willed to John on the death of Frank had an ancient cocky-gate into these back lands which John had just left there. He had no idea why Frank had access to this back property, or if he ever used that access. It must have been there for a reason. John thought that Frank's original settler family owned all this valley at one stage, but he never did ascertain exactly how much. It may have included these back paddocks as well.

John decided to risk a trip into this land through this gate on horseback. He retrieved his old rifle scabbard and rifle that he had not used for years, just in case. In the old days of his first arriving, John often encountered the odd fox, many rabbits and occasionally, the rare wild dog. Most of these were rarer now, after years of attending to their existence. He entered the place and headed slowly up the gentle slope until he attained the first ridge, some distance into the paddocks. He gazed around in some wonderment. He had never investigated anything this side of the road, he had no reason, other than curiosity, to do so. John did not realise that there was quite so an extensive a valley this far in from the first little creek of his irrigation plot. The more remote ramparts were some distance from his domain, so he was unaware of what was there. He headed off north to the steep hills in the distance. The valley floor was covered in much more vegetation than he was used to on his properties. It was far more natural than the rest. There were many mature trees and much scrub about.

Eventually, as he approached the barrier of cliff-like hills, John came to a small river. It was flanked on the north by what was basically a sheer wall of a near-vertical barrier. This blockade, a lowset ridge extending all the way along this part of the land, was a single mass of exposed rock-face and enormous boulders gleaming in the shimmering light. The vegetation was sparse on its face, and consisted only of straggly bushes, shrubs and grasses that clung to a precarious existence in the harsh steepness, lack of soil and the glare of the western sun beating down on it incessantly.

Prior to his arrival at this point however, he had traversed an amazing and extensive expanse of what appeared to him to be a natural pasture of almost lawn-like appearance and consistency. It was covered in scats and some evidence of old cattle droppings. Most of the evidence pointed to kangaroos and wallabies, and probably wombats as well. Frank had said in the distant past that some of the valley was as if it had been prepared for their arrival by the existence of so much pleasant pasture-like country, also a possible result of the original Aboriginal inhabitants keeping it that way by means of fire-stick farming to encourage the roos to graze there, easier to hunt. It had been a long time since any real domestic stock had wandered over this remote nirvana. John wondered why no one utilised this wonderful asset. It was rather difficult to get at, but not insurmountable, especially these days.

John was enthralled at what he had stumbled onto. He ventured a long horseback ride along this pristine paradise, marvelling at its almost primeval beauty. He headed west more towards where the new proposal was being considered for Roger. The creek was quite deep in some places, he wondered what was lurking in its depth. Then he stumbled on an amazing scene. He was so enraptured by its revelation that he dismounted his horse and began to explore while the animal grazed contentedly on the surprisingly lush, though short, grasses.

What he had run into here was the ruins of a small hut. It was very old, possibly an early herdsman's or shepherd's hut, a long way from civilisation. The only giveaway to the unobservant was the crumbling remains of the small stone fire place. Small plants had ensconced themselves in some of the crumbling crevices and collapsing mortar joints. It would not be too much longer before the entire edifice was returned to its genesis on the fertile plain. On closer inspection, there was evidence of several exotic trees of some sort, located close to the ruins. They were gnarled, wretched, barely alive after decades of neglect and in their last throes of life. The old shack would have been a very lonely existence, but it was next to the deep waterhole of the quietly running little stream in its path to the junction of more rivers further west. John marvelled at the tenacity of the early pioneers. He thought his original life-style was isolated.

More poignant however, was the clearly observable evidence to the wary eye of what appeared to John as an ancient grave site. He wandered over to the area some distance from the old ruins. It was long abandoned and partially overgrown and had not seen a visitor, other than the roos, for many years. There was clearly one early headstone and possibly two other sites. They were set within a crumbling and barely surviving low-set rusted iron picket surround. The headstone showed evidence of fire attack and was slightly skewwhiff. However, surprisingly, John could make out with some difficulty, and the scratching assistance of his pouched knife, most of the inscription that had been deeply chiselled into the rounded-top stone, hoary with age and lichen.

He had difficulty reading all the script, but he finally decided that he had deciphered enough of the grave stone to ascertain most of the brief story therein. It appeared to him that the stone was for a child aged ten, a girl name Charlotte Finney, who had died, possibly, according to the inscription, from appendicitis. The date appeared to be about 1885 or 1886. He marvelled at the touching sense that a poor little child died, probably in pain and fear, so long ago from an illness that was so easily cured today, if the medical services were available. He assumed the other two sites could be her parents or other relatives. John found it quite emotive and he pondered the ephemeral nature of his brief existence on this earthly plane. These poor souls were once vibrant humans, now not even remembered by a single person, and probably not even recorded anywhere.

As he knelt there beside the last earthly reminder of a forgotten soul, he was struck by an overwhelming sense. John lingered there in the tranquil serenity of the total and complete isolation of such an idyllic calmness. He felt at that moment at one with the universe, the connection between himself and all creation and the honour of being blessed with the insight and the gift to perceive such an amazing moment. For the briefest of time, he felt completely alone with all of the wonders of creation, as if he were the only soul in existence. He gazed about in wonderment at the scene presented to him in his loneliness, and the perception of the world dissipated before his eyes. In the near total silence, the only sounds he could hear were the distant gentle munching of his contented horse and the soft jangling of the tack, and the occasional chirrup of some unknown water life. What did they perceive of the troubles of the blighted world outside this nirvana. In the middle distance were many small kangaroos and wallabies warily but calmly surveying him, but still fully employed in their timeless activity as if he were absolutely no threat and, for that brief moment, belonged inside this scene.

John slowly arose from his position of contemplation

and wandered slowly over to the creek. For some reason, this entire length of the stream on this side had no riparian vegetation other than the lawn-like grasses that bordered its bank in profusion. The far side of the narrow creek abutted the sheer face of the steep wall of jump-up that formed the northern boundary of this hidden vale. Here there were small flowers in among the grasses. In fact, the entire paddock was distributed with tiny little colourful flowers of some sort, growing in scattered profusion amongst the sea of manicured greenery. The stream was narrow but quite deep for most of its length here. It had a moody darkness about it as it ran silently and almost motionlessly through its long course. The surface was tranquil and broody, only slightly disturbed by the incessant and manifold small aquatic life that scurried across its surface in pursuit of he knew not what.

He was suddenly struck by the sense that he knew nothing of all this, his total ignorance of all these matters was overwhelming. There was nowhere on all his own properties that had ever engendered such an awesome sense in him. There was no evidence of man-made creation in view here, other than the proof of our ethereal nature by the single tombstone. There were no fences, no buildings, nothing; except the horse.

John was loath to depart this spot that had so entranced him. Reality slowly reasserted itself upon his reasoning, and he reluctantly walked over to his nibbling horse and mounted him, taking in one last longing look at this enchanting interlude. Then he headed towards the west to investigate the lay of the land nearer to where the new enterprise was being discussed.

John traversed some interesting country through there. He finally came into some more heavily wooded areas in rougher country and it was here that he discovered the next surprise. John was a tee-totaller. He did not drink alcohol or smoke – never had. He was even more ignorant and unconversant with matters relating to any form of drug use. But he was pretty sure he knew a marijuana bush when he saw one. Towards the most western extreme of his travels in the neighbour's property, the land merged into rougher and much hillier country, carrying a heavier cover of bigger and more mature trees. In amongst these older gums and wattle shrubs, he saw scattered in a random kind of pattern many starkly greener and totally different forms of vegetation from the usual native species.

John wandered through this enormous grove gently navigating the undergrowth to ascertain the extent of this endeavour. There were not all that many specimens here, just scattered at random amongst the natural environment. John could see no evidence of any cultivation, no sign of harvesting facilities and no indication even of any vehicular access. He wondered if this was a remnant or an active cultivation. The plants all appeared to be very healthy, but he knew nothing of their reproductive processes. They may just be the remnants of an abandoned effort from some time back. He was rather nervous at being here amongst all this evil. He headed back towards the Cross place and the ridge where the pines might be planted.

The next day, John went into town to visit Tom Grady's old firm again. It turned out that they were a wealth of information on this owner, and had done a bit of research for John. The name of the owner was Peter Lawson, nicknamed Henry, and was well known in the district. He owned several properties in the area, mostly cattle, and was also a renowned horse and carriage exponent, being involved with show exhibitions and country show competitions. John knew of him once the name and pastimes were mentioned, but did not know him personally. Peter Lawson also ran one of the smaller hotels in Cooma, so was an established businessman.

John went back to his car to think for a minute. He decided on the spur of the moment to attempt to contact Peter if he were at the hotel, while he was in town. It was located up one end of the highway, a little out of the centre. It was now only late morning, so trade should be docile at the moment, John surmised.

John had never ever even set foot in a public bar. He was a bit sheepish at this first effort. He went up to the bar and asked if Peter happened to be in. He was not, but the barman knew where he was, and it was close by. John set off to find him in another office further down the street.

Peter was leaving as John met him. After introductions, Peter invited him back to the pub to chat. They went to a small office at the rear of the place that Peter used as his own. John was a little nervous, as he did not like to ask permission after the event. Peter was a big man, not quite as tall as

John, but much heavier, almost obese. He had a very firm handshake. John began,

'Peter, thanks for your time. Look I own the land next to your large block on Bull Flat Road, out towards Shannons Flat. You know it?'

'Yes, I'm familiar with that block. I don't get out there much. Why, is there a problem?'

'No, no.' said John rather hastily. 'I do apologise in advance for not contacting you earlier, but I want to ask you something.'

'Sure. What is it?'

'I don't use the scrubby ridge next to your place at the road, but a young bloke wants to grow trees on it and I'm kind of thinking that I may give him permission. But you see, I did some investigating a few days ago and, I'm sorry to say, I rode into your place to check a few things out on our boundaries and inside a little.'

'That seems okay. Is all well there for you then?'

'Actually, Peter, I wouldn't have bothered you over it but I wanted to ask you something. You see, I actually ventured right over to the river where the bluff is at the far northern end. You familiar with that bit?'

'Ah, sort of. I don't go over it much. I occasionally send out some boys if I need to muster the scrubbers out there. I haven't been there for years now.'

'Okay. Here's the thing.' said John, 'In my ride over to the river, I came across the ruins of the old hut, and the grave of the young girl there. I was rather taken with the whole scene. I'd like to ask your permission to visit it occasionally. I found it most impactful just being there. I'd ride over. There'd be no interference with your stock. How do you feel about that?'

'You know, I didn't even know that was there. No, no worries. Tell me about it.'

John went on to describe the scene. He tried to emphasise that it was non-descript and nothing much to see, hoping to keep others away from it, and keeping it for himself. Peter was enthralled. He again gave his blessing for John to visit as much as he wished. To conclude matters, Peter asked casually,

'Everything seem in order there'

'Yeah, nothing of note. I did not ride over much, but all seemed okay. Well, thanks for your time. It was nice to finally meet you. Catch up later.'

With that, John departed in good spirits. It dawned on him during the conversation that Peter probably never went out there. He simply sent out a few blokes to muster and so on, they could be responsible for the crop. It was rather small for all intents, and that would account for there being no vehicular access to the site. Best not to rock the boat as they probably used it for themselves alone, hopefully.

John was grateful for the permission. He did over the years, visit the grave site at irregular instances, but gained much solace from the serene experience of the remote little drama it all entailed at that spot. He never mentioned it to anybody, not even Livinia, that the dramatic tranquillity and detachment engendered by the whole isolation of the sad little story even existed. He pondered and hoped that he was the only living person to know of its existence. As for the marijuana, he never visited that site again and hoped it all died a natural death.

As he sat in his tranquil and comforting lounge, contemplating all these reminiscences, he often wondered whether the solace, and part of the attraction of that private little interlude he obtained from the forgotten grave and old house, was not in some way a subconscious acknowledgement to his own lost son Brendan, who was buried in the little church cemetery on the road back to Cooma, not a private site at all, unlike the little girl over the road.

In his contentment, his mind drifted back to the two most fascinating people he had encountered. He felt privileged to have had the opportunity to interact with them. He pondered the meaning of the divergence in character of people. Jessie was simply astounding. Graham Longley was so enigmatic, so mysterious, especially considering his apparent late arrival into the sheep industry. He pondered that conundrum.

Graham woke very early as usual. The day was calm, warm and pleasant. He gazed out the large kitchen window that gave him an almost uninterrupted view of all his property to the east. The house was set high enough to avoid nearly all the garden shrubs that were planted about this part of the house. The shearing shed from here was situated some distance away to his right and further up the slope, so it did not particularly interrupt his paddock view, but he could see it comfortably from here. He could survey most of this part of the near-road grazing with much surety. Graham was not a gardener. He begrudged having to mow the lawn and often utilised a few tame sheep to do that task. He was certainly not interested in the nuances of the shrubbery that Gloria probably agonised over. As for the trees, they were now on their own.

The original property that was selected in the early 1840s was a very large holding. The entire area was covered in moderately dense native eucalypt forest and the occasional large more grassier areas that the original native peoples had maintained with their fire-stick management. This encouraged parts of the land to be an attractive pasture-like environment that was conducive to the accumulation of mobs of kangaroos and wallabies – easier to hunt in those conditions.

To arrive at the state that the land was now in required much hard work and years of endeavour to clear the land of the bush and the timber – all by hand using axes and hand-saws. The early pioneers had no knowledge of the impact their efforts had on the situation and indeed they were of the opinion that the fewer the number of trees the better and the more grazing that was available for their sheep. As he became more attuned to the world of nature, Graham often surmised at the now lost ecosystems and the flora and fauna that must have been obliterated by the totally ignorant early settlers. If the impact they had on the ecologies with their late-coming and inadequate equipment, he often tried to imagine what impact the coming of the Aborigines had on what was then a pristine and human-less biology with their advanced hunting ability and equipment, not to mention the introduction of the dingo. Still, he often also recalled with a sigh of resignation that you cannot make an omelette without breaking eggs. There were still many survivors of that earlier cohort, mostly roos and wallabies, plus, along the softer parts of the river banks, many wombats, and of course a multitude of birdlife.

In the early 1950s, the large property, which according to the maps and plans that John and Gloria Wheatley left behind for the new owner, whomever that was, (they did not know it was to be Graham), which was called *Wolstongrove*, was subdivided. It was split into six separate properties. The original homestead was allocated only 5,500 acres, but included the house. The adjoining block comprised 7,500 acres, but that had the shearing shed. That was the block that Graham's aunt and uncle had purchased. It had no dwelling, that is why they bought the place in relatively nearby Captains Flat, until they could build out here. The Davidsons, Graham's other neighbour to his south, was about 7,000 acres. The Johnsons, it was Bert who had the cattle, was 10,000 acres and there were two more smaller blocks further up the river that only comprised about 5,000 acres each. All the boundaries ran roughly east-west and for some distance back off into the distant hills. By the time anyone reached the later blocks further along the road, they were many kilometres from Graham's home.

Graham knew most of his immediate neighbours, including those roughly opposite, and there was a certain camaraderie existing among this group, especially as most of them used his shearing shed. This was not the case with Graham's other immediate neighbour to his north. This neighbour bordered the boundary fence on what was John Wheatley's place, now Graham's. John had never mentioned that neighbour much in all the dealings that Graham had with John Wheatley over the years of working on his place while he tried to learn the ropes. The few obtuse references to that neighbour were often couched in derogatory terms and he often just referred to the woman owner as 'feisty'. To Graham, 'feisty' usually was a euphemism for 'bitch'. As John was such an amenable and docile character, Graham was reluctant to initiate any interaction with this new neighbour, and they seemed to be independent of the shearing facilities of this side of the fence. Though John usually commented that they ran mostly cattle on their extensive 'flats'.

Graham was of the habit of checking his boundary fencing on a regular basis, something that John was more tardy at doing. Graham could drive most of the way inside his own property around all his boundary fencing, once he crossed the river at the one point that almost any vehicle could navigate that option on his place, especially when it was low-flowing. He rarely struck any problems as there were no trees actually in any proximity to his fencing, so the only issues usually arose with animal damage or the effects of aging infrastructure.

In his now more observant mode, he noticed that there were several repairs in the fenceline along the boundary with this 'recalcitrant' neighbour. They all seemed to be in fairly close proximity to one of the few clumps of mature gumtrees that were extant on his place, a place where there was a lot of bare earth where the sheep had habitually camped under the shade over many generations. These repairs were also distinctive for two reasons. A lot of them appeared recent. Another reason was the repair method. The wires appeared to Graham to have been cut cleanly and then rejoined, not snaped by any strain on the wires which showed a different characteristic. That in itself would not normally incur any suspicious thinking except for the joining method. It was simple, primitive and amateurish twisting of both the wires through each of the joining loops – a particularly lazy and ineffective joining system prone to rusting and re-breakage. The other reason that struck Graham was that John Wheatley would never use this sloppy method on his fencing. He had instructed Graham on and shown him the much better and more effective method of using the figure-of-eight tie that, if a strain were exerted on the wires, the knot would only pull tighter on itself and never break. Graham was suspicious about these strange occurrences in this area.

This neighbour's property was not visible from most of Graham's place as he had to ascend the gentle rise between his house and the place to his north. When he first ventured over the low rise and surveyed the neighbour's property, he was struck by the vista. Graham's house was located on a double slope. From the roadway into the property, the land sloped gently down all the way to the river which was located a good kilometre or more into the property. There was also a gentle upward slope from the shearing shed and the house towards the north that culminated in a gentle crest some distance from the house. The boundary fence was just over the other side of this crest. From the top of this little rise was laid out the vista of the neighbour's place. It was an expansive and breathtaking panorama.

During his early working days with John Wheatley,

Graham never really took in the real magnificence of this panorama. He was still a very naïve and relatively unobservant new-comer when it came to matters rural, besides, he was usually totally engrossed in the job at hand when he was associating with the co-operative and instructive John Wheatley. He simply had no real interest in other matters. That had now changed with the advent of all his gained knowledge and experience immersed in the world of nature. He viewed that vista now through much more informed and interested eyes.

Graham was struck by the sight. His city mind was slowly bending to the siren magnetism of his enforced immersion into the world of close connections with nature and the bush. The view from the top was of a pastoral landscape that extended almost to the extreme distance of his view. The roadway from here into town also followed the gentle rise and fall of the topography. As it crested the gentle rise, it deviated moderately off to the left and down the other side in an enormous curve that was almost unnoticeable to the unobservant driver. Graham never gave it a moment's thought why the road did this. From the road, this view was also invisible. He could now see what impact the topography of the district had on influencing the construction of the road. There, laid out in all its glory was a huge and expansive dead-flat plain that stretched as far as he could see. It was almost as if it were deliberately constructed. It was dotted all over by numerous black and red cattle, with a sprinkling of Herefords. There was not a single tree or even a bush on it, nothing but endless pasture. Running through the near right of it was the clear evidence of the Shoalhaven River. For some reason, Graham now knew instantly what he was looking at. His sensitivity to his new environment was shining through.

He instinctively and confidently leapt to the immediate conclusion that this extensive and valuable pastured asset was the result of aeons of time and the natural construction of a huge lake of some sort. He gazed off into the far distant north. Sure enough, there in the distance was a low range of hills. It struck him as logically as day and night. The only way such a huge expanse of fertile dead-flat country could be created was by being at the bottom of an enormous lake that was probably there for millennia. The epochs required to facilitate the creation of such a sight must be enormous. The soil was probably metres deep, comprising silt, debris, organic matter and rubble that settled on the bottom of the waterway. This would be the product of the mighty Shoalhaven River and the passage of endless time. If he could have followed the river from here, he knew he would come to a point in the distant range where the river had broken through in the past or where it finally took a bend to escape this captivity. He was totally enthralled.

Graham was until now unaware that this asset and natural gift existed. It was mostly invisible from the road, and its extent was not evident from that position. The best way to encapsulate the grandeur of this spectacle was from a vantage point such as this. He was also unaware of exactly where the owner of this property accessed their house and where that was located.

Graham had two unpleasant interactions with the owner of this grazing paradise. The first one occurred about three months after it was sold. A letter arrived in the letter box addressed to J Ransom. It was on a letterhead from a solicitor's office in Queanbeyan, but not the one that Graham used. Graham was nonplussed by this arrival, as it appeared to him to be a scam or a try-on by that particular neighbour. The letter was a little intimidating and lengthy, but in essence, it was a bill for the new owner's contribution to the common boundary fence that was erected along that location, it amounted to more than $5,000.00.

Now Graham knew that John Wheatley had done a lot of work along that fenceline, as Graham had helped him in doing some of it. It was one of the processes that he had used as a learning experience not that long after he had acquired the property from his late aunt. Graham learnt a lot about fencing. John had provided all the timber posts and all the labour. The joint costs only covered the wire, the droppers and the star pickets. Graham also knew that the neighbour was tardy in payment of their share and quibbled incessantly. Another indication to Graham of the 'feisty' nature of this person. He never did find out the final outcome of all that carry-on.

Graham decided to approach his own solicitor in Queanbeyan, Mr Deane. He wandered into the office around midday and asked if he could have a quick word to Mr Deane.

Mr Deane offered him a quick chat between appointments, for which Graham was very grateful. The essence of his discussion revolved around the character of the letter-writer.

Mr Deane was circumspect about any criticism, but did volunteer that that firm had a certain reputation around town and was known for being less scrupulous, shall we say, than was considered professional. Its main business centred around family law disputes, minor property conveyancing and small compensation claims, not fields that Mr Deane aspired to. Graham got the impression that that firm was not very highly thought of in legal circles. It was run by a woman of dubious reputation, just the sort that would appeal to the person that he calculated his newly-acquired neighbour would desire if deception were contemplated.

That evening, Graham rang his friend Peter Knuckey from the law firm that handled his devastating divorce saga in Sydney. After hearing all the details, Peter offered to address the issue with a letter of his own, on his letterhead, sent to the doubtful firm in Queanbeyan. Graham was delighted that Peter was prepared to do this for him, but insisted, this time, on paying him for his professional advice and assistance. Peter reluctantly agreed.

The substance of this tome was rather severe. Peter used his legal practice's own impressive letterhead and wrote a lengthy note addressed to the small legal firm in Queanbeyan. The message centred around the facts that the fence in question was completed quite some time ago; that the original owner had constructed the entire thing with no input from the aggrieved party, all at his own initial expense with delayed and disputed agreement as to the final amount. The new owner to whom they had sent the letter of demand may be an out-of-town party, but had intimate knowledge of all these matters and was totally conversant with all the details. There was also an eye-witness to all the above. The letter concluded with a statement to the effect that this appeared to be a fraudulent attempt to extort money from the new owner whom the Queanbeyan firm may have erroneously assumed had no knowledge of the facts. Any further contact with the recipient client would result in legal action and a call to the ethics board of the lawyers' association. Graham assumed that a small-town legal firm of doubtful character would shudder at receiving a threat from a large and establish Sydney city legal office.

The demand from the neighbour for this money seemed to have arisen in the mistaken assumption that the new owner, one J Ransom was ignorant of any facts. This had arrived before Jessie had the land that was registered in her name changed from hers to Graham's, as he had asked for the delay in order to protect the Wheatleys from any embarrassment. Graham never heard anything more about that ruse again. He assumed it rankled with his neighbour.

The second interaction was a little more serious. It followed on in some ways from the first incident, but a little later. Graham was always suspicious of the apparent fiddling that seemed to have occurred on this length of fencing. He was conscious of the exact number of repairs. When he discovered what he considered an apparently more recent one on one of his regular boundary inspections, he decided to act.

He was now suspecting that these people were possibly stealing his sheep, an issue he had never contemplated. Then he recalled a couple of incidences of lost and wandering lambs, their mothers could not be found. No evidence was ever discovered of mauled or mutilated sheep. He was unaware of any dog problems out here despite the region being extensively surrounded by national parks and reserves. He did have plenty of foxes, but they never attacked mature fully-grown ewes, only their lambs if they could. These were the lambs that Graham usually got the two boys to raise and kept about the house to reduce the grass.

Then one night, he heard the dogs barking and there must have been a disturbance somewhere nearby. He had the thought to investigate the repeatedly repaired fence. It was relatively early in the evening, there was a full, bright moon and the sky was clear and calm. He grabbed his point 22 rifle, wondering momentarily whether that was a good idea, but took it anyway, as it had a magnificent infra-red military-grade night scope, a gift from the wonderful Jessie Summers. The other thing he grabbed was a hooter. This was a small hand-held device that John Wheatley had used to scare off the birds, mostly cockatoos, from his rather excellent orchard, one aspect of the new owner's areas of neglect. It made a particularly and devastatingly loud noise. He thought that it might startle anyone loitering about suspiciously.

He snuck up the rise and peered over the crest. Sure enough, there were what appeared from here to be two horsemen and they were inside Graham's property. He skirted the ridge and entered closer by using the clump of ancient eucalypt trees as cover and was able to get very close. There was a big mob of sheep camped all about and close to the fence, many with young lambs. They were alerted to something unusual. The two people had cut the fence, he assumed, and were folding it back into their place and making a quite large entrance area in order to shepherd the flock, or at least some of them, into their side of the fence.

Graham was able to sneak up very close to the action and survey the scene. He finally decided to act. He let out a huge and explosive trumpeting of the hooter. Pandemonium ensued. Firstly, the two horses, which were standing close to the fence but inside Graham's side of the fence, bolted in mad panic straight up the fenceline towards the road many hundreds of metres to the west, their reins dangling and flaying about in the air. The sheep all arose as one and darted off in the opposite direction towards the river and the open paddocks, bleating and stampeding in confused mayhem. The noise had disturbed a great collection of quietly nesting birdlife which used these trees as a refuge and nesting site. Graham could even hear the dogs back at the house barking wildly as well. The two horsemen stood startled and peering in the direction of the horrendous disturbance. Graham stood stock-still, not moving or saying anything, hidden behind one of the enormous gumtree trunks. There was now deathly silence descending onto the scene as the retreating horses disappeared along the fenceline and into the depths of the night. The sheep did not stop until they were almost out of sight, well clear of the house enclosure and nearing the banks of the river. The two riders were totally confused. Finally, one of them spoke.

'Is anyone there?' she asked.

Graham did not answer. He was amazed to discover it was a woman. Then he remembered that the people on that property were this feisty person and her two daughters. Maybe it was they that were doing this themselves. Again, the question,

'Is anyone there?' she asked a little more loudly. Still no answer. They began to talk among themselves. They were in real trouble here. Their horses were gone; the fence was still cut open and laying all over the ground and they were obviously a long way from anywhere. Graham could slightly hear their conversation. They were wondering if it were not just an alarm of some sort and that no one was there. Worst of all however, was the loss of their transport and, apparently, all their repair equipment being carried by the now gone horses. They momentarily considered trying to recover the horses. Then one of them was heard saying something along the lines of let's close this gap in the fence and hightail it out of here before someone responds to the alarm. It was agreed. They quickly reassembled the damaged fence as best they could and then just began to hurriedly retreat from the area back down the slope and into the enormous flat plain that was their home.

Graham was delighted. He had foiled their plans; he had

the evidence before him and their horses were well and truly ensconced in his place. They could not ask for them back as that would immediately implicate them in the act. He tried to secure the fence enough to wait for daylight when he would conduct the proper repairs. He wandered back to his house very contented.

Next morning, quite early, Graham went up to the damaged fence in the old restored Land Rover to begin the repairs, before any stock discovered the damage and decided to wander. What he discovered annoyed him rather immensely. There was a couple of cut-and-repair points in the fence where gripples as well as amateurish knots had been used, which he had noticed and which originally alerted him to the potential of shenanigans. But things appeared to have advanced considerably from those apparently earlier attempts. To his surprise, the fence had not been cut this time, but instead, someone had arranged a neatly disguised system of camouflaged hooks that simply needed to be unhooked and re-hooked at a suitable wooden post to obtain the outcome. It was really quite ingenious. Then the thought struck him, that if they were so clever, why would they arrange for this deviousness to be perpetrated in so close a vicinity to the house. It would have made much more sense to have done this way up the other side of the river, miles from the house, and where no one would see or hear them. It must have something to do with this huge encampment that the sheep utilised around the clump of ancient gumtrees. He would need to inspect the rest of the fence very carefully all the way up to the back boundary.

Graham removed several hundred metres of repaired fencing, including the hook-up system and replaced it with completely new fencing. The old stuff may be useful out at Cobar. It took most of the early morning to achieve this feat. Then he returned to the house.

Graham then rang Jackson Faulkner for advice and a discussion on the matter. Jackson had some sage guidance. Then Graham rang Thomas Summers out at Auvergne Station to discuss it with him and maybe get Jessie's opinion of the situation. Jessie suggested that he carefully remove all the tack from the two horses, if he can corral them, using soft gloves in order not to remove any of the fingerprints from all the equipment. She would contact the stock squad in Cooma and see if she could arrange for them to attend his property and secure prints from the gear. Graham agreed.

About midday, Graham went off to try to find the two horses, carrying a pair of soft cotton gloves. He eventually found them quite some distance from the events of the previous evening, still carrying all their gear and dangling reins. He did not like horses much, he was a little afraid of them, but he thought that these two might be tame enough for him to gather them up and take them back to his yards at the house to remove all their gear. This he finally did, with quite some trepidation, but, surprisingly, they were fairly docile once everyone decided there was no threat from either party. He slowly walked them back to his house yards, all the time growing more confident in their demeanour and acquiescence in being attended to.

He finally got them into a small stock yard near the house. He shut them in and left them for a few minutes to settle down. Graham had never even been on his own with horses, let alone attended to their unsaddling and removal of reins and halters. Graham set up a place in the machinery shed using two 44-gallon drums and some planking between, where he could stow the removed gear in such a way as to allow for fingerprinting to occur, yet prevent contamination. Now all he had to do was await Jessie's results about the stock squad's request for investigation. In the meantime, he would like to release the two horses into the nearby paddock adjoining the house here, but barely visible from the road.

Jessie, through her extensive network of contacts, managed to persuade the Cooma stock squad to attend to this matter. Graham was exceedingly pleased. They would be there the next day. In the meantime, Graham could now thoroughly inspect the entire length of the boundary fence, on foot, to see if there were any other anomalies occurring.

That afternoon, Graham walked up to the corner post of the boundary that commenced at the road and slowly inspected the entire length on foot. All was in order until he had crossed the river and proceeded several hundred metres up along that fence. Then he discovered a replica of the hooking system he had encountered near the large clump of trees. There was also evidence of activity occurring both sides of the fence. Surely, they were not stealing sheep from here as well. He was horrified. Maybe, as John Wheatley aged and became less active, they perceived an opportunity to pilfer stock. Who knows? He would fix this rupture as well. Simply by repairing it, it would alert them to the fact that he was now aware of their activities. Not the sort of action from a nice neighbour.

Next morning, Graham thought that he would try to re-capture, or at least encourage the two horses back into his house yard for the Cooma stock squad to inspect if they so desired, not a task he relished. They were still in the larger of the house paddocks this side of the river, so he knew where they were. He approached them in the paddock and they did not flee. They were actually quite docile and displayed curiosity rather that fear. He even managed to pat one of them, the smaller of the two, which also proved to be a smaller animal than he was used to with Sophia and rather a passive and compliant little beast. She was a lovely little mare. Graham had no idea about her age. He also discovered that the pair of them rather enjoyed the odd feed of oats and a few of the other products he had about for his rams and sheep.

The stock squad arrived about ten-thirty in a large van and immediately began their investigations and capturing all the prints they could access. They were very personable and pleasant people and Graham got along with them with no problems, all the time trying to think what he could ask them while they were there. When they had completed their investigations inside the shed, and advised Graham that he could now use any of the equipment that he desired, he led them to the pair of horses in the stockyards near the house.

It turned out that both the police officers were experienced horse people and from a country background. They were slightly amazed to discover that both the horses had no branding at all on them and no distinguishing markings. They advised Graham that they most probably were born and raised on the property that they had come from, not all that an unusual occurrence. There followed a long discussion about the implications of the last few days, and any obligations on him regarding the two animals and all their saddlery and saddle bags of gear. They advised him that they would be investigating the prints and then get back to him in due course. They also took photographs of much of the gear and also of the rolled-up fencing that Graham had removed from the fenceline.

That evening, Graham again rang the Faulkners to see if he could yet again impose on their expertise and if Sophia or Jackson, when next passing by, would be able to drop in to give their opinion on the quality of the two newly acquired horses on his property. He was still of a mind to keep them. Jackson leapt at the request, stating that he had an employee who was a one-time farrier and horse handler. He would get him to accompany either Sophia or himself to his place immediately. Jackson was suddenly astonished to also discover that Graham now lived on the property, not in Captains Flat, a fact that, up till now, he was unaware of. That was because Graham had been most circumspect about Jessie's benevolence towards him in buying the Wheatley place after Graham had saved her life in front of his own place after she was abducted.

Two days later, Sophia, Jackson and their horse man Brian, paid Graham a visit. The visit was not entirely in connection with the appraisal of the horses either. Both Jackson and Sophia were very keen to discover how Graham had suddenly seemed to acquire the place next door with the old original homestead on it, considering that they both knew that Graham was, shall we say, mildly cash-strapped with all his family and property commitments.

The Faulkners were delighted for Graham that he had managed to acquire this place, and were very keen to find out all the details. Sadly, Graham was rather guarded about that issue and they were unable to find out very much at all. Never mind, that can wait in abeyance for now, as the main object of the visit was to peruse the two horses.

Graham had corralled them again in the house paddock stock yards. The trio gave them a thorough inspection and then passed on their verdict. The little mare was quite a nice animal, about seven years old and in rather good nick. She had been well shod and well fed, and had at least two foals. Her teeth were fine and her confirmation was adequate for the farm work Graham might have in store for her if he decided to keep her. The other horse, a gelding, was about nine and a little bigger and more muscular than the mare, but again, was in good condition. His teeth were also fine and he appeared to be used to a lot of riding and handling.

All the saddlery was old but well maintained and serviceable for the sort of work it would encounter on this property, and it was suitable for the two animals that it was used on. The overall conclusion was that these two animals would be an appropriate acquisition for Graham's enterprise – and of course, the price was right. Maybe the old saying *you don't look a gift-horse in the mouth* applied here.

Graham rang his solicitor in Queanbeyan and made an appointment. It was arranged for ten am. Graham arrived early and waited in Mr Deane's office. Graham entered the office and sat in the now familiar seat opposite the large and tidy desk of Mr Deane. Graham commenced by asking,

'Mr Deane, you recall that incident with the request for payment for the fencing on the old Wheatley place?'

'Yes.'

'Well, there's been a development since then.'

'Oh, really? I haven't heard any more about it.'

'No. I bet you haven't.' said Graham firmly. 'There's a good reason for that. With all due respect for you and your firm here in Queanbeyan, Mr Deane, I arranged through a firm in Sydney to drop that lady a little note. She would have been chastened, even rebuked by that receival.'

Mr Deane stared at Graham in silence, a little baffled by the direction of this conversation.

'Before we continue Mr Deane, you might like to peruse that little tome.'

Graham opened his manila folder he had taken out of his brief case and withdrew a two-page letter from it. He then handed it over to him in silence. Mr Deane read very carefully the contents of that letter. Then he raised his head and peered at Graham, saying,

'That certainly would have stymied any further action on that issue.'

'It certainly did.' replied Graham. 'However, another more serious matter has subsequently risen. It is in the throes of being attended to, but I want you to know all about this one too.'

'Oh, what's that then?'

Graham went on in some detail to explain the saga of the sheep stealing and the methods used to accomplish that end, and how it was discovered. He also went on in more detail about the effects of all the criminality and that the Cooma stock squad was involved. Then Graham stated,

'A senior uniformed detective inspector from Queanbeyan, I believe a Mr Townsend, arranged to get a warrant and visited that property with several other officers and conducted a search of the premises, the stock yards and all the stock. I believe they discovered anomalies regarding some of the cattle, but mostly they were looking at any sheep on the place, of which there were many.'

'How did you arrange to get Mr Townsend to be involved? He doesn't normally do that sort of thing.' asked a puzzled Mr Deane. He was familiar with the name Townsend; as he was a member of the same Masonic chapter in town. Graham remained silent. Mr Deane stared deeply at Graham. He cast his mind back to the very first time he ever met him. He recalled the man he encountered struck him as a failed surfie; slothful, over-weight and unkempt on arrival. He also did not come across as very coherent. Then, many months later, he came in again – a completely different man. It was as if his twin had taken his place. He was erudite, alert, toned-up and much better presented. The change was miraculous. Now he was sitting here in front of him describing how he appeared to have been able to arrange for a senior police officer to be doing routine hack work over a relatively minor matter. He was thinking that he must have some impressive contacts somewhere.

'I also believe that Mr Townsend paid a visit to that legal firm in Queanbeyan.' continued Graham. 'I expect that will keep that particular personage in line for a while. There is a lot of on-going activity in regards to that particular rural property as well.'

'Why are you telling me all this Graham?'

'I want you in the loop in case things develop. I also don't mind how much of this is spread about town regarding that despicable little bunch of crooks masquerading as a legal firm here in town. You may have gathered Mr Deane; I do not normally hold the legal profession in high regard, present company excepted.' Mr Deane simply nodded non-committedly.

There was a lot more to play out in the life of Graham Longley and his move to his new abode.

# CHAPTER THREE

n the meantime, Jessie Summers had had another attempt on her life. This time, the culprits had made the fatal error of actually arranging their rendezvous outside the front gate of the reliable Graham Longley, allowing him to intervene.

Jess was severely rattled by her abduction of many months ago now, at the instigation of Bales, John Summers' disreputable son-in-law, she suspected, or his associates. She had no definite proof, but again suspected him. She doubted that Stolt, the crooked Assistant Police Commissioner, with a long history against her, was involved, though he definitely wanted her dead too. For some reason, she felt an overwhelming gratitude and debt to her fortuitously placed saviour, the remarkable Graham Longley. If not for him and his timely intervention, at his isolated property along the Shoalhaven, she had no doubt that she would not be here.

Jess now surveyed her fractured life with more emotion and sentiment than she had ever previously done. She was not sure whether this was for the reason that she came so close to death, yet again, or whether this was because, as she aged, she was becoming more conscious of her own immanent mortality and all that entailed.

Jess was also becoming more mindful of the impacts on her happiness by the actions of others. Though each new iteration of her disrupted life offered her new challenges, seemingly always accompanied by new and greater attainments, she was aware that each one was preceded by traumatic actions from someone else. This someone else, she recalled, often seemed to be the same person and for the same reasons.

To her, the most devastating event was always the first one because it was so shocking and distressing for the young Jessie MacIntyre. That was her unceremonious removal from her first mentor in Newtown, Donald MacIntyre at the innocent age of just thirteen. Though she grew enormously from that interlude that attended her remarkable existence in the remote Kimberley, she still regarded it as traumatic and undeserving, especially for one so young. And this was all at the hands of the crooked, yet esteemed, cop, Mick Stolt.

Then again, fifteen years later, she was once more ripped away from her hibernation-inspired comfortable life by the self-same personage and his organisation. The devastation of that event lingered in her mind forever after. Then there was the near-death of her loving husband at the hands of the same people again when Thomas was accidentally shot at the Cooma saleyards in another abortive attempt to remove her from the scene. Now this recent attempt that almost succeeded with the kidnapping from her own home at Auvergne.

Jess had learnt a great deal from the events resulting in the removal from her life of the notoriously corrupt and colourful legal representative that went by the name of Geoffrey Bales. He was married to the elder daughter of John Summers, Audrey, but she knew for certain that he and John were basically sworn enemies. John detested the man intensely, though for totally different reason from Jessie. John Summers had very little inkling of the depths of the evilness of his unwelcome son-in-law. Jess was appraised in some considerable detail of his wickedness, stretching back to his equally despicable father, another reprobate judicial figure of some note. The full depths of the depravity and corruption of the senior Bales was possibly not even fully recognised by the junior Bales, as Jess had access, through Donald MacIntyre and Inspector Ian Knuckey, to much more information that was, unfortunately, mostly hear-say and scuttlebutt gleaned from around the traps of the more erudite and alert coppers from the bad old days of Sydney's crime scenes before it was more openly cleaned up following some bad press. The pair of them were far too cleaver to get directly involved.

That Bales was removed from her life so soon after her attempted abduction and her subsequent saving at the hands of Graham Longley, was a great relief to Jess, but it initiated a train of events that had major repercussions. Firstly, Jess learned some serious information consequentially from the now departed Bales. Secondly, because of the violent nature of his demise, it was widely assumed that he was severely tortured in order to extract information from him relating to matters criminal. Thirdly then, it was now also widely speculated as to what the nature of that information was and, more importantly, about whom. As the Bales' tentacles stretched far and wide, Jess was one of the names that was gathered up in the net of the exhaustive police investigation, as some of those within the police force of more dubious background might be involved within the results of Bales' blabbing.

Shortly after the demise of the shady Geoffrey Bales, came another major and serious death. Someone finally decided to remove the notorious and controversial and lately retired Assistant Commissioner, Miko Stolt. This resulted in an even wider and much deeper police investigation. The list of suspects was a large one. Many people in the criminal fraternity feared his knowledge, as did quite a few within the police itself, as Stolt had surrounded himself with many like-minded cronies, some with dirty hands. Stolt would have this knowledge held within his mind, just in case.

Stolt also had some very loyal subordinates, a small cadre of senior people who would owe their success entirely to his mentoring and/or possibly because of their deeds carried out for him, sometimes just as insurance for Stolt. There were some very nervous people living in these dangerous times.

On the death of Stolt, his most loyal and devoted underlings located his hitherto secret files on the people that he feared or despised the most; near the top of that list was the name of Jessie MacIntyre.

Stolt's death had made huge headlines, not the least at its brazenness. Then there were the Morangill deaths, closely following on from that. They were a notorious criminal family of long-standing, but these deaths were at first not associated with this act on Stolt. It was thought that some sort of turf war or gang rivalry had erupted, but Stolt's death was unable to be involved in any way so far. What did matter however, was the fact that serious police resources were dedicated to the investigation of the death of a senior officer.

Stolt kept secret files on the MacIntyre case, among others. Once these files were discovered and her whereabouts possibly revealed, steps were instigated into the possibility of getting her. Once all this was underway and that she may also now still be alive and living under the name Jane Ransom, a name that appeared in his secret files, it was soon exposed that a Jane Ransom also owned property around the Cooma area and a unit in Sydney. These were now under serious surveillance.

Some of the most senior officers of the NSW police force owed their not inconsiderable advancement to the controversial Stolt. One of these was now in charge of the case to find this woman and bring her to justice, or preferably, just eliminate her as Stolt had hinted. This officer had been privy to many confidential conversations with Stolt, such that he was inculcated with the poison disseminated by the evil Stolt that Jessie MacIntyre was the perpetrator of the original killings in Newtown and associated with the once disgraced detective Ian Knuckey, not to mention many other devious crimes that Stolt had managed to implement onto her.

He always avoided disclosing the inconvenient facts about her age at the time or that she had proven herself unable to be the perpetrator for several reasons, one of which was her decidedly left-handedness. Stolt was ever-mindful that it was Jessie MacIntyre who was the only witness to his killing of those officers on that night that was still alive. He had eliminated all the rest. The new man in charge of this sordid affair was now consumed with anger at the callous death of his mentor and protector in the force, and acknowledged inwardly the desire of Stolt's to eliminate this woman, not merely arrest her. He was of a like-mind now himself.

He had made some headway. Firstly, he had established that she was now possibly married and living on a property south of the rural country town of Cooma. He had also discovered her bush block in the name of Jane Ransom and the address and had set in place a scheme to arrange for her to be eliminated via a cunningly-devised scenario that would be carried out by a collection of accommodating lower officers. It took some considerable thought and planning, and several options presented themselves to this man. He was an Assistant Commissioner in charge of, among other things, still-open but old cases. His name was Assistant Commissioner Barry Whitehead. He had a reputation within the force of getting results, sometimes with what were regarded as dubious means. He was not averse to 'arranging' things so that results were achieved. He now planned on taking care once and for all of this pestilential person that had so haunted his erstwhile mentor Stolt. It was all set in train.

They had thoroughly investigated the layout of the Auvergne property via drones and helicopters disguised as surveying sorties and ascertained all the options. This option appeared to be fraught with difficulties. However, the huge isolated bush block that she seemed to visit frequently, and usually *alone*, offered many tantalising opportunities. She had though, so far been unsighted at the bush blocks and also unseen at her Rushcutters Bay unit for some time. But at last, she was confirmed as being at the address in the isolated and rugged bush location out from Cooma. This might be a suitable opportunity to strike. It was arranged.

When Jess visited her tranquil and heavenly peaceful bush setting, which she now did on increasingly more sporadic occasions, she usually drove there in her Land Rover Discovery Series 4. This was the one she bought to travel to her Rushcutters Bay unit after the altercation with Thomas over her television appearance. It was far more comfortable than her older Toyota Landcruiser Troopy 76 Series which she had purchased to leave the Kimberley in. She normally garaged the Discovery at the small house just inside the adjoining property that she bought next door to her original block. Here she would swap into a much more suitable and more rugged vehicle, an old late 1970s Nissan short-wheelbase Patrol that was unregistered. It was a dirty white colour. It had large knobbly tyres and a ragged black heavy bullbar that had been used to ram things in the paddocks. It had seen better days, but was admirably suited to rough bush-bashing and to getting her from here to her even more isolated original bush block over the next little hills and rough tracks. There she could move onto her old GMC and travel all the way up to her almost inaccessible eerie on top of the range in the enormous parcel of adjoining land that she also owned.

Barry Whitehead had established that she was at last actually located alone at her remote land, so he gathered his men who were on short notice to be ready for a secret but vital task involving a notorious criminal that needed attending to. When every detail was in place, he acted. Jess was confirmed to be travelling along the rough gravel road from her place heading for town mid-morning in her white Discovery. All was set.

The incident in question occurred as she rounded a gentle bend that eased off to the left slightly and that traversed a part of the country where the road was bordered on the left by a high batter cut out of the long ridge that rose up from the road to some height up the hills to the left. On the right-hand side, the ridge had dissipated into the low gully that drifted off to the right and ended many metres below the road in the little creek that followed the valley floor, along with the road, all the way from past Jessie's place until it finally joined another little creek that eventually flowed into the Murrumbidgee River many kilometres further west.

Here's the thing though. About a kilometre before this planned happening, Jess was almost ambling along the road. She was a gentle and conservative driver, after years of travelling along very isolated and rough gravel tracks in all sorts of vehicles. Suddenly, a small wallaby jumped out from the passenger's side of the road and darted across to the creek side right in front of her. Jess did not see it immediately, as her car had, for her, a rather high bonnet extruding in front of her close vision. She hit the brakes and just missed colliding with the fast-moving little animal. However, a couple of small plastic containers on the front seat slid off the passenger's seat and onto the floor which was already strewn with assorted paraphernalia that Jess left on there for easy access.

Jess did not like untidiness or clutter. She did not mind dirt, she had never in her life ever washed a car or a truck, but she did not like mess. She wished to retrieve the two containers immediately. She slowed the vehicle to a crawl and undid her seat belt. She had trouble reaching them. She waited till she was in a short clear spot on the road in an attempt to retrieve them again. She may even have to stop. She came to the fateful bend in the road.

Jess was only really half paying attention at this point, but suddenly and without any warning, there was a loud bang, an explosion, followed by a massive jolt that flung the vehicle violently over the edge of the road. The explosion had been placed such that it occurred under her front passenger side, causing the vehicle to thrust itself forwards over the bank, tumbling slightly nose first onto its bonnet and then rolling several times and coming to a shuddering halt in a tangle of trees and bushes that lined the edge of the little creek. The massive and heavy Discovery had landed on its roof, leaning slightly towards the driver's side such that the driver's door was wedged firmly blocked. The car had immediately burst into flames on its first impact and burnt furiously, igniting all the immediate shrubbery that it had landed amongst. There were several minor explosions coming from under the bonnet of the mangled heap as the vehicle was engulfed in a huge fireball and diesel fuel burnt furiously and running into the small creek, lighting up anything that the flames contacted. No one could have possibly survived this *accident*.

Jess lay stunned on the soft ground unsure of what had just happened. She lay slightly bruised and covered in sandy clay-coloured soil, facing the burning remains of her treasured Land Rover furiously blazing away below her many metres down the moderately steep slope to the gully below. She quickly looked about her. She was totally confused. Suddenly, she realised some of the intent. She lay mostly unhurt smack-bang in the middle of the biggest wombat tunnel entrance she had ever seen. She had seen plenty of wombat holes, the whole region was awash with them as they lived in the vast mountain country all along the creek banks over the whole district.

The car had been violently flung to the right off the road. It immediately hit a large boulder, one of a string of rocky outcrops that lined this part of the country adjacent to the gravel track that was the road out here. On impact, her driver's door was sprung open and she was ejected with some force from the vehicle and landed just below the rocky outcrops. Over the countless centuries, the little creek had flooded up to this level and deposited metres of soft sandy and gravelly soil all along the valley floor. This was ideal wombat habitat, as it allowed them to burrow into this soil for some distance, providing safety and protection.

She quickly wriggled backwards feet-first into the depths of this monster tunnel until she was completely inside. She remembered at the first instance that the door had sprung open on the first roll-over impact on that large rock outcrop and she had been half flung out and half fallen out at the jolt. She was unsure how this had happened, and in such a short time available. The car then bolted on down over the rocks and kept tumbling over and over and the door was closed each time it hit the ground. An observer on the other side of the road and above her would not see her exit on the initial tumble. She lay prone and trembling for a few seconds. Then she heard the voices.

There were eventually about seven men there in dark-blue overalls with no markings on them, if they were all dressed as the only one she glimpsed from her tunnel. He, incidentally was heavily armed with side-arms. She heard one man referred to as sergeant and sir many times and there was a general consensus that this plan had gone better than expected. They were speaking in a hurried manner and with some urgency. A late arrival confirmed that he had the pictures of the woman clearly showing it was she before the 'accident'. They stood around admiring their effort and praising the leader for such a welcomed outcome. Someone commented, 'Whitehead will be pleased at last.'

Then someone began barking orders. Firstly, he clicked on a two-way and said almost in front of the hidden Jess,

'Okay, Fenton, bring the vehicles around.' A 'Roger, Sarge' was all she heard.

Then she heard at least two large diesel engines from up on the roadway. The sergeant then asked the men there to attempt to put out the burning bushes, but not the car, as he did not want to attract unnecessary attention from passers-by, or any locals that may be able to detect the smoke. There was some noisy activity on the roadway. The sergeant then ordered,

'Bourke, Floteteli and Sangi, go up and help Fenton and Gomez to fill that crater up with dirt.

They carefully examined the scene to ensure no one escaped the crashing and burning vehicle and they remained briefly to ensure it totally burned itself out and was destroyed in its entirety. They were slightly disappointed that they could not definitely confirm the death by seeing a body, but were convinced that no one could survive this inferno. Several pictures were taken of the damaged vehicle. The sergeant then said to the remaining men down by the creek, 'Let's go boys, don't want to hang around here any longer than necessary.'

Then the sergeant and the last man by the creek headed back up to the road. There was a little noise from up there while they were doing whatever it was that was required, apparently to repair, or at least disguise any evidence of things occurring on the road surface. Then she heard the distinct sound of at least two large, probably four-door, four-wheel-drive utes or wagons depart the scene and total tranquillity descended onto the area except for the now gentle crackling of the wreck in its isolated and remote deathbed. Apparently, the smouldering ruin and the smouldering vegetation could all be left to someone else's attention.

Jess waited sometime before attempting to venture out. She was rather stiff and a little sore here and there, cold and shivering slightly, but otherwise all right. She glanced at the remains of her erstwhile faithful old companion and set off on the walk back to her eyrie. Luckily, it was only about six kilometres away.

Jess kept to the bush as much as possible in case someone came along. Nobody did, but she was still cautious. She made straight for the little cottage where she normally parked the now destroyed Discovery.

It was now several hours since this latest attempt on her life. She was still queasy and shaking slightly. She was totally bewildered as to what to do and where to go. She was distraught at the loss of her beloved Discovery and its fondest memories. Her unsettled sense of nervousness and anxiety was beginning to be countered by a growing degree of anger and rage. Her fevered mind was still confusedly racing while she considered her options. And who was this Whitehead who would be so pleased with her demise? Were those men police? Or were they some criminal organisation? Though the term 'sergeant' would indicate the former.

Jess had plenty of time to think about her plight on the long lonely walk back to her cottage. She wondered if her place was under surveillance or not. She was beginning to formulate a scheme; the rudiments of thinking were becoming clearer. Firstly, whoever the perpetrator of this little exercise was, they were now apparently convinced that she was definitely dead. That gave her one advantage over them at this stage. They might just be a little more careless now about divulging information about this incident thinking she were dead.

Jess wanted a lot more private time alone to consider all the options and analyse the situation and all the known facts before she revealed herself as alive. Where to go for this task? If whoever it was that carried out this little exercise, they seemed to know a lot about her and her movements. It surely cannot be anybody associated with Bales. Just as surely, it cannot be anyone associated with Stolt, though that is the most likely source. Jess needed somewhere to hide in safety and undetected while she figured it all out. The only place that sprung to mind was the one place that her persecutors hopefully were unaware of – and that was the abode of Graham Richard Longley – a man that Jess found totally reliable and discreet. It also occurred to her that it was probably very fortuitous that she had changed the name of Graham's property from her name as Jane Ransom into his at the new house block in enough time for any property search now not to reveal her name as appearing there.

It was very late in the afternoon and darkness was now rapidly descending as Jess was getting close to her property along the deserted and winding bush track that passed for a road this far out from any towns. She decided to delay her return to the premises until as late into the night as she could. The old Nissan Patrol was sitting in a small single wooden garage. The keys were hidden in the garage as well. About midnight, Jess snuck up to the doors and quietly opened them after retrieving the large key from under a rock at the far side of the building. It was a little noisy, but she hoped that no one was here in surveillance. She quickly checked out the old solid wooden garage. It had very solid doors, heavy wooden construction and it was well secured, probably a hangover from the previous owner's concern from being so close to the road. There appeared to be no interference with this structure, so at least they had not apparently attempted to enter this shed and put any form of tracking devises on the old Nissan.

She removed the old car and closed the doors, relocking the massive padlock and re-hiding the key. She drove out of the place without any lights until she was well clear of the premises and out onto the public roadway. Although the car was unregistered, she had little worry about being harassed at this time. She headed for the farm of Graham Longley. She hoped he was still living alone out at his property. He had advised her that the two boys were now living away from home at university up north studying agriculture and now only visited during semester breaks. He hopefully should still be alone.

It was quite a drive to the Longley property. Jess was some distance out of Cooma on this block and then she had to get to the Numeralla Road to head north towards Braidwood. It would be some time before she arrived at the Longley place, if the old Nissan made it that far – with an overnight stay somewhere.

When she had almost arrived at Graham's place, Jess parked the old Nissan some distance from the entrances to Graham's two properties, one entrance into the shearing shed block that he originally owned, and a near-by one that lead into the house block that she had only recently purchased for him. She tried to ensure that there was no one else there and that the place was reasonably deserted. She tried to think whether the people attempting this assassination would have ever been able to ascertain if she had any connection to Graham. She hoped desperately that that were not the case. She recalled that behind Graham's house there was a large open machinery shed that he did not have enough equipment to completely fill, as the previous owner had sold off a lot of his equipment. She thought that sometime in the dark she would drive into his house paddock and park the Nissan in one of the vacant bays.

Graham spent almost every day alone on his now rather large property. He always had plenty to do. He usually worked basically from sunup to about sundown every day on some aspect or other of his extensive pastured enterprise. He normally came back to the house about sundown and fiddled inside for a short time then went to bed fairly early. His days of late-night carousing were well and truly behind him now that he was so physically employed and accompanied by so much personal responsibility.

His realm was exceedingly quiet. The only sounds he ever heard were caused by only one of two things: either the products of the source of his wealth; his sheep, or the results of the interactions of his domain with mother nature, of which there was ample evidence in this isolated part of the world. So, when he was woken in the early hours of the morning by the distinct sound of a rather noisy large diesel motor entering his house area, he was very wary. The dogs had a little episode, but that seemed to dissipate rather quickly when nothing else occurred. He did always keep a point 22 calibre rifle and two shot guns, a 4/10 gauge and a larger twelve-gauge very handy, especially when he was alone.

The vehicle seemed to drive past his house and he was sure it actually entered his large machinery shed. That could mean that the driver was familiar with his property. He was very wary. He remained quiet and alert, but made no effort to leave the house or put on any lights. Nothing seemed to happen for quite some time. He was very confused. Was it one of the boys coming home mid-week?

Jess had parked deep inside the large shed. She sat trembling and bordering on emotional collapse at the never-ending assaults on her life and happiness. She absolutely hated having to impose on anybody else, but she could not think right now of anybody that could be removed from her sphere of known associates any better than the reliable and dependable Graham. She wondered if he had heard her arriving in the loud old Patrol. She also wondered how she was going to explain all this to him a second time; and who else to tell and when; Thomas for instance. She clearly recalled how calm and realistic he was in their last encounter of this nature. He had cooly summed up the scene; he had determinedly carried through the appropriate plan of action and he had firmly ensured everything was in order. She felt in no condition to be achieving that right now.

The dogs had barked initially at the noisy disturbance, but they were now basically quiet and settled again. Graham finally decided that he better investigate this matter. He grabbed the smaller 4/10-gauge shotgun and a handful of shells and quietly proceeded out the back to the dog pen. He quietly roused them again and unlatched their gate. They were now fully alert again. He gathered them up and slowly edged towards the machinery shed. There was a bank of light switches just inside the nearest wall. He flicked two of them. Instantly two long fluorescent tubes briefly flickered then burst into life.

Graham was confronted with a complete mystery. There in the far corner, well ensconced deep in the recesses of his shed was a completely unfamiliar large dirty old short-wheel-base off-white massive bush wagon of some unknown make, at least to him. The driver was still in there, he could clearly see that someone was just sitting in the driver's seat not moving. He began to wonder if it were not maybe a neighbour who had misplaced their directions in some inebriated stupor and sought refuge in this not entirely unfamiliar spot for them.

Graham cautiously began to advance towards the vehicle when nothing happened when he put on the lights. He gathered in the dogs to be right near him. He tapped the barrel on the rear of the dusty car gently at first, and then with a little more force. The driver opened the door and half stumbled out of the car and propped themselves against the side and advanced gingerly towards the rear of the car.

Graham was shocked to see the familiar personage of his rather recently acquired new best benefactor and, may he assume, fondly admired friend and supporter. He propped the shotgun against the rear of the car and rushed over to the dirty and dust-covered frame of the distraught Jessie Summers. He helped her to stagger away from the car and assisted her to a near-by small drum on which she sat with some awkwardness. She was now a little teary. He could not at first speak. The dogs stood wagging their tails awaiting instructions. They slowly sidled up to the not all that unfamiliar person. She absently patted their willing heads.

He sat beside her holding her dirty and shaking hand. She just sat there in dazed bewilderment gently shaking and dropping the occasional tear. Nothing was said for some minutes. Then, after several minutes, he said to her,

'Come inside.'

She got up tentatively and followed him unprotestingly out of the cool shed, switching off the lights as he went, and activating the small torch he had with him, and into the house via the back door so he could secure the ever-faithful dogs. He escorted her to the kitchen table after switching on that light. She sat silently down at the table and laid her grimy face onto her equally grimy sleeves. She began to gently sob. He was mortified. 'Cup of tea?' was all he could say.

She seemed to nod slightly. He touched her accessible arm gently and slid over to the bench and put on the jug. He prepared a pot and retrieved some of the wonderful home-made scones that his doting mother made for whenever she could.

He sat down again at the table. The jug boiled, he got up and made the tea. When it was all set on the table he said,

'Jess, have some tea. There are some scones if you'd like.'

She raised her head and looked at him. Her pain was obvious.

'What happened?' he asked.

She lowered her head and blinked a deliberate and exaggerated blink as the moisture dribbled down her face. She did not know where to start. She looked at him again, saying,

'Graham, they tried again.'

He touched her arm a second time in sympathy.

'Have you got some pencil and paper?' she asked.

He got up from the table and retrieved a small pad from the sideboard. He sat down again and poured her some tea. She took the pad and began to write. She kept looking up into the walls as if trying to recall something and then writing it down. She did this several times. Then she looked at him again. She took a sip of tea.

'Would you like to have a wash?' he asked

'Yes, shortly.' she replied.

After a short time of sipping tea and nibbling a small bit of scone, she said that she might just wash her hands before any-more. She went to the small washroom just inside the back door. He took the opportunity to peruse her notes. It was just a list of seven words, he assumed some could be names, and a couple of 'unknowns'. She came back after washing her face and hands and sat down again.

'Do you want to tell me what happened, or would you rather wait till later?'

'I was driving back from my bush retreat when my car was blown off the road by a bomb. The inexplicable way I survived is miraculous. But they think I'm dead, burnt alive inside my destroyed Land Rover. These are the names of some of the men that were there'

'But how did you get this information?'

Jess began to explain her drama. The more she got into it the more animated she became. The full extent of her unbelievable survival finally began to dawn on her. Eventually, after Graham let her unburden her tortured soul, he said that Thomas should be informed. Jess insisted that that was not a good idea right now. She wanted time to think about it and devise a plan and decide what to do and whom to inform. Besides, she reasoned, if it were the police, she bet that they had all the Summers' properties bugged. No, she must think about it when she was less distraught.

It was nearly morning by the time she was returning to the more normal Jessie Summers that Graham knew. By the time they had finished talking enough for Jess to have calmed down emotionally, the sun was well and truly up. She agreed to have a shower and he would provide her with some clothes to go on with.

Graham was too alert now to go back to bed, so he thought

about his day. It would depend considerably just what Jess wanted, and indeed, needed to do. He would first of all attend to her needs, then maybe leave her in peace while he got on with things.

Jess was a long time cleaning herself up and came out dressed in some of Graham's better clobber. She sat at the table again and he prepared her some breakfast.

'Shouldn't you be telling Thomas where you are?' he asked.

'No. Not yet.' she replied rather emphatically.

'Won't he be wondering where you are?'

'Probably, by now. But I need time to think about all this. I have a potentially huge advantage right now. See, they think I'm dead. They are convinced of that. I heard them say so. But, crucially, I have these name, something they will not have factored into their thinking. I think I'd like to try to contact Ian and get him to investigate who they are before they have time to try to hide any evidence that may still be laying about.'

'Well, you can do that here if you like.' he countered.

'No.' she said deliberately. 'I'd bet whoever is behind this has got Ian's phones all well and truly bugged. And probably all the Summers' phones as well. How else would they know all my movements so well, well enough to pull off this little stunt.'

Graham was beginning to be slightly amazed at the quality of Jessie's returning alertness and the clarity of her deductions and thinking. This was something that was out of his ken. He realised that she would probably be well-versed in this kind of circumstance occurring to her, as she probably had, unfortunately, much practice and experience.

'I am lucky that you are alone at the moment Graham. How long will that be the case?' she asked.

'The boys are away at present, and their granddad sometimes comes out here Friday arvo. Why do you ask?'

'Well, I don't want to interfere with your life any more than is necessary. I also don't want anybody else to see me at the moment.'

'Okay, then what have you in mind?'

'The first thing is to contact Ian, but not on any phones. Then I want to secret myself away somewhere very private where no one can locate me.'

Graham's first and immediate thought at that suggestion was, of course, Cobar; and the poor Butlers. He was thinking that they would reason that he only considered them as some kind of refuge for all the persecuted and mistreated that came his way. Then the thought also suddenly hit him that the Jessie Summers he knew was not the sought of overt conversationalist that might fit in with the garrulous and lonely Fiona Butler. Also, he was aware that Jessie Summers was a very worldly and sophisticated person who had a checkered history dotted with both fame and infamy, and, apart from being reticent, she had these unusual auras and mannerisms, one of which involved a mesmerising, penetrating and often piercing stare that definitely unsettled and often disturbed the recipient. The Butlers would almost definitely find her a most difficult guest.

Fiona Butler was not a sophisticated woman. She was probably poorly educated and came across as so amiable and innocent when it came to worldly matters, that Graham was not all that sure that Jessie Summers would find her company all that riveting. Fiona was garrulous, shy and yet introverted, especially when it came to people that were 'different'. Jessie Summers certainly was 'different'. Her countenance could come across as very severe.

'We could consider Cobar.' said Graham rather tentatively, almost hoping that that suggestion was anathema to her.

'What exactly is at Cobar?' she asked.

Graham went on at some length to explain the situation of the Cobar property and the family that lived there. Jess was not dismissive of this idea. He tried to raise any issues he perceived as arising when considering this suggestion, including what he euphemistically referred to as her 'checkered' past *vis-à-vis* the sheltered Butlers. Jess thought about all of this for some time. Then she said,

'Graham, if I were to go out there, I would have to go there in another guise. I suggest that I can always pose as an Austrian tourist or student or whatever and that would completely mask my true self from everyone.'

'But how can you do that?' he asked.

'I speak fluent German Graham. I learnt it from Werner as a child and then from years with George on Milbark.'

'I didn't know that.' he responded, a little amazed. You certainly could pass as a German or an Austrian with your appearance.' She made no response. Then he added, a little sheepishly,

'That could then account for your…,' he paused, 'shell we

say, rather introverted and reclusive manner.' She looked at him knowingly. She was fully aware of her inability to socialise very well.

'How would I get there?' she then asked.

'I would have to take you.'

'I don't know.' she said with a sigh. 'And how can we contact Ian if we don't want to use phones?'

'I would have to take you there myself, or speak to him myself. I could try to see Ian in person as I do go up to Sydney a bit to see my daughter Sally and Peter Knuckey, his nephew.'

'That might work. But I don't want to impose on you too much.'

'For you, Jess, I would gladly do that, or anything else you thought you needed.'

'Thank you, Graham.' was all she said.

Jess tried to stifle a yawn. She was slowly getting drowsier and less alert as the whole potential plan was beginning to take shape. Graham suggested that she go to bed in the back guest room that was rarely used by the family. She would be safe there until she was more fully recovered and they could decide on the next action to be required. Jess was shown into the far back small room and left to herself. Graham wandered back to his kitchen deep in thought.

Jess slept right through the day, most unusual for her. Graham spent some time contemplating events and all the possible ramifications and different scenarios that this situation offered. He was prepared to do anything for his friend. There were no reports on any news services about her accident or that she was missing. The way Jess described the whole scene and the apparent planning, it could be some time before her burned-out vehicle was even discovered. He was conscious that Thomas would be very worried and then devastated when he learnt the truth of her demise.

Jess did not arise until well into the early evening of that day. She still looked a little frazzled and passive after her ordeal, but that was understandable. Graham thought that Jess would ultimately probably prefer to be shunted out to Cobar while she got the people in Ian's Commissions to investigate the names she was going to supply. Graham had spent some time trying to concoct a suitable story about Jess to thoroughly disguise who she was in order to be able to ensconce her out in the wilds of the far west. He needed a convincing story as to why this rather sophisticated and elegant woman was desirous of spending some time in that atmosphere. At this point, she did not even have any of her own clothing at all, or any identification or any money.

Graham had raided the wardrobes of the boys trying to find some passably suitable clothing for her. It was difficult, but he came up with a few items that just might pass muster.

Jess sat at the table almost in a kind of distant daze. Graham offered her some tea. He was looking at her with a discerning eye. He had the weirdest sensation. He tried not to stare too much at her, but in her pre-occupied state, she was more vulnerable to perusal. He suddenly thought of his late Aunt Alice, who had bequeathed to him this bizarre lifestyle, dragging him from the depths of despair and desolation. What strange karma had led him to this point. Jessie Summers was a ravishing and stunning woman, even at this age. He was thinking of the two most glamorous women in his circle. Sophia Faulkner was a young but very cultured and elegant person. He marvelled at her class, and her talent. Jessie MacIntyre was such an enigma. Sophia was an all-round classic beauty with perfect features – she seemed genetically gifted. Jessie MacIntyre was so very different yet also so stunningly perfect. Unlike Sophia, who seemed whole in her perfection, Jess had at least two very distinct attributes which added to her appearance, and caused the eye to wander. That was her absolutely stunning blue eyes, and the disturbing stare that could emanate from them, not always deliberately intended for that effect. He had seen her intended threatening stare unleashed. It was devastatingly effective. She also had, even at this age still, a most dramatically perfect set of teeth. Even Graham had been distracted by their flawless state.

The other fascinating aspect that differentiated these two women from each other was their attire regarding jewellery. He had seen Sophia decked out in stunning and elegant long earrings, accompanied by graceful and expensive pearl necklaces and other striking pieces, especially at some of the evening affairs that he had attended. He had never seen Jess in any adornments at all. He had never seen her with earrings, rings or bangles. She did not even seem to wear a watch – nothing at all on her personage.

But it was her stunning eyes that often distracted the observer, and the mesmerising attraction they engendered within others. He recalled the few comments that Tony, his late neighbour in the Captains Flat cottage, made about her eyes, even as a child in Newtown. Their steely, severe and penetrating gaze could confuse those in conversation, such that they would lose concentration. Tony often spoke of her angelic and adorable existence when young. But then again, Graham recalled, it was exactly that striking difference of her appearance from others that had attracted the attention of her first saviour, Donald MacIntyre. If she had not stood out, he would not have recognised her aura from the milieu of others bustling about the markets.

Graham thought about his aunt again. Then he thought about his departed and tortured late wife. He still wished to honour her memory. He never considered these two women in a romantic way. In many ways, they were too perfect for that lowly consideration. He realised that he regarded the pair of them more as works of art – living masterpieces – but nevertheless as art. He did not hold the perceived threat of Ophelia in anything like the same awe, or respect; she was a decided hazard. He could admire these two women with no fear of any involvement other than that which they themselves initiated. He wondered at the miracle of their paths crossing, something that would never had happened in his previous life. With no threat of any complications, this had made these associations so much more pleasurable.

Graham looked at Jess still. He was thinking about the demise of the notorious Judge Bales the Younger. His death had apparently set in train all these events that followed.

There were so many criminal and corrupted police in fear of what he may have revealed that all sorts of 'insurance' was being perpetrated on all sorts of people. He wondered if Jess had been caught up in the net of criminal retributions and needed disposing of, just in case. He knew that she had knowledge of all manner of criminality from her dark days of Newtown, and subsequently from Ian Knuckey's investigations. He still held suspicions of her involvement in the death of Bales, but was not prepared to offend her by asking. Somehow, he just could not see that in her.

He was just as quickly thrust back from his musings and into the present dilemma. Jess was looking at him. She asked,

'Can I get to Cobar?'

'I will gladly take you.' he shot back.

'How will we achieve that without causing problems?'

'Leave that to me. Now, by the way, I have been thinking about this a lot. We may have struck a real stroke of luck here.'

'How do you mean?' she asked.

'Well, while you were asleep, I rang the Butlers at Cobar just to say hello and see what was what. I spoke to Fiona for some time; I sort of laid the groundwork here. I did mention you in a roundabout way. It appears that Sid, her husband, is away at the moment down at her father's place. The old man lives alone out on that property and, Fiona was telling me, neither she nor her brother is able or willing to take over the lease. So, the old man is destocking the place and eventually surrendering the lease back to the government. They plan on probably moving him into town to be nearer

Fiona. Apparently, the conservationists have an eye on the place. Anyway, the thought struck me that you could go out there as an Austrian tourist, or whatever, who has just lost all their luggage and papers in a robbery. We met up in Captains Flat when you were staying at the neighbour's place. Now you are waiting for all your new papers to be reissued from the embassy and the Australian people. I thought while you are waiting and unable to do anything, you could visit Fiona. What do you think?'

'Brilliant! Instead of a tourist, I could be on a study tour and am keen on authentic outback experiences which I am having trouble finding. How about that?'

'Yep, brill. You come up with whatever is convincing, as long as we agree on the same story.' said Graham. 'Listen, if we are going to do this, we better get a move on. If you are ready, we can leave today.'

'You sure?' she asked.

'Yes, the sooner the better. You give me those names and I'll call in on Ian Knuckey on the way back from there so he can start to investigate.'

'I don't suppose you'd have a spare laptop?'

He did not answer. Graham stood up from the table. He stared down at the demure figure of Jessie Summers. He said to her in that not unknown to her firm and decisive tone,

'All right. First things first. Let's get you to Cobar immediately. Then, on my return, I will go straight to either Peter or Ian Knuckey with these names. What do you say?'

'I think so.' she simply agreed.

Graham organised a few things. He told his parents that something had come up and he needed to go to Cobar and would they mind attending to the farm house and the dogs for a few days. He retrieved a spare laptop as Jess requested and then departed in his ute with Jess to Cobar.

# CHAPTER FOUR

With the return of Graham from his hasty sojourn with Jessie out to Wilingubra Station, and after visiting Ian Knuckey on the way back, he spent some time contemplating the results of that visit. Graham sat at his new kitchen setting, thinking. This was a far cry from the tiny and cramped little kitchen in the old cottage of his aunt's in the cold village of Captains Flat. He still remembered that sad little setup. He recalled often his gloomy and melancholy arrival at that strange arrangement that fate had seemed to impose on him at the behest of that distant and very vaguely remembered old aunt. He still marvelled at the whole proposition. Who had instigated this upheaval in his meaningless former existence? And why was he plonked down in that weird place that he still squeamishly recalled that he detested so vehemently at first. And why did he seem to gradually succumb to its siren spell and began the process of not only succeeding at the new paradigm, but actually enjoying the encounters and the slowly-won achievements?

He marvelled at the long line of occurrences that emanated from that original acceptance of the challenge offered. His only regret in all this adventure was the melancholy awareness of Jenny. For some reason, Graham never had the thought of his late wife ever stray far from his awareness. He wondered why this was so. He always felt the desire to honour her memory and her existence in his former life. For this reason, he had no yearning to replace her, despite the pain and trauma that she imposed on him. In some ways, that aspect acted as a deterrent to his ever succumbing to another in his life. He recalled often their time together before the children arrived. In many ways, they were the catalyst for her disintegration. The two boys seemed to have suffered no ill-effects at all over all that disaster. Not so Sally. Graham never lost the feeling that Sally held him in quite some distain because of it all. She was always reserved and distant in his perception. This may partly be because of her own personality, but he was sensitive to her detachment towards him. He never mentioned the fact to her of her arrival being the genesis of the destruction of their happy life together – that might be a step too far.

Despite the reverence he held towards his only true love, he was also mindful that in no way would she ever had fitted into this new life that he now led. It was not all that new a life either really. He had been living this encounter now for many years, and thoroughly enjoying it – even without her. He often gazed out the expansive window and over the panorama that was his very own empire of this wonderful existence. He marvelled at it all and was ever mindful of its blessings bestowed upon him by whatever means.

The other marvel in his life was the weird existence of Cobar, what was that about? And why was that included in the parcel from fate? He found himself considering that conundrum often, and the people that came with that aspect. It had a major impact on his being. It had again been instrumental in having a serious influence on his existence, with Jessie the latest recipient of its benevolence. Now there was another incident arising from that connection, and his latest sojourn out there. It involved the lovely Fiona.

Fiona Butler had a younger brother. His name was Xavier Jennings. The Jennings owned a station further out from Cobar and much further south. It was desolate and barren country and was originally a moderately successful enterprise given the harsh conditions and the extreme nature of the climate, but its viability diminished over time as economic conditions changed. Fiona met Sid Butler in an unusual set of circumstances, considering the sparseness of the population. Fiona was raised in these adverse outback conditions, so was not daunted by, or averse to, the offer of a marriage to a relative local.

Fiona and Xavier's father, the holder of the leasehold on their childhood property, was conscious that his children would probably not wish to follow in his footsteps out on the farm. As he aged, he was also aware that the property held little attraction for any other grazing activities, given the desert-like conditions. He was seriously contemplating surrendering the lease back to the government, as there had been approaches from several groups to try to obtain this acreage and convert it to a nature reserve by trying to rehabilitate the stressed vegetation and removing all domestic stock. There were also some concerns surrounding the issue of feral animals, though not so much with invasive weed species, and their impacts on the very delicate nature of the environment in such harsh conditions.

With this in mind, Xavier, and for that matter Fiona, had attended schooling in the larger towns with the aim of attaining some form of qualifications to ease them out of rural living and probably into a more urban existence. Xavier gained some advanced learning in the fields of finance and management.

Graham, and for that matter, his father Richard, had actually met Xavier once on one of their visits to the Butlers in their earlier days of visiting. Graham rather liked him, what little he had to do with him in this relatively brief encounter. He was struck by the diffident, unassuming and restrained nature of the young man, but realised that, as Fiona's brother, they could possibly be very similar in nature. He was quite a handsome young man and obviously used to heavy manual work.

Xavier found country-town life not entirely to his liking, so when Fiona asked Graham while he was entangled with the visitations of Jessie out there if he knew of any employment opportunities of a more rural property nature back his way, Graham felt more than obliged to facilitate her request, considering all she had done for him and his friends when they needed sanctuary. Xavier had accumulated a modicum of savings and was in a position to support himself for a short while if needs be while he looked for more attractive rurally-oriented employment in a more developed area. His father had also contributed a substantial sum towards his sustenance, realising that the property was not going to end up in either of his children's hands.

Graham offered Xavier a casual farm-hand's job with accommodation with himself while he hunted around for something more permanent, as there was always plenty that needed doing on his extended grazing enterprise. Graham was mindful that he may not always be in the position to afford the luxury of an employee, especially if there were a downturn. Xavier proved to be adaptable, willing and competent at all aspects of the scene and Graham was tempted to try to employ him permanently.

Things drifted slowly by, but Xavier was finding it difficult to locate a rural position as economic conditions seemed to be slowing down. Graham was pleased enough to keep him on as he was proving very useful indeed and all the rest of the family liked him, and found him most amiable.

The first incident in the entanglement that was, in due course, about to unfold, occurred late in the year when Xavier had been there for several months. Sophia was driving along the road into town from her property when she spotted the flock of sheep in the middle-distance heading slowly away from the homestead towards the east. This normally would not have piqued her interest as anything untoward, except, this fairly large flock was being shepherded by the usual dogs she could clearly see even from this distance, but, most unusually, being tailed by a man on horseback.

Sophia knew for certain that Graham was almost terrified of horses, especially big active beasts such as she rode. She was wondering if he had attempted to overcome this aversion and was trying his hand at this pastime. Sophia slowed down and observed the activity from the road side, but then decided to venture into the property to check if this were the case. She knew he had acquired those two horses some time ago now from the crooked neighbour, but was not sure what the outcome was of that acquisition. Maybe he was still holding onto them and even learning to ride one of them.

Sophia pulled up at the homestead gate that led from the house into the original shearing shed paddock and tried to attract the attention of the man that she assumed was Graham. He did eventually see that someone was at the house, so wheeled the horse around and slowly cantered back to the house.

Sophia deduced that this man was riding in a manner that indicated that he was not a novice. Surely Graham could not have mastered that trade so readily and admirably. She was puzzled. This could possibly not be Graham. She was unaware that he had any employees as she realised, he was not overly endowed with spare cash for such an indulgence. As he got to the gate, he drew in the reins and dismounted in a style that also indicated to her that he was practically an expert. She was then a little surprised to realise that it was not Graham. Maybe it was an accommodating neighbour that was helping out.

Xavier approached her with the snorting horse following him as he pulled gently on the reins. It was the gelding, the larger of the two that she had inspected when Graham first indicated the issue with the neighbour.

'Morning, miss.' he said. 'Can I help you?' His voice was gentle and dignified, and he spoke in an educated manner.

'Sorry, no' she replied. I thought that it was Graham out in the paddock. I did not mean to interrupt you out there.'

'That's all right miss.' he said. 'Can I tell him you called?'

'No, it's okay. I'll catch up with him later, thanks all the same.'

'Very well.' was all he said.

Sophia drove off a little confused and slightly embarrassed at her interrupting proceedings for all the wrong reasons. When Graham got home from town, Xavier informed him that he had had a visit from a young woman in a large off-white vehicle. When Graham enquired about her demeanour, he was informed that she was petite, polite, well-dressed and blonde. Graham deduced that it was probably Sophia. He would attend to her later.

The follow-up to this little drama occurred a couple of weeks later. Jackson Faulkner rang Graham to invite him and his family to a small pre-Christmas party at their place for the staff and the Faulkner family and a very few special chosen friends that they knew. Graham Longley admirably fitted the criterion of 'special chosen friend'. Graham did, however, decline the offer of his own family attending for a couple of reasons, but asked pointedly if he could instead bring a mate along that he thought that the Faulkners would like to meet. They of course agreed.

On the appointed day, Graham and Xavier travelled together in his ute to the party. Xavier was a little nervous about all this new experience and unsure how he would fit in with so many strangers there. The party was to commence about mid-afternoon and go on into the evening for those in a position to stay the distance. Graham was anxious for his new friend to mix in with the local gentry, as it might just open doors to a more suitable and permanent position with much better prospects for so talented a person than Graham could ever offer. Graham found Xavier very useful and productive, but he was not ever going to be in a position to offer him anything commensurate with his ability and knowledge. Besides, he had his two boys in the wings, and he hoped that they might follow on from him and eventually take over the running of the property, if that were their eventual desires. All indications at this stage were that that was exactly what was planned to occur.

On their arrival at the Faulkner's huge palatial homestead, there was already plenty of activity occurring about the grounds. Graham and Xavier headed for the front door and were greeted by a familiar employee whom Graham knew well. They were directed into the house and through to the back where the barbeque was all underway.

Jackson spotted Graham and wandered over to greet him. Simultaneously, Sophia also saw him and bounded over with some liveliness. Graham greeted them warmly, then introduced them to Xavier Jennings, Fiona Butler's brother, from the outback of New South Wales. Jackson was delighted to meet the brother of the wonderful Fiona. Sophia greeted him warmly, if not a little sheepishly, still slightly embarrassed by her interruption of a few weeks ago. She gently chided Graham for not informing them that he had such a distinguished guest at his place. Graham simply replied, with a slight grin on his face, that he knew they would find out soon enough. Jackson asked Xavier to accompany him so he could introduce him to Edith, his wife. Graham was delighted that Jackson took so much interest in his new friend.

Graham and Sophia had a chat. She asked him about Xavier. She also commented on his horsemanship and other matters and then asked Graham if he had attempted to ride either of his apparently newly-acquired steeds. Graham explained some of the developments concerning the long-drawn-out saga of the recalcitrant neighbour and that, yes, he was still in possession of the two wonderful animals, and that he was learning to ride the lovely docile little mare with much assistance from Xavier. He was rather pleased with himself over that particular skill as he unusually almost bragged to her of his miniscule attainments in that field. It did rather fill him with quite a sense of achievement to feel that he was on common ground on an issue he thought that he had no chance or desire to accomplish at the beginning.

It turned out to be, as anticipated, a rather pleasant and enjoyable time spent in the company of such a distinguished family and associates. As the evening progressed, Xavier adjusted to the camaraderie and became more at ease with his new companions. They departed the scene quite late in the evening, after a very pleasant sojourn. Nothing untoward seemed to eventuate. That, however, was not the case. The seeds had been sown for major developments.

* * *

In the meantime, things were moving on the Jessie front. Graham had hinted at the potential of his bringing out this Austrian visitor who had lost all their documentation when he contacted Fiona while Jessie slept. As Fiona was warm to the idea, Graham suspected that if he just turned up at the place, she might receive Jess with no qualms, possibly delighted with the added company, female at that, while Sid was away at her father's property.

As he and Jess decided with some degree of urgency, rather hurriedly to remove her from society and ensconce her out there for a short duration, they set off that evening with as little preparation as possible. It took about two and a half days to arrive at the house itself, as they had left at such an awkward hour. Graham drove all the way to Cobar before attempting to stop. Once there, he made a few adjustments.

Firstly, he had grabbed as much cash as he could muster from a small stash he kept on hand for emergencies. It amounted to about two thousand dollars. When he pulled up in the main street of Cobar, he rummaged about in his coat and pulled out an envelope. He turned to Jess and said,

'Jess, here's an envelope with two grand in it. I'm goin' to Woolies now to get some stuff. How 'bout you come with me an' get some items that you want, like tooth paste etc, an' leave them with me. I'll pay for all that. Just up the street there, is an op shop.' he said, pointing out the window. 'Why don't you then go up there and see if you can buy some suitable clothes for yourself. We can't just rock up there with you with nothing at all.'

She looked at him, and said, 'Thank you Graham.'

They alighted the car and went up the street.

Graham was some time in Woolies. Jess was able to buy for herself some rather presentable shirts and trousers, along with some other items, including a reasonable hat and sun glasses. They then departed town for Wilingubra homestead. They arrived there about three in the afternoon. Fiona was alone. Graham thanked her profusely for accepting a visitor at short notice and he introduced her as Annika Weiltze, an Austrian tourist with an interest in outback environments and ecosystems, working at an environmental centre in Austria. She had all her belongings stolen from a room in a city apartment, while she was visiting Captains Flat with a friend from town. She suspected an inside job. He really appreciated her being able to stay out here while all her papers were being replace from the embassy and the Department of Trade in Canberra. With no papers, or a car, it was impossible for her to move about for the time she was without them.

The two boys arrived home late in the afternoon from school, so Fione would have some daytime company while Sid was away and the boys at school. Graham only stayed for one day. He hinted that he had much to do back at the farm. He departed very early in the morning and drove straight to Woy Woy and to Ian Knuckey's apartment. There followed a most intense conversation. Graham filled him in with as much of the information that he had from the distraught Jessie. His main aim however, was to give to Ian the list of names so he could immediately start investigations. Graham departed as soon as he could.

Ian Knuckey was stunned by this latest development. He could not believe that she was still being persecuted and hunted by whomever. He thought that that might have abated now that both Bales and Stolt were dead. The first thing he did was contact the most trusted members of his investigation teams, especially the Integrity Unit. Ian was now of an advanced age. He had achieved mostly what he wanted to achieve in the earlier days of his re-instatement to the police circles. He well understood that, despite his long years, he was nearing the end of his usefulness and ability to continue in this work. To that end, he had ensured that he was able to ensconce an honest and most reliable senior man to oversee the continuation of the clean-out of any corruption still prevalent in the police and the legal system. He was gradually handing over to this man and his small team, the leadership of this important work. It was to this man that he now turned to ensure this was handled with the utmost urgency and discretion.

The first priority was to arrange for an instant arrest of the named officers that Jessie had provided. Accompanying that process was the imperative of also securing all their office and desk material to see if there were any trail of evidence for the actions that were perpetrated on Jessie. At this point, they had an enormous advantage, as the people committing this travesty all assumed that Jessie was dead. It was all arranged for the next early morning. This had proven a tricky manoeuvre. The Integrity Unit was often able to carry out procedures independently of the rest of the general police force, if they considered circumstances warranted such a move. Jess was so paranoid about the level and extent of either plain old-fashioned corruption or at least, gross inefficiency and dereliction of responsibility within the force, that she tried to persuade Ian and his heir, Detective Inspecter Garth van Heiken, to carry out the operation with as little notification as possible. The fewer people that knew about it the better. That directive included the Commissioner and her deputies. Garth van Heiken was a dour man of severe countenance. He was notorious for his honesty and protocol adherence. He had a rocky climb up the ranks because of his devotion to morality and procedure. When Jess hinted at her doubts about who was trust-worthy, through the medium of Graham, he acknowledged her concern and proceeded with almost no notification to anybody.

Ian Knuckey knew exactly who Whitehead was. That was

a Barry Whitehead, an unsavoury character that Knuckey had little respect for and who in return had little time for all this integrity nonsense. He could quickly enough collect the other named officers, Fenton, Burke, Floteteli, Sangi and Gomez. He was unsure who the 'sergeant' she heard referred to was, but could quickly enough figure that out. That left only one unnamed officer, the one she heard referring to some photographs confirming her attendance in the vehicle before it was destroyed.

Ian was also familiar with most of these names. He had suspicions already about some of them, but, as usual, there was no hard evidence of wrong-doing. He was also aware that at least Stolt, if not others, had gathered a cadre of like-minded persons about him and were also suspect in many matters. He knew for a fact that Jessie had always insisted that it was Stolt that had shot the two officers in the Newtown shop, and she was there. She now also knew from the late Tony, Antoine, also from Newtown days, the former neighbour of Graham Longley's in Captains Flat, that Stolt was responsible for the demise of Donald MacIntyre and Werner, plus the policeman that had accompanied him in the raid on Jessie's home in Australia Street. She now also knew of several others that she had gleaned from her dealings with that fiend Judge Bales. Though most of his inside information related to the judiciary and not so much to the police.

Ian's mind was racing. He must arrange for the actions to be swiftly carried out and well-co-ordinated. If he could arrange for these men to be isolated from each other and questioned, he figured that they might just leap to the conclusion that one of them had squealed on the rest. That way, they might all just open up and reveal all, especially if the photographer was at this point unknown and still on the loose.

It was all arranged. It was a massive operation involving multiple teams co-ordinated to all strike at three am and to escort those arrested to separate lockups. There was pandemonium within the police force; rumours were rife and scuttlebutt was ubiquitous. No one really had any idea what was happening or why these men were all arrested. The Commissioner, a female promotee of doubtful ability, was livid when she was informed after the fact that these actions had occurred without her knowledge or authorisation. The essential aspect of this action also involved separate teams thoroughly searching any relevant offices and desks.

By midday, the personnel of the police force were in total bewilderment. All the required targets were detained and all their areas searched. Barry Whitehead was escorted to his office by van Heiken himself and one other and requested to open the locked safe in his office. Therein was discovered the most prized piece of evidence that Knuckey could imagine – the list prepared by non-other than Stolt himself containing multiple names – right near the top was: Jessie MacIntyre. Beside her name – to be eliminated. He was ecstatic.

To this point in time, no one had even discovered the burnt-out vehicle, so there were no reports of a missing Jessie Summers yet or of a potential accident. Jessie had indicated that it was well secluded and isolated with little traffic in the area, besides, it was also a very steep drop to the creek bed there. Thomas Summers must still be contented that his wife was still staying over at her secluded eerie hide-out in the mountainous region away from his home.

Ian Knuckey was finally able to contact Jessie out at Wilingubra. He obtained a private mobile of a friend and rang her the next day to advise her of the outcome and the progress to date. She was also very pleased with the results. Ian then rang Thomas at Auvergne to inform him of developments and to assure him that all was well, she would be home again in a few days.

Jess stayed with Fiona for four days. She spent all the daylight hours with her, as Sid was still away with her father down south. During this time, there were a couple of developments regarding the isolated and reclusive Fiona. Jessie spent an inordinate amount of her evening time on her little laptop supplied by Graham. Fiona was curious as to what occupied her for so long. As Jessie seemed to be conversant with computer matters, Fiona asked her if she could assist her with some issues she was having with her new machine, as she had only recently acquired one as a means of her pursuing a newly-developing pastime, that of writing down her thoughts as an isolated country woman with the possibility of seeking publication.

Jess was intrigued that Fiona would be pursuing such a pastime. She certainly was keen to advise her in any way she could. Jess asked to peruse the output in order to offer any advice.

Now Jessie Summers was definitely *not* a literary reviewer

or commentator of any note. The number of novels Jessie had ever read over her long life would barely cover the fingers of one hand. Jessie had written many novels herself, but as she read so little, she had no yardstick or benchmark to use as a measure to gauge her ability or her place in comparison with other well-known and successful authors. At school, Jess was an above average student in all fields, but not necessarily particularly outstanding at English. She did, however, have a very good grasp of the subject, and her exposure to the mind of Norman Woods, the absconding Earl from England in her days at Milbark, and some of his rare classic publications sharpened her ability in that field.

Jess clearly recalled her first attempts at writing. It was with the short, trashy, cheap novels as Jane Ransom, aimed at the less discerning audience and predicated on simple, quick and open romantic themes. That endeavour spurred her on and was the genesis of her growing desire to achieve at a much higher standard. She attempted that ideal by producing the far more brilliant and startling output that culminated in the hugely successful iteration known as George Norman Thaler. On his demise, she could not assuage the burning desire to produce high-quality novels, so her final iteration in that field resulted in the enigma that was Catherine Holbrook Seymour. She still dabbled in that arena to this day.

She had no idea where the stunning quality of her brilliance in wordsmithing came from, but as for the stream of fabulous storylines, she did know of their source. She still had endless details from the enormous store of information from the classic mind of Norman Woods, plus the tails of the outback cattle industry from both Peter Taylor and Stuart MacIntyre.

Jess wrote to please herself. She wrote in a manner that reflected her personality and the way she would express her thoughts if she were more verbose. That this style was attractive to others was a bonus to her, not a form of a marketing ploy. In fact, her literary success and the consequential financial benefits were never central to her thinking, and that she had attained such notoriety and achievement was a constant wonder to her. Jess was very conscious that her ability to judge other's output was constrained by these perceived restrictions and weaknesses. She was very wary of commenting and remarking on any personality traits that others proffered to her for judgement. In fact, that offer was never really forthcoming before in her life.

Jess was able to give her some advanced instructions on how to perform the tasks she desired on her new laptop. Jess spent some time explaining how to set up her work in book-form format and how to arrange for the programme to automatically continue on in that form. Fiona was most pleased.

Jess asked if she could see some of her output as it amounted to a considerable quantity. Jess was rather impressed with the extent of that output. Fiona had obviously put a lot of time, effort and thought into this pastime. To Jess, it was rather more than just the girlie jottings of an unsophisticated rural lass with a limited literary ability. The writing was in a simple, innocent, almost naïve style, but struck her as genuine and sincere in its message. The content of course was basically unique and genuinely knowledgeable.

She encouraged Fiona to continue on with this project and hinted that she might be able to enquire about any possibility of publication. Jessie implied that she had a friend who might just be interested in this work. Would she be interested herself? Fiona was chuffed at that suggestion. Jess said no more at this stage to her. She did however, purloin a USB stick copy of her work, hoping to show it to a publisher or two in the city.

On the fifth day, Jess got Fiona to drive her to the Cobar airport and she arranged for a flight back to Sydney. Jess had fabricated a story along the lines that her papers from overseas had arrived and she wished to retrieve them as soon as possible. She would be in touch again soon in appreciation for all her efforts for Jess over this week. In Sydney, she met Thomas and they returned to her apartment at Rushcutters Bay. Jessie was VERY angry. She had never been this angry over all the attempts and the interference and impacts on her life from usually the same source. She was going to try to wreak retribution, havoc and revenge this time. She had been angry now for about one week.

Jess rang Ian Knuckey to discuss their next move. She did not care now if any of the phones were bugged. That was probably unlikely now if Ian had started any form of dissemination of facts to anybody.

Jess suggested that they begin by attempting to get the Commissioner of Police, the police minister and the Premier in one room and go from there, as she hinted to Ian that she had access to more information that was not publicly available. There was still no word for why these officers were arrested and no one had any suspicions. The vehicle was finally located after information from Ian, but, on its recovery, there was no evidence anywhere of a body inside or nearby. Supposition that marauding animals could have disturbed the scene was considered a possibility.

The Premier was informed that he may be required to arrange an urgent meeting with his police minister and the Commissioner over a rather serious matter that would impact his government and the police. He was advised that, although the details were sketchy at this stage, he should convene this as soon as possible or information would be disseminated to the public that was very detrimental to them all.

He finally agreed to this suggestion on the provision that he was informed fully why this was deemed necessary. Jess agreed to do that. The meeting was convened immediately. The Premier was a little disconcerted that this apparent travesty necessitated his attention, but, at the urging of van Heiken, and to some extent, Knuckey, he was encouraged to convene this meeting as Jess had indicated that she had access to much more information that was not in the public domain and she was threatening to release to all and sundry if she were not heard first. She may be persuaded to hold off doing that if she were guaranteed to finally receive some action over these life-long grievances.

The meeting was scheduled for eleven am. There were quite a few attendees, many hangers-on that Jess would later deem as unnecessary. They were all waiting expectantly for the proposed addressees, named as DI Garth van Heiken and possibly Ian Knuckey. The topics were listed as highly confidential and controversial matters pertaining mostly to the actions of some police officers that were going to impact severely on the government.

At eight minutes past eleven, there was still nobody coming into the room as listed and the overall state of affairs was now getting jittery and annoyed. Then the conference room door opened and two people entered, DI van Heiken and a strange woman that nobody except Ian Knuckey knew. DI van Heiken took a seat that was vacant on the near side of the table while Jessie stood close to the door surveying the scene. The man next to the Premier bade her to enter and be seated along the table near van Heiken. Jess just stood there. There was a momentary bewilderment among all those seated at the table as nothing seemed to be happening. Then Jess spoke, in a soft, clear but commanding tone that was easily heard in the sound-proof room.

'I am not here to socialise. I do not need a seat. This will be brief. My name…' there was a momentary lull. Then Jess continued, 'My name… does not matter. I may be known to some of you with long memories as… Jessie MacIntyre.'

Jess paused to ascertain any reaction. There was little. Then she continued,

'On the eleventh of this month, certain officers of this repulsive and, may I say, tainted organisation known as the New South Wales Police Force, yet again attempted to kill me.'

There was slight rumbling in the room, but nobody spoke. Jess continued,

'This is at least the third or fourth time this has happened.' Jess paused as she scrutinised the room. There was a deathly silence. 'It better be the last. For decades, you have known that that despicable personage known as Assistant Commissioner Stolt was a thorough crook. You did nothing about it. Instead of firing him, you promoted him. It is well known that he was personally responsible for the shooting murders of those two young policemen in Newtown in 1980. It is well known that he is responsible for the demise of Donald MacIntrye, as well as Werner Rhinhartd. It is well known that he was responsible for the destruction of the career of Inspector Knuckey here. He is also responsible directly for the death of Constable Hindler from that Newtown debacle through the agency of the Morangills. He was also responsible for many other crimes that I know about, but apparently, you either do not know about or decided to ignore.'

There was a momentary silence. Jess wandered along the length of the table scrutinising them all again. She turned and paced back along the table. Then she began again,

'Worse than all this, this crook then went about establishing his own cadre of like-minded thugs using the disguise of law-enforcement as a means of promulgating heinous crimes and assorted rorts, for decades – for decades. I have here in my hand two lists. One is in the handwriting of Stolt himself of the people he wants to eliminate. It is rather lengthy. Many have already been eliminated. Near the very top of that list is my name. Assistant Commissioner Barry Whitehead is his chosen protégé. He is the latest in a long line of assassins after me as well as others.

'Those officers arrested last week were carrying out the orders of Whitehead. It is only by the hand of God that I survived that attempt. The other list is a list of corrupt and doubtful judiciary figures working in cahoots with this inside evilness. This list is not generally known widely. I got it from the horse's mouth, so to speak, directly from the corrupt Judge Bales junior.' There was a long pause. Then she continued, 'I say junior, because his father, Judge Bales senior was a notoriously corrupt individual, again nothing ever having been done to bring either of them to judgement. That these two individuals have been eliminated is vastly overdue, but not surprising, given the circles in which they moved and the kinds of people with which they mixed.'

'Now, here's the deal. I will give you one week from today to sort this mess out and start arresting all these crooks, or I go public with these lists and assorted other stories that I have accumulated over a lifetime of dealing with your crooked lot of cops and legal systems. I assure you, this will not end well for any of you, so the sooner you get on with it, the less the damage will be to the cops, the judiciary and the government. Mr Knuckey here has access to a lot of the details, as does Mr van Heiken.'

The Premier looked totally bewildered. He stared at the apparition standing defiantly along the lengthy conference-room table. Then he turned to look at the police minister and, when she returned a glazed look of total puzzlement, he turned to the Police Commissioner. Her countenance revealed even more bafflement. He then turned to Jess and asked, rather pointedly, 'Sorry, who are you again?'

'That is irrelevant, Premier. All you need to know is that I am not bluffing and that I have access to interminable details about your rotten force, and a lifetime of cover-ups. All you need to know is that it better be fixed this time or all hell is going to break out. Mr Knuckey here will be dealing with this matter, along with Mr van Heiken.'

Jess then turned her angry and penetrating gaze towards the Police Commissioner and said to her in a slow and deliberate manner,

'And I better not hear anything more about removing another of your perceived senior threats from any of the investigations I want to see instigated here either. Your treatment of the former Assistant Ben Richards was a disgrace.'

With that, Jess turned decidedly towards the door and exited, leaving them all in total bewilderment at what had just transpired. The Premier turned to Mr Knuckey and asked,

'What the hell just happened here?'

Ian Knuckey cleared his throat, and delayed his response. Then he began,

'Mr Premier, that was the famous Miss Jessie MacIntyre – yes the real Jessie MacIntyre. If you don't know her story, look it up. She is the only witness still alive to the murders of those two policemen killed in Newtown in 1980. She was there and saw then inspector Stolt shoot those two men. She is privy to an enormous amount of dirt on the police and the judiciary, going back decades. How she came by the information on Judge Bales, I don't know, but it is startling and devastating. The connection between the police and the judiciary is stunning and going to cause you all a lot of trouble.'

'What details? And what do you suggest we do about it?' asked the Premier.

'She has given me some names and cases that were suspect at the time, but that she has managed to find out more detail on. The connections between crooked cops and the judiciary are a revelation, even to me. I will pass on these names to the Commissioner here.

# CHAPTER FIVE

Jess was used to visiting her spacious apartment located at Rushcutters Bay. It was a relatively conservative unit situated on the fifth floor of an older but prestigious and very secure building with some views across the harbour and towards the city. It had a north-easterly aspect and was quite airy and bright. It was also quite an expansive unit, possessing two large bedrooms and a large dining/lounge room. It also possessed a smaller room that was designed as a study. It was here that Jess tended to do any creating in which she was engaged while staying there in Sydney. She did not always just go up there to work however. She really did rather love the whole atmosphere of the vibrant city and all its attractions – and for her there were many.

However, the sanctuary status of this possession was now greatly diminished. After the latest devastatingly traumatic attempt on her life, Jess acknowledged that those out to get her knew that she also owned these premises. They seemed to be aware of all her details. She felt totally betrayed and vulnerable with this fact a reality. She sensed that the security of the place was compromised. She felt now destined to never having the haven that she deemed it to originally be.

Jess gave this dilemma considerable thought. She was of a mind to dispose of this asset, but would miss the facilities and the novelty of the city environment. She was in no position to simply replace it with another in the same name. Jess came to a rather rapid conclusion that, if she wanted to experience this diversion, and have a sense of separate security from her rural abode, she would have to purchase another amenity in a totally different name.

Jess had a separate bank account in the name of Kimberley West, a hangover from her now long-departed Milbark Station days back in the Kimberley district of Western Australia. It was yet another of her litany of deceitful little acts perpetrated on the unsuspecting Stuart MacIntyre. How she managed to escape from her devastating trial with that name intact and undetected, she often marvelled. It also contained a sizable chunk of her substantial income. She considered that she could possibly try to buy another apartment nearby in that name as she thoroughly enjoyed the atmosphere and the sanctuary of this kind of digression.

Another consequence of the latest attempt on her life was the loss of her beloved Land Rover Discovery Four. Although it was now aging, it had been a pleasure for her to drive, especially on the long trips from Auvergne to the city. She was loathe to replace it immediately, as the latest models were a lot more modern and electronic, and computer-controlled, not an aspect of driving, especially rough bush driving, of which she was particularly enamoured. In response to that dilemma, Jess had resurrected her even older Toyota Troop Carrier, a leftover from her sojourn when departing the Kimberleys for the last time. It was rather cumbersome for city driving and a trifle slow, but the big diesel engine was very economical on the long trips. The only real concession she made to the changed circumstances was to replace the knobbly bush tyres with more suitable ones designed for the highway. Then an incident occurred that hastened her thinking along these lines by an unfortunate encounter with the despised police yet again.

It had been a month since the attempted assassination of Jessie when this occurred. She had taken to attending her Rushcutters Bay apartment alone for some diversion and relief from the strain of it all. She had tentatively been considering buying a completely new unit, as everybody seemed to know about this one. As usual, Jess arrived up there in the early hours of the morning and always departed her unit well after midnight in order to avoid any traffic and to arrive home to Auvergne in daylight hours, after all, it was at least a six-to-eight-hour drive, depending on stops. This timeline was exacerbated right now by the fact that she was using her old Toyota Troopy, which was slower and noisier.

The very first time Jess utilised this method of trying to

attain some digression for her tormented soul, a harrowing incident occurred to her on her return journey that had major implications and led to hastening a development that she, at first, did not fully contemplate to any form of completion.

As usual, Jess departed the unit at about two o'clock in the darkness of morning. When she reached the unencumbered serenity of the M5 motorway well past the airport, she tended to relax a little and just let her mind wander, and, maybe create. It was not long after she had gained the comfort of the easier driving along the M5 that the incident occurred.

The speed limit on this stretch of the motorway was normally 110 kph all the way to the Canberra turn-off. Jess was a conservative and careful driver, and usually in no real hurry to get anywhere. She normally travelled at about 95 to 100 kph for several reasons. This evening, Jess noticed that for some distance behind her was a single vehicle travelling in her direction from behind and catching up to her with some speed. The problem was that this vehicle had its lights on high beam, and they were particularly bright and annoying to her for some distance.

When the vehicle did not rapidly catch her and overtake, she slowed down some more to 80 kph, trying to encourage the car to pass. This did not happen. The car seemed to slow down as well and remained behind her. She was getting jittery, as there were almost no other cars on the highway going south.

Finally, after about three kilometres of this, the vehicle pulled out from behind her in order to overtake her. Jess thought, *at last*. But, after the car had passed Jess, it entered her lane and slowed down again. Jess flashed her lights, including her spots to indicate that she had been inconvenienced by the other's high beams. But instead of moving on and leaving her alone in the welcomed darkness, the vehicle flashed its hazard lights and then activated a siren and flashing blue and red lights emanating from inside the car and externally along the grill. It was an unmarked police car. Jess was horrified. She did not trust any police, if that was what they really were. And she was basically alone out here, because of the hour. She was very angry, again, and fearful.

The car pulled up in front of her lumbering Troopy as Jess moved to the left-hand lane. It was a dark, late-model sporty-type small sedan of indeterminate make, at least Jess could not immediately recognise it. All of its available lights flashing garishly for all and sundry to observe. She awaited the arrival of whomever. Finally, a shortish and, Jess thought, rather plumpish figure emerged from the vehicle, sporting a surfeit of assorted paraphernalia about her already generous middle and donning a cap of some sort and almost waddled over to her side of the car, wobbling awkwardly, Jess thought, just like a ruptured duck. Not a very auspicious advertisement for the vaunted New South Wales Police Force, if that were what she really was. Jess wound down her window slightly and waited, exhibiting mounting caution following her interaction with this mob on the back roads near her bush block. The officer, a woman with a garish and gravelly voice, began to speak, but Jess cut her short by saying,

'Have you got your bodycam on?'

There was no reply. The police woman stared at her slightly. She had a round puffy face and very short hair. Jess, being seated in her Troopy, sat at quite a high position, almost towering over the woman, approximately at her eye level. Then the police woman said,

'Turn the engine off please, and show me your Licence.' Jess noticed that the woman seemed to lean in towards her deliberately and purposefully. Jess asked again,

'Have you got your bodycam on?'

The woman again looked puzzled, but replied,

'Yes madam. Engine off. Licence please.'

Jess wound up the window, then opened the large door, the policewoman having to move aside as she did so, the big diesel still purring away under the bonnet. She climbed out of the driver's seat and closed the door. Then she turned to the policewoman and said,

'Why have you stopped me?'

She replied, 'You were observed to be driving erratically. Can you please turn off that motor. And may I see your licence please.'

'No.' said Jess, ignoring her demand to turn off the engine. 'Explain to me your definition of driving erratically.'

'You were driving at under 95 kilometres in a 110 zone and then dropped down to 80, causing a driving hazard to other motorists.'

'And what other motorists would that be then?'

'Your licence please.' she demanded again.

'No. You mean it is now unlawful to drive *under* the speed

limit? Ask me why I was *driving erratically* as you put it.' There was no reply. Jess continued in place of a non-response.

'You realise that you followed me for about five kilometres. That whole time, your lights were all on full high beam. Don't tell me you did not know that. Have you any idea how distracting that is? Talk about driving erratically. Have you any idea what that does to my night vision? Mate. And in case you haven't noticed, this is a heavy four-wheel-drive. It is cumbersome and slower driving is much more suited to its design. It is not designed for the bitumen. I tried desperately to get rid of you by slowing down. You finally decided to pass me, and I even flashed my lights to tell you your lights are on high beam. My thanks were to find out you are an unmarked police car sculking about in the dark harassing innocent travellers with your haughty attitude of superiority and entitlement over others.'

'Licence please.' was her only reply.

'Did you hear what I was just saying? No. You got Buckleys mate. You are not seeing my licence. You have no right to harass the public at two am in the morning for simply driving under the speed limit, and you with your lights intimidating other users.'

'You were observed to be driving erratically. I am now demanding you provide me with your identification or you can be detained.'

Jessie's blood was now boiling.

'You and what army, mate.'

That seemed to startle the officer. In response, the

policewoman began to reach down to her side. Jess was alarmed at that development, and she responded with, 'If you draw your Glock, you will end up in that gutter.'

The officer hesitated and withdrew her arm, she was not much taller than Jess herself. Jessie's countenance was now very intimidating and her voice was resplendent with menace and threat. Jess noted the officer's identification number and had already noted the number plate on the vehicle. She then said, with a genuine menacing tone,

'I am now leaving. I suggest you do the same, before someone really gets hurt. And you better have kept your bodycam on mate. You're going to need it.'

With that, Jess turned her back to the officer and opened the door of her Troopy. She then got into the car and simply reversed it away from the police car and slowly drove off as the officer moved hurriedly out of the way as Jess drove past her retreating body.

Jess was furious. She was more annoyed and angry than she had been for many a long day. She was shaking and felt quite queasy. She knew that she would have to calm down or she really was going to have an accident. She drove on in a daze, all the time half expecting another interaction with more police, this time probably with more backup. She felt quite ill. What Jess did not know at that precise moment was yes, indeed, she had already called for more backup, but during the previous half hour, there had been a fatal triple car accident on the M7 involving a B-double as well. There was also a dangerous car chase occurring at the same time in several western suburbs close to these highways. Jess would learn this from Garth in due course. She did wonder why the police had not attempted to intervene again with her travels. They had allowed the incident to drift into abeyance following the triple fatality and the concurrent car chases, but had already contacted the Cooma precinct as they had all her details. Garth, in due course, also put a stop to that source of enquiry, much to their confusion.

When she had travelled some distance out of the city proper, there was the first real rest area on the road south. It was well utilised and popular with travellers. Jess pulled into this rest area and wandered about for a while. She still felt quite ill. She had a small sandwich which she habitually prepared for the long trip home, and a cup of tea from her thermos. When Jess reached the Canberra turnoff, she stopped at that small rest area just past the turnoff and rang her newer contact in the Integratory Commission, Garth van Heiken.

There were two major repercussions out of this encounter, one professional, one personal. The professional one involved the unfortunate officer that tried to impose her authority on an innocent member of the public. There was hell to pay the next day after this seemingly innocuous occurrence on the near-vacant M5 motorway at two am.

Garth van Heiken was also furious when he was informed by an emotional and near broken Jessie Summers in the early hours of the new day while she was parked on the lonely road to Canberra. She wanted retribution, but more than that, she wanted heads to roll, serious heads. She was not going to be thwarted and denied this time. She had already made major contact with the Sky News television network, where her original attempted assassination was sensationally revealed in all its gory details and huge ramification emanated from that revelation. She had warned the Premier, the police minister and the bumbling Police Commissioner that she would go straight to the press if nothing was done, and nothing *seen* to be done – in one week from that fateful meeting in the Premier's office. Little was in evidence of action being done, or in any case, seen to be done. The Sky News people had a field day with all this information at the time. Jess had already contacted them over this latest shattering episode.

The offending highway patrol officer was detained mid-morning from her flat in Western Sydney and taken straight to the Police Commissioner's office building in the city to await developments. She had no real idea what was really wrong, but surmised it must have involved that altercation on the M5 at two am. Her vehicle was impounded earlier in the day to undergo a thorough mechanical check. Her weapon was seized, and, more importantly, her bodycam evidence was also seized and examined.

Finally, late in the afternoon, she was summoned to the office of the Police Commissioner. In attendance were her supervising officer, two others and, importantly, Garth van Heiken. He seemed to be in control of the interview. He began, tersely, by asking the constable to be seated, then said,

'Do you know why you are here?'

'No, sir.' she replied.

'Now I want you to consider very carefully your answers here constable. Do you recall the incident this morning at approximately two-thirty am on the M5 motorway where you apprehended a Toyota Troop Carrier with one female occupant?'

'Yes sir.'

'Why did you pull that vehicle over?' he asked again rather tersely.

She was a little nervous and reluctant to reply. Finally, she responded, rather brusquely and with an air of authority,

'The vehicle was travelling erratically. I suspected possible intoxication, plus the vehicle flashed its lights at me. I try to dispense unbiased and even-handed policing and enforce the law to my best ability, sir. If I think I detect wrong-doing.'

'By erratically, you mean she was travelling well under the speed limit?'

'Yes sir. That often indicated an intoxicated driver.'

'Well, for your information, that particular driver would find that accusation rather offensive to say the least. As for driving erratically, I'll let you know that that woman possesses a road train licence, for an eighteen-speed manual gearbox, and learned to drive on an ancient crash box. She has enormous driving experience. She is anything but an erratic driver.'

'I would not know that, would I sir?' she asked disrespectfully.

'Well, you know now Constable. When you were informed that she tried to dispose of you following her because your lights were on high beam, why did you not just simply acknowledge that explanation and thank her for the advice, and move on.'

'My lights were not on high beam sir.'

'You deny your lights were on high beam? Consider your response carefully constable.'

'No sir. Not to my knowledge.'

'Well, that is interesting. You may very well have just dispensed your version of unbiased enforcement on the wrong person.'

'She also was unco-operative and threatened me.'

'Consider yourself lucky that was all she did, Constable.'

The others in the room turned a quizzical stare at Garth.

'What do you mean, Sir.' asked the puzzled officer.

'That woman could have put you in a wheel chair, Constable. Threatening her with your sidearm was not an advisable move.'

'I deemed it appropriate to ascertain her sobriety and in attempting that process, she showed no effort to comply with my lawful request to see her licence. She was belligerent and threatening.'

The Commissioner intervened at this point, supporting the seated officer in front of her. She began, sarcastically,

'We can't have members of the public just going around threatening the police Detective. Can we?'

Garth responded immediately, and with some venom,

'And we can't have the police force just going around threatening and intimidating innocent members of the public who are fully,' he paused, '… fully, obeying the law. Especially *this* member of the public.'

'And just who is this special member of the public that seems to have captured your support so vigorously?' asked the Commissioner, a little nervously.

'Never mind that right now. You will find out soon enough. When this blows up in all our faces. The fact is, that this particular member of the public was committing no crimes other that being in the sights of a now suspect officer.'

He continued, looking at the constable seated nervously in front of him,

'You realise that we have listened to your bodycam constable?'

'Yes sir. That will back me up in this point.'

'Do you really believe that, officer Babibe?'

'Yes Sir.'

'I can see we have a serious problem here Commissioner.' he said, turning to face the bewildered chief again.'

Garth van Heiken sat momentarily in silence, while the others observed this little drama unfold with amazement. Then, with an air of total disgust and annoyance, he promptly ordered her to be taken away to be further interrogated. He advised that he was still awaiting the results of the mechanical checks and confirmation of the bodycam conversation in full. Then he said,

'I can't believe this mess. It's not four weeks since the last kerfuffle. Not four weeks. She has already released that program on Sky News about that. I can tell you here and now that she has also already contacted Sky News over this incident, including a full transcript of the entire affair. Is there no rest from the troubles that you impose on this woman?'

With that comment, it began to dawn on the room just whom they could be talking about over this mess. No wonder she did not want to reveal herself to someone she could not be certain was even a *bone fide* police officer.

The Commissioner was amazed at that comment. She enquired,

'Well, she can't have our full transcript, DI, can she.'

'She doesn't need our stuff, Commissioner.' he blurted. 'You don't think this woman doesn't have full copies of her own of all these painful interactions. I only hope she does not doctor anything in there to make it worse.'

'She has her own copies?'

'Of course. What do *you* think? Do you blame her?' he responded rather angrily.

The room was filled with deathly silence. They all knew what trouble was brewing over this latest injustice. There was a lot more to play out in this saga yet.

On the personal level, this incident had a significant impact on the private life of Jessie Summers. She was devastated by the whole affair. She never discovered whether this officious little pestilential policewoman was a plant to torment her, or just another of her interminable unpleasant interactions with the police.

She spent much time contemplating the entire affair. She concluded that she may have to dispose of the much-loved apartment in Rushcutters Bay entirely, much to her gross disappointment. After much thought, Jess came up with some dramatic options. She passed them by the sympathetic Garth van Heiken. He agreed to instigate the most favourable options that he was capable of legally achieving.

He and Jess spent some time together and finally came up with a plan that satisfied her desires and that he was in a position to achieve. He agreed to her suggestion of issuing to her a brand-new driving licence in an altogether different identity. She had decided on the name of Kimberley West. The reason for this choice was that she already had an operating bank account in that name, a secure source of income from her novels in that name and, if she had a matching licence, she would be able buy a new apartment in that name, a name she hoped was untraceable to her. Besides, Kimberley West was not that rare a name, it could easily be several other people, muddying the waters. Jess also arranged for the registration of the old Troopy to be re-issued with new plates. These details were then hidden in secured data, not for general use.

Jess did a lot of research, culminating in a few trips on foot wandering about the area reasonably close to the area where she was now very familiar. When an apartment within a kilometre of her Rushcutters Bay unit was hinted to possibly being available off-market to the right person, Jess investigated. She had placed her name on a couple of agency off-market lists hoping to avoid all the hassles of inspecting open properties and bidding against others.

The agency that she ended up dealing with realised that

this woman had some class and was possibly very wealthy from a couple of her comments. Her requirements were quite specific. When, a few months later, the right place that may appeal to her was touted as coming onto the market, she was contacted.

The place she was finally able to purchase was almost perfect for her needs. It was located just around the corner on a nearby headland that jutted out from the bay into the blue waters of the harbour. It had views across the harbour, mostly eastward towards the heads, with a slight view towards the city. But more significantly, it was a later constructed building, catering for a specific kind of clientele. It was an extremely secure building with a huge underground facility that consisted of two-car accommodation, and a large storage cage underneath coupled to the garaging site.

Being a luxury establishment, it did possess a strong security element that reassured Jess that her investment in this lifestyle would be as protected as possible, considering her infrequent visits. This was not a monetary investment, but an asset she acquired in order to be alone, private and secure from intrusion.

This unit also came with some physical attributes of considerable benefit to the lifestyle Jess sought. Apart from the size and scale of the construction, it had an open parking area outside the building if she ever arrived with the roof-rack loaded beyond the height of the entrance to the underground parking. But more importantly, it also came with parking facilities for two vehicles, plus, significantly, a rather large lockup cage underground that catered for a considerable amount of storage facilities for the owners. Many of the cages were occupied with such items as small boats, antique vehicles, motor cycles, much valuable furniture and assorted other equipment, depending on the whims and hobbies or indulgences of the relevant owner.

The building itself was located on a prominent small headland and at a height well above the harbour water level. Nevertheless, Jess was mindful that this facility may be prone to flooding if conditions were severe enough, though it was supposed to be flood-free. That was really of little import to Jess, as she stored almost nothing in her cage, it being nearly entirely empty apart from a few boxes of no real significance. This was in total contrast to all her fellow lock-up holders, most of whom crammed much material into their respective cages.

The reason for divulging this detail was because things were about to change in a significant way for Jess, and it all involved her visitations and activities associated with this attractive routine.

The plan was that Jess would try to visit this unit as often as possible. It was difficult, as Auvergne station was a large property with a diverse and demanding workload and it required the attendance of Thomas for most of the time. Jess did not like to visit the place without Thomas, not because she did not wish to be alone, that factor was indeed the opposite, but because, as she was married to Thomas, she felt obliged to be near him as his wife as well as a working partner in the farm activities. Thomas was not quite so enamoured of the city scene and was much less enthusiastic about going there. This was not the case with Jess, who absolutely loved the whole idea of the place, despite her antisocial approach to life – she felt alone and happy even in the midst of so many thronging people.

Furthermore, Auvergne was primarily a fine-wool producing property, mostly with high-tech procedures. Jess had little interest in the sheep side of the property, which, considering that that was its primary aim, was a slight anomaly. The property carried some commercial flocks of open-range sheep, but also a small herd of beef cattle on the rougher country. Jess was originally employed by Thomas to manage the cattle side while he tried to master as much as he was capable of achieving of the technical sheep-breeding program. Over time, as Jess assumed she would be moving on, she had encouraged and supported the employment of at least two of the increasing Summers clan offspring to ease her way out of the need for her presence.

Jess became far less important as time drifted by, to the point that Thomas could manage without her. Her marrying Thomas was not an eventuality she had ever contemplated. It had been a shock to her to learn of his affection towards her and an occurrence that she had never considered. These assorted little details meant that, in essence, Jess could be away from the station with little impact on the day-to-day workings of the place. She could therefore visit the new unit as often as she desired, the only consideration being its impact on her husband, Thomas.

In the first six to twelve months following the latest harrowing attempt on her life, Jess found solace in being alone in the confines of her Rushcutters Bay unit, and then, latterly, the new one that she acquired with much searching, which she found an unusually cathartic exercise. The new unit was destined to impact hugely on her life subsequently to its purchase.

Jess was enthralled with her new purchase and was very keen to spend some time there, but she was conscious of deserting Thomas and his desires to have his wife alongside him for all the normal property activities. He was also mindful that she had had a traumatic experience and was accommodating to her desires to alleviate any of her lingering distress.

Jess was able to visit the new unit about once a month or so for up to a week at a time. She spent some time removing all her personal items from the old unit and much of the furniture that was suitable for the new one. She initially utilised the spacious storage cage in her basement for any bulky items, but eventually basically kept it entirely empty. She would, in time, soon enough sell the old original Rushcutters Bay unit in her name of Jane Ransom, severing her last known contact in that name. This now new situation was about to lead to an amazing development.

Jess made no effort at all to meet any of her neighbours and, because of the deliberate design of the complex, this was a situation that was easily achieved and maintained. The only chance for her to ever interact with any of the other residents was if by chance they ever met up in either the garaging facilities or by the lock-up cages – not a very likely occurrence. The cage next to Jessie's on the right was crammed full to the brim. It was not overly well lit in the cavernous confines of the darkened basement, so the contents were not all that discernible to her, just that it appeared to be chockers. She could determine, however, that the contents seemed to predominate with mechanical items; tools, car- and body-parts and boxes of assorted paraphernalia of some sort. The other neighbouring unit was also fairly well occupied, mostly with wood-working machinery, such as routers, and small piles of assorted fancy timbers and chunks of tree pieces.

The first time Jess accidently and annoyingly, bumped into the right-hand side neighbour, it had a huge impact on her future. The people that owned that cage were down there one morning when Jess went down to retrieve some small boxes of ornaments after buying a new display cabinet. Her cage was by now almost empty. She perceived that the neighbour's cage area was well lit up, so she almost returned to her apartment. She decided however, to proceed to her cage, hoping that the brightness was coming from somewhere away from her own enclosure.

She unlocked her large padlock and the noisy jangling of the excessively heavy chain alerted the occupants next door to her presence. She returned to the cage gate with a large box and prepared to place it outside the cage and to lock it up again. She was startled to discover a couple emerging from their side and shuffling over to greet her.

They were an elderly couple, well dressed in casual gear and chatting about their things inside the cage. They saw her and the woman said a polite hello and smiled a friendly greeting to her. Jess responded with a mere nod. The lady passed a few more pleasantries and seemed to be a lovely person. Jess was not in the mood to socialise and was not very receptive to her advances. While the neighbour's cage was so well lit up, Jess tried to make a more determined attempt to scrutinise the contents of their cage and was bewildered by the quantity of items that seemed to be pertaining to an antique vehicle of some sort that was within this cage. The fact that it was a mechanical collection slightly piqued her interest.

On realising that the contents may be related to things mechanical, Jess decided to be a bit more polite and at least acknowledge the couple, as they were actually very personable. They slowly got to chatting. It transpired that the couple were long-time residents of the complex, since its construction, and his pastime in his retirement was to restore this antique Rolls Royce. He had all the parts and all the interior was all restored, it was just awaiting its re-assembly. Sadly, he had been taken seriously ill and now was unable to complete this task. They were at a loss as exactly what to do because the man did not want to die leaving his wife with this mess and a cage full of stuff that was hard to dispose of. A thought suddenly flashed across Jessie's mind. This could be an amazing opportunity to indulge in a really time-consuming and enthralling assignment, filling in any spare time she had while staying up here in Sydney.

She suddenly looked at them in a different light. She

scrutinised them more thoroughly now and raised her level of sincerity to a much more serious attention. They had a long chat. Finally, Jess asked tentatively,

'Maurene and Harold, I was just thinking. Would you be prepared to sell me all this material pertaining to the Rolls?'

Harold looked at her then at Maurene. He was momentarily lost for words.

'What do you want for all the parts and the tools in there?' asked Jess.

'It's worth a lot of money, but not in that state. And it is very difficult to organise a removal.'

'Is it all there?' asked Jess.

'Yes, it's all there. I've had all the upholstery done, all the panels are prepared and just about all the mechanicals are repaired or replaced. All the glass is wrapped up and over there and the tyres are very good.'

'How much?'

'Considering all the trouble in moving it and the difficulty in finding someone to buy it in this state, I'd take about fifteen thousand for it. It is worth a hell of a lot more than that.' said Harold.

'That includes everything?' asked Jess.

'Yes.' replied Harold. 'Why would *you* want to buy this?'

'I would enjoy the effort of assembling it myself.'

'We'd help you as much as we can to move it all dear.' said Maurene.

'Why don't we just swap cages?' asked a more animated Jess.

The couple looked at each other.

'Why not!' stated Harold. 'Let's just swap cages. You can move your locks to this gate and we can move our lock to yours.' His mood had changed most noticeably and his demeaner was becoming much cheerier at this prospect. Jess finally said,

'I'd like to buy all that. Are you happy with fifteen thousand for it all. I can deposit it directly into your own account if you wish.'

The deed was done. Jess simply removed her small collection of boxes to the new cage, swapped locks and the Doolans ended up with a brand-new empty cage and huge peace of mind. Jess was delighted with this turn of events. For the first time since the attempted murder, she finally felt a sense of purpose; a feeling of doing; employment of use, and she enthused at the mere prospect of the new endeavour. Jess began by doing a complete inventory. She found all the necessary manuals and was impressed with the quality and quantity of the tools that were there. Once Harold discovered just how competent a mechanic Jess was, he was delighted to become involved with the little his declining health would allow. He was staggered at the amount of time Jess was prepared to spend on the project and the rapid rate at which it progressed. Harold Doolan was totally unaware of the solace and diversion this small activity was to the still fevered persona of Jessie Summers. For some reason, Jess was still traumatised from her recent escape, far more than she had from previous attempts, and immersing herself in this project went some way to helping her from reliving all those horrors.

Jess had never before worked on an item which possessed such mechanical and engineering elegance and sophistication, especially for the times in which it was manufactured. The more she delved into its intricacies, the more she admired its refinements; its sheer power and grace. It was a 1937 Rolls Royce Phantom III four-door hardtop. She marvelled at the massive 447cu inch V12, nearly 7340 cc of meticulously engineered power, so quietly delivered. This one had a four-speed manual gearbox, something she found incongruous in such a luxury car. There was synchromesh on gears 2, 3 and 4 plus an overdrive which was contained in the gearbox. She could not wait to see it running.

Maurene was so pleased that her sick husband had this wonderful diversion that he could attend at the times that he could manage, despite the irregular and limited times Jess was actually there. She often came down to see how it was all going, bringing morning or afternoon teas occasionally. It was during one of these diminishing attendances of both the Doolans that something of major significance occurred.

Jess knew that he was dying and trying to finalize his affairs. Maurene mentioned in passing that they were trying to sort out their boatyard. Jess had heard it mentioned once or twice before, but its significance was missed by her in the scheme of things. She thought that maybe they owned a small boat of some sort and that was the extent of it. She certainly had no interest at all in anything nautical, especially if it floated. Jess then asked of the old couple, that she had begun to grow rather fond of, and more out of politeness rather than any real interest in the topic,

'What's wrong with your boatyard?' thinking they meant a small boat in somebody's storage yard. Maurene proffered,

'We own a small slippage and salvaging yard over the bay dear, including lighterage barges, we have had some offers for it, but they are from developers and a crooked local councillor. We are trying to find someone who'll keep it as a business for the tenants we have there, they have been there for years, since the 1920s, one of them.'

'May I ask where it is?' she asked, again really more out of respect for their obvious concern over some matter to do with this yard.

'Certainly dear, it's just over the next bay. I'll tell you all about it as it was my grandfather's. It's the one near the yacht club. It's called the Hindmarsh Boatyard, that was my grandfather's name.

Jess was suddenly intrigued. Her interest was slightly heightened at the mention of the commercial aspects of this bigger object than just a small boat. Maurene spent some time describing the business to her. It was obvious just how much it all meant to her and she was emotionally attached to the whole thing. Next day, Jess went over there to have a look around and see what it was all about. She rather liked it. For some reason, this surprised her that she found it so motivating.

That afternoon, Jess contacted Garth van Heiken about an issue with a neighbour friend of hers and the troubles they were having with authorities. Maurene had hinted at some fraudulent and corrupt local councillor's involvement in trying to close down the site and resume it for public use.

Jess did recall, with the mention of that fact, that she had read about some problems in the local area with dubious local council people and attempts to close small businesses and residential buildings for more public access. This must be one of those sites. Garth agreed to investigate and to get back to her, as a favour. Jess emphasised to Garth that this enquiry was on behalf of one of her elderly neighbours living in her new apartment building, and that there was no urgency about the request.

This he did almost immediately. Maurene was right. There were moves afoot to try to resume this site. Both the local council and the state government were in cahoots in trying to obtain this valuable property. The talk about town was that it was being resumed for the greater good, but in actuality, it was really being sought by the suspect local mayor for his own benefit. There was a hint of state government influence, council corruption, but, worst of all, there were also hints of law enforcement involvement in the harassing of the owners and of the tenants, things such as stand-over tactics and protection rackets. The criminal undertones intrigued Garth van Heiken. Garth gave Jess a comprehensive briefing about goings-on at that site.

Two days later, Jess knocked on the door of the couple in the building they shared. When they realised Jess may be genuinely interested, they gave her more details and the name of their solicitor if she were keen to proceed any further. Their solicitor was an old family friend of theirs, and, they assured her, very reliable and trustworthy. Jess was not so sure about that, but, as she had no access to any legal services, she thought she might just try him out.

The solicitor's name was Karl Lukas. He was an elderly man, very personable and friendly and acknowledged to Jess that he was indeed a long-standing family friend of the Doolans, and had been their legal representative for many years. He looked at Jess in a deep and thoughtful manner, carefully appraising her. She was a little nervous at his assessing her; she hoped his interest did not extend beyond real estate. He was quietly spoken and slow of pace; he struck her as very diligent. They chattered meaninglessly for some time before he seemed to get serious. Finally, he stated,

'Ms West, I have spoken at length with the Doolans over your interest and at some pains over many years dealing with this particular property. I sense that you may have slightly more than just a cursory interest in this place. Are you genuinely interested in possibly buying this property from them?'

'That depends. I certainly have more than a passing interest.'

'I would wish to be honest with you Ms West. There are issues here that I feel you need to understand.'

Jess just nodded in cautious dread. She may know some of these already from the information divulged by Garth.

'This shipyard in particular has been on and off the market now for many years. The Doolans have owned it as a family since early in the last century. They have had several offers over the last few years. These offers ultimately usually come from basically the same source. You see, Ms West, the local mayor and councillor, a Mr Chung, is very keen to get his hands on this place, in fact the whole site. He has made life very difficult for the Doolans, knocking back approvals, delaying submissions and doing all he can to damage the site with council activities.

'The Doolans are loyal to their tenants. There is a slipway, some industrial barges, that's the Hindmarsh Boatyard; a rather good restaurant, that's the Exeter House, and a small block of four very old units on the far side. Mr Chung wants to remove all that and possibly place a huge multistorey unit block there, or even a casino, all under the guise of returning the resumed land to the public for recreational use. He has access to some state government clout as well, and we fear he would finally succeed in that aim if he gets hold of it. The Doolans cannot hold out much longer. Mr Doolan is dying of cancer and Mrs Doolan is now too old and exhausted to carry on this vendetta and struggle that has evolved to this point. As you probably know, the Doolans have no children.'

'No, I did not know that Mr Lukas. That topic never arose with us.' she interjected as he paused.

'Yes. Their only daughter died of MS at a relatively young age several years ago and they are now alone. They are keen to sell to a suitable buyer at a discount if that person or group can offer some assurances that the status quo may remain.'

'I did not know that either. What is the price they are asking? We never actually got that far.'

'Before we go any further Ms West, there is one more issue you should be aware of. There is a lot of pressure on the state government to either resume that land or convert it to public use if the opportunity arises. There is also a lot of resentment from local residents about that industry operating in that prime spot, so close to the yacht club. You may have noticed that there is a bike-path all the way from the city to Watsons Bay, with that spot the only real interruption.' He paused to gauge her reaction. Then he continued, 'This property, as it stands, is valued at about one hundred and thirty-five million. But to the right person, it could be acquired for considerably less, say one-twenty million.'

'Explain to me again the issues as you see them associated with this place, Mr Lukas.'

The solicitor went on to explain again and further.

'There have been incidents around the businesses there that I suspect are the results of the councillors who want it gone. There are possibly big plans for that block. I have not always told the ailing Doolans everything that happened – they have enough on their plates with his illness and her infirmities associated with old age. Both the businesses there are quite profitable, but many of the locals now want that site cleared away and the industries removed from that expensive area. It is one of only a few remaining slipways and barge sites left so close to the working harbour. I think that the local residents would be mortified if they knew that Mr Chung wants to build a multi-story apartment block there, no matter how luxurious – and possibly a casino – of international standard. His reputation would not necessarily allow for him to be involved, but he has extensive connections within the Chinese community, and I fear, Ms West, with the Chinese criminal scene, if you get my drift.'

Jess found all this information tumbling from the congenial Mr Lukas most fascinating. She liked the site when she secretly visited it and found the boatyard rather charming. The fact that it had doubtful goings-on associated with its existence intrigued her, as she was always keen to thwart oppression and coercion of the vulnerable.

Karl Lukas was an elderly man, about sixty-five, well dressed and quite dapper. Jess suspected that he was of foreign extraction as he had the slightest of accents. He was measured and slow in his deliberations and appeared to be genuinely forthright. His practice was not a large one, he seemed to have one or two younger solicitors under him, but essentially it appeared to be a small semi-solo practice. He seemed to be specialising in family affairs with occasional forays into tangential issues arising in connection with whatever family complexities arose. Jess found him most agreeable.

Mr Lukas offered to tee up a site inspection for her if she were genuinely interested. This she reluctantly agreed to, realising that if she were going down this track, she better investigate it thoroughly. Mr Lukas suggested that they disguise the fact that this was possibly a prospective purchaser inspection in order not to alert the people that seriously wanted this place for other purposes. Jess fully agreed, suggesting that she be introduced as a representative of a management company with an interest in the management rights to the whole site. It all sounded good.

It took Karl Lukas only a couple of days to tee up all the right people. He arranged a meeting for a week's time. That included the owner of the shipyard, the owner of the adjacent restaurant and most of the tenants of the small unit block. An inspection was arranged.

Jess returned to Auvergne for a few days before returning in time for any inspections that were arranged. In the meantime, Jess again contacted Garth and passed on to him all the new information she had gleaned from Mr Lukas, emphasising that this information emanated from her elderly distraught apartment neighbours. Garth was able to gain much more information about the suspect Mr Chung, the connections he had and involvements with shady characters and public servants. His connection to doubtful police contacts was of concern to him.

Jess returned back to Sydney a day before the arranged meeting. On the day, she tried to dress as she assumed an upmarket office agency representative would dress, accompanied by a neat note pad. Mr Lukas arrived firstly at the shipyard. As the businesses were all on the one title he parked near the slipway and could then access the other properties from there. The first one to talk to was the owner of the shipyard.

This was Jessie's first surprise; the owner of the shipyard was wheelchair-bound. He was very proficient at manoeuvring it and had obviously had a lot of practice. His name was Barry Upton. He escorted them about and gave a good description of the layout and the operations of this enterprise. Jess took it all in and after about twenty minutes they prepared to leave.

'Any questions?' asked Karl.

'Yes.' said Jess. 'How'd you end up in a wheelchair?'

Karl looked askance at her then at Barry. He was immediately and confidently responsive, replying with total frankness.

'I had an accident as a child and am paralysed from the waist down. It does not interfere with my life too much though.' he said as he stared straight up at Jess.

'I believe you and your family have owned the shipyard business since the 1920s.' said Jess.

'Yes, that's right. One of my ancestors went into partnership with Mr Hindmarsh for years, before buying out his business interests in this yard. We have owned the lease since then.' replied Barry.

'I see. Good, now, what is wrong here on this site? What needs attention? And what improvements would you like done here?'

Karl was impressed with the forthright and authoritative way this had suddenly turned. Barry stared up at her and began with a litany of items that needed attention; things that had been neglected and improvements that he wanted. Out of this long list of items, Jess gleaned two things. One, the uncertainty surrounding the lease position *vis-à-vis* ownership and long-term planning, and two, the interference with operations caused by the constant attention of the megalomanic council.

Jess had a final good look about, then they bade him farewell and moved next door. The same procedure was followed at the

Exeter House restaurant. The owner there was a well-known three-hatted chef with quite a reputation in the Sydney sea-food field. His name was Ian Ellis. It transpired that the issues were much the same. Then they moved onto the small block of harbour-front units. Three of the tenants were there and Jess got a good feel for their issues as well.

After this inspection, Jess asked for a few days to think about it all. She really liked the idea of owning this little parcel of land, as she found the shipyard of particular interest. Jess looked at her bank account under the name of Kimberley West. It held a lot of money, a very lot, but not quite one hundred and twenty million dollars. She might just have to transfer heaps of her excess cash from her other names. She thought about it all and decided to call back to see Karl Lukas and make a proposition to him.

Three days later, Jess returned to the solicitor. Her position was such that she desired to make the following offer: she did not want anything registered in the name of Kimberley West, or any other of her aliases; she wished to use a company name with a postal address; but she could offer the requested one hundred and twenty million dollars – in cash. She knew that this was an amount below the real value of the property, but it came with considerable challenges – challenges that Jess was in the mood to tackle, given her troubled mind with matters of a different calibre, plus, she might just be doing the tired and troubled Doolans a kind of favour if she could save the place as they wished it to remain. Also, Jess had a lot more relevant background information from a co-operative Garth van Heiken about her possible adversaries associated with this purchase than the beleaguered Doolans had access to.

Karl Lukas contemplated the offer. While he thought that it was a trifle low, he would pass it on to the vendors. The other issues he could accommodate through his legal abilities if the sale were agreed. The Doolans found the offer acceptable, especially considering their circumstances. They rather liked the young woman they had come to know, and the prospect of all the businesses remaining as is was favourable. It was all agreed. Karl did all the paperwork; Jess was happy with the title arrangements and she was the proud owner of the industrial site on the harbour. It certainly was a completely different lifestyle from her usual rural retreats on the Monaro. It had the added advantage of reducing her hugely excessive cash reserves that she really had no idea what to do with that was substantial and beneficial to anybody else.

What she had asked for and what was agreed to was the following: Jessie wanted the whole title of the land registered in the name of Michael Price Investments. She claimed he was an expatriate tourist charter-boat operator, who owned and operated a very successful tourist charter-boat company located on the island of Cyprus. This was a particularly lucrative pastime, catering for the summer tourist season on the Mediterranean. The company of Michael Price Investments was then to be registered as a wholly-owned subsidiary of another company called Tampinyeri. She thought that sounded sufficiently confusing and misleading. She would have to be registered as the sole owner of the holding company, but asked Karl to be the legal contact for her affairs, to which he agreed.

Jess had to re-assess her position. She was spending a lot of time trying to fully restore the beautiful 1937 Rolls Royce. It took a few weeks for all the legals to be finalised to the satisfaction of all. The sale had so far somehow remained a secret. Jess let another three months go by, mostly at Auvergne tidying up all her other matters before devoting her time to the new project. When she felt the time was right, she began. So far, Jess had not made one mention of this to Thomas. She was following her usual path of secrecy and, essentially, deceit, when it came to her life and affairs, and divulging this information to her loved ones. She had a very long history of this kind of deception and intrigue – very long indeed, stretching back to her days as a young woman on Milbark.

Finally, Jess could delay her revelations no longer. She had made extensive inquiries into the state of the land tenure there and the council restrictions. She found Karl's office most obliging in these matters. Somehow, the sale of the site had eventually leaked out, probably from the Land Titles Office, so the secret was out, though the identity of the new owners was a mystery. It was thought that it was a conglomerate of overseas buyers who sought to redevelop the site. Jess let them think whatever they wished. Apparently, Mr Chung was beside himself with rage.

On a later visit up to her new unit, alone again, Jess rang Barry Upton at the slipway one morning and requested a visit at a time that was most suitable to him, preferably when no one else was there. He agreed to the Saturday afternoon. Jess caught the bus to her new project and wandered into the yard around two o'clock. Jess slowly walked about checking out the outside of the place. The yard itself was a bit of a mess, with neglected outbuildings suffering from years of uncertainty and damaged infrastructure similarly neglected. The piers required some new piles and recapping and some of the jetty decking was shoddy. There was an air of slowly advancing deterioration culminating in languor.

The office, main boatshed and workrooms were all located in a slowly crumbling clinker-built weatherboard building that was located right at the water's edge, with the sliprails and jetties and some piers jutting out into the harbour. The whole surface area of this side was covered in old tarmac and bitumen, with parts also in concrete. The boatyard was at harbour-side water level, but the yard stretched inland for some many metres before it abutted the roadway embankment, a major arterial thoroughfare above. Against this embankment was a long-neglected, ancient crumbling wooden shed extensively covered by an equally ancient huge spreading Port Jackson Fig tree. It was obviously many years since the inside of that poor shed had seen the light of day, the doors being split, sagging and inoperable. There was a very old concrete ramp with concrete rails embedded in it located opposite the shed that was once used to drag up small boats onto the bank in order to work on them. Jess wondered at its history.

Barry saw Jess wandering about the yard and came out in

his wheelchair. Jess greeted him with a faint smile. He was expecting someone else. Jess sat on a crumbling and splintery hardwood log that served as a seat gazing around. Finally, she spoke,

'Barry, nice to see you again. How have you been?'

'Yeah, great thanks Kim.'

'Barry, we need to talk. You have plenty of time?'

'Yes, sure. I wasn't expecting you to turn up this arvo, I thought the new owners themselves were coming. We've seen nobody here for some time now.'

'No, that's right, but I am representing the new owners, Barry.'

Barry stared at her confused. Jess saw his confusion and went on, 'Yes Barry, they bought this place from the Doolans. I wonder if I might ask you to keep that little bit of information a secret, if possible, please.' He just nodded.

'Now Barry, that shed, what's in it?'

'It was extensively used before the war. I haven't looked in there for years, probably long before my father died. There would be some old tools, maybe old motors, old cars and other equipment. Obviously, we don't need whatever's in there. It used to be used with an old winch or a tractor to haul boats up from the water there.'

'Well, I might attack that myself with your agreement. Let's go inside and talk about things.'

With the assurance now of possibly a more permanent and long-term lease arrangement, with more stability, many long-neglected improvements could now be implemented. Barry faced the future with a much happier and more confident outlook than he had had for many years. During the next week, Jess went through the same process with Ian at the restaurant next door.

Four weeks later, on her next visit from Auvergne to the new unit, Jess again visited Barry. She asked him if he would mind if she attended to the shed. She planned to demolish it and possibly extend it a little and restore that area to a usable space. He had no objections. She saw in it a potential place where she might be able to clandestinely hide things if that need ever arose, and, possibly, another little project for her away from the farm.

Jess employed an arborist to check out the old fig tree, and remove some obstructing limbs in order to be able to demolish the shed safely. Then she found an old man with a small truck that did odd jobs about the city area and employed him on a casual basis to do all the heavy demolition work slowly so that nothing was damaged and the interior contents could be rescued and stored if they were worthy of that goal. His name was Sven. He was a large man, very tall and strong, though possibly not highly educated, but he spoke fairly good English.

Once the obstructing limbs were removed and the demolition could begin, Jess was keen to see what was in there as the two damaged doors were finally able to be removed. As Barry had intimated, there was a sizable collection of old tools, many heavily corroded, several different engines and shelves of various assorted marine-oriented gadgets and equipment, plus old ropes and chains. There was evidence of a once usable sink and bench along the wall furtherest from the tree, and beside that, parked up along the back wall, full of assorted piles of junk, was a sight that sent Jessie's heart racing.

She could not believe her eyes. Despite its present state of total neglect and abandonment, she could clearly make out that it was a very old Land Rover short-wheel-base car. It was grimy, the tyres were dead flat and it had some minor damage to the body. Because the panels were all made of aluminium, it was rust-free. She could tell it was an early model simply by the headlights being still set not in the two mudguards, but in front of the radiator and totally covered by the metal grill. It was backed into the shed, so she could also see that it had a prominent winch bolted to the front bumper with a small cable attached and that it was unregistered.

Jess was suddenly filled with thoughts of all the possibilities; her mind was racing. She was nearly finished the Rolls Royce under her unit, and her writing was occupying her evenings, but this would be a project that she would really love. Then she realised that it probably belonged to Barry or the company. He may not want to part with it. She tried to get a better perspective of the old vehicle while it was still so covered in mess. She then asked Sven to clear all around it but to leave it alone until she spoke to Barry. Her enthusiasm was waning. She spent some time just staring at it, hoping she had not got too excited for nothing.

To delay her potential disappointment, Jess fiddled in the shed a little longer supervising the removal of everything from the battered building. In mid-afternoon, Jess ventured over to the main structure to consult Barry. He was occasionally coming over to inspect the gear that was being removed from the shed. Jess found him in his office. She informed him that she was making progress and that she had found this old Land Rover in the corner. He said that he would come over in a minute and have a look.

Shortly after, he wheeled himself over to the shed and looked at the gear being accumulated outside, before deciding what was useful and what was not. Then he peered into the evolving openness that was becoming the inside of his neglected shed. Jess asked,

'Did you know that was there?'

'Yes, I was aware it was there, but didn't think you would be interested in that.'

'What's it's story?' she asked.

'Well, I vaguely remember it. It was here when I was young. Dad bought it when he was in England, just after the war. It had just come out in production then. When he saw one, he was so impressed with its possibilities that he ordered one straight away to drag all the boats up from the water up that ramp.' he said, pointing back to the railed concrete ramp at the water's edge. 'As you can see, it's pretty steep and short. We used to have an old tractor to do that and before that some of these old winches you found in the shed. Dad had it shipped back here in the late forties, when he came back from England. We don't use that ramp anymore, since we got that better one nearer the workshop.'

'Do you want it?' she asked.

'Well, not really. I don't want it to use here at all.'

'Could I buy it from you?'

'You can have Kim, for free, if you'd like it. Why would you want that?'

'I'd love it. You sure?'

'Sure.' he said.

'Can I have that in writing?'

Barry smiled, and wheeled his chair smartly around to return to the office. He hastened off, grinning and saying,

'No worries.'

Jess was delighted. She followed him up with his agreement for that in writing that afternoon. Jess now surveyed the vehicle with a new eye. If it could be hers, she wanted to remove it safely and secure it, preferably in the workshop out of harm's way. She looked at the tyres, they were dead flat. She wondered if she could inflate them enough to move it out of the shed and manoeuvre it over to the workshop. It reminded her fleetingly of the time she first discovered the old GMC 6x6 in the Milbark Station shed.

The progress on the shed was steady. Sven spent about a week after everything was removed in demolishing the building and removing the debris to the tip, or to a recycling yard he knew of. Once the site was cleared, a new extended concrete pad was laid to add a metre or two to the area of the shed and new plumbing work installed to allow for a toilet, a shower and a decent sink. The power was reconnected.

A new metal shed was erected on the site with a narrow rain-water tank attached and the gutters lined with leaf-proof coverings to prevent the excess of leaves from the massive tree blocking them again. Luckily, the plumbing and drainage from the old shed were still serviceable to allow for the new installations to be used.

After about a month, the new replacement shed was up, the gear that was to remain was put back in and the old Land Rover re-installed in its old spot ready for Jess to work on if she wished. Barry was impressed with the new arrangement, but really had little use for this facility anymore, so was only too pleased for Jess to utilise it to her heart's content. He did notice that she seemed to have arranged it so that she could actually sleep there if she wished, but that was her affair.

The problem for Jess was that she now had a spacious and airy place to restore this old vehicle, a task she relished every time it was offered, but little access to all the tools she would need. She had all she needed back in the unit block near Rushcutters Bay, but no means of transporting it, other than the cumbersome Troopy. She could get to and from the new site by public transport, or even by her new electric push bike, but in order to supply tools, she might have to break one of her most treasured conditions; that of not driving her bulky Troopy about town. This presented a challenge for her – one she would have to overcome alone and on the quiet. Of course, she could also just move the old Rover back to her new unit.

Jess arranged with Barry for basically her exclusive usage of this new shed while ever she was working on the vehicle. He was a little stunned at her persistence and her emerging ability at this task – an outcome he did not see coming. In light of that fact, he agreed for her alone to have access to the facility, so she maintained the only keys to the locks. This allowed her to come and go weekends and, as Barry had noted, sleep over in security if she so desired. Jess then discovered that, once she was well established, that she could actually ride almost all the way there on the bike paths around the harbour, so she had invested in an electric bike, most convenient.

In the meantime, Jess had not neglected the restaurant next door. Once the ownership issues had been finalised and appeared to be now long-term, Ian Ellis elevated his facilities and carried out much-needed upgrades to his kitchen as well as the dining areas. This restaurant was located in an ideal location for taking advantage of the wonderful harbourside vistas, despite its being next to a small commercial business. In fact, in many ways, the yachts and cruisers that were often moored along the shipyard jetties and up on the sliprails added to the maritime atmosphere of the scene.

Jess got to know Ian very well. He was eternally grateful to her for allowing him to enlarge his business and increase his celebrity and reputation within the culinary scene. He kept her secret that she was working for the new owners of all this area, and on the many occasions that she might work late into the night on her new restoration project, he would offer her free late-night dinners on the quiet in a secluded corner of his flourishing establishment.

The restaurant was a rather large structure. It was a late-Victorian wooden building, high-set on short stumps at the front, which faced the harbour. It had many ornate ornamental features of that age and at least three large brick chimneys visible from the outside. It was well-built, and well maintained externally and it had originally been a guest house and inn for the travelling and holidaying public of that era. It possessed over-large all-circling verandas which now doubled as part of the dining facilities. The metal roof was a pale green colour. The back of the building was basically at ground level as the block rose slightly from the water's edge to abut the roadway behind which, at this point, had descended from the heights behind the boatyard to a lower level. This allowed for much easier entry to the block from the road and also allowed for an extensive car park behind the restaurant.

In front of the building was a large area that was once grassed. It was now used as an alfresco dining area with appropriate attractive coverings for sun or light rain protection. This establishment possessed its own jetty, allowing for charters and ferries to attend to the business if so arranged. There were the rudiments of a beach front, but the harbour water-level was usually too high for that to be of real use. Between the restaurant and the shipyard was a line of aged Norfolk Island pines that mostly hid from view any of the activities of that outlook and its adjoining car park, which was much smaller than that of the restaurant. The old unit block of four units was located at the extreme eastern end of the holding, and sat almost on the harbour waterfront. Here the road had reduced to barely above sea level and also was now very close to the water's edge.

The progress to restore the old vehicle was slow, as Jess

had limited access to all the tools and equipment she really needed, plus her time was so scattered between life-styles. But this was a decidedly enjoyable labour of love for her and the city travel in many ways added to the fulfilment she felt in the advancing achievement.

The increasingly obvious improvements to this site and the loss of its acquisition by certain parties were grating with them enormously. They were incapable of reversing this outcome at present, but Mr Chung was nothing if not determined. There had been a few suspicious incidents at the site over the last few months once things settled down. Jess suspected she knew the source, but had no way of proving it. The police were hamstrung with their investigations because the perpetrators were very proficient and professional in their criminal trade. Jess kept right away from any interaction with the police.

In his anger and frustration, Mr Chung was plotting a final serious blow to these Aussie interlopers that had thwarted his desires on gaining hold of this parcel of land, right from under his nose. Try as he might, he could not find out who actually owned the site. This information was hidden behind a wall of legal and administrative hurdles that he could not penetrate. He just kept coming up with the same tight-lipped solicitor's office, which was immovable. The owning company was not a publicly-listed entity, so there was no avenue for information there either. Mr Chung would have to deal with this blockage in his usual manner. What he did not count on were two things. One, that Jessie was increasingly spending the nights there after working on the restoration, if she were in town, and secondly, he had no idea of the calibre of the person he was planning on messing with in the guise of the individual formally known as Jessie MacIntyre.

On another front, Jess had now completed the restoration of the 1937 Rolls Royce. She got it registered, though only as an historic vehicle, as she did not plan on ever driving it as a normal car that much herself. She was now fully occupied on the Land Rover. This had stretched on for some period and Jess was spending more time at the shed overnight, whenever she was in Sydney. This fact would lead directly to her next drama.

The Land Rover was proving to be quite a profitable endeavour. Barry Upton was demonstrated to be correct in his assessment of the vintage of this vehicle. It was almost one of the very first off the production line. Jess was able to confirm these suspicions by some judicious inspection and checking up on the style of these early versions. It turned out to be exactly as Barry had intimated. It was a Land Rover Series One 80 inch. It had a full grill bar, not a t-shaped version. The steering bars were visible, there were no sills along the base, it had gate hinges on the doors, so they could actually be lifted off, it had flat side-panels, there was a pin on the floor to engage four-wheel-drive and a red knob.

The components of the engine were cast aluminium, steel being difficult to get in the conditions at that time in post-war Britain. It had a chimney-type oil filter with a screw cap on top. It had a bypass oil filter – a large silver can type – with pipes. The top rocker cover was in one piece of cast aluminium.

There was no breather on the top front, it had a small breather at the back. There were also no mushroom caps on the top of the filler and rocker cover. All these were note-worthy in confirming its identity and authenticity, important for accurately pinpointing its age and year of production. Jess was beside herself with pride in gaining hold of such a treasure. There was a metal plate screwed onto the firewall under the bonnet, that also gave much valuable detail.

From Barry's recollections, his father had returned to England in 1940 to join the RAF. He was a spitfire pilot of some note, being highly decorated with a Distinguished Flying Cross, the result of the sinking of a small enemy ship in the channel by dropping a bomb down its funnel. He had remained in England after the war until 1950 to help with the reconstruction works, as he had extensive experience in waterfront activities. It was here that he encountered the first Land Rover. He was so enthralled with its potential for his own business back in Sydney, that he ordered one immediately and waited for it to be shipped out, he accompanying it himself. Barry did recall in his early days its use about the water's edge hauling up small boats from the water to the bank to be worked on.

This information was significant because it had a big impact on what was about to play out. Mr Chung was ropeable that firstly, he had lost the opportunity to gain the prized block of land on the harbour-front, but secondly, that some bunch of round-eyes had outsmarted him. He was so furious at this loss of face, as it was well-known about his desires, that he determined to wreak retribution, such that the land must surely either come back on the market, hopefully again off-listing, or even better be resumed by the state government with the aid of some of his contacts, and then silently allotted to him, via his proxies. He was so sure he had worn down the invalided Doolans with his constant antics.

He decided to organise vengeance. It must look as if it were either an accident or a fault of some kind, and that he could not possibly be involved. On the desired evening, he organised a noisy party and gathering at his palatial and gated residence with many selected guests. There would be many witnesses that he was at home when the incident occurred. His pretentious abode was securely fenced with high walls such that most of the property was invisible from the road. It was a secretive and reclusive dwelling. It was also a fated gathering; many would not survive the night.

Whenever Jess was in town, and that was becoming less frequent now, and she wished to work on the Land Rover, she worked late into the night on her project, as it was nearing completion. She would often then go over to the restaurant late in the evening and secure something that was surplus to requirements or left over from excessive catering. It worked well for everybody. This night, she had finished up after midnight, but, luckily as it turned out this time, she did not wander over to see Ian. Whenever she did go there, the clientele was usually dwindling to a few late-night revellers and the place was winding down. Jess often stayed later and chatted to Ian and some of his staff. This night, she did not do that.

The shed had two large opening doors for total access to the place, but also on the hinged edge of one of the doors was a single opening small door that allowed ingress without opening the large doors. Jess retired to the shed through this door. About Two-thirty, Jess heard a clinking sound outside the shed and voices, she did have very good hearing. She replaced her old overalls and put on her soft leather gloves, grabbing a heavy shifter just in case. She carefully opened the small door, as the shed had no windows. There were two men just a short way from her shed in the dullness offered by the enormous Port Jackson fig tree, giving them some protection from any wayward lights about the place. They were whispering and discussing things in a rapid fashion, as if deciding on the procedure.

The large fig tree was the abode of many forms of wildlife, and there were often mumblings and murmurings abroad in the enormity of the huge refuge offered by its limbs. In the still of the night, though there was a slight sea-breeze, and amongst the various disturbances offered by mother nature, Jess was able to open the door and peer out without being noticed, despite the door opened outwards, and the two men were engrossed in their planning.

She quickly determined what she thought was afoot. The two men were carrying plastic jerrycans and one small metal one, and had already appeared to have placed several close to the boathouse. Jess made a split-second decision. Luckily, the two of them had their backs to her and the shed as they discussed their tactics, pointing and waving arms about in their excitement. She was able to creep up behind them and gave the nearer one an almighty whack on the back of the head. He fell instantly, crumpling at her feet. The second man, so surprised by this action, turned to see what had caused the ruction. Jess crashed her left leg forcibly and viciously into his right knee, dropping him instantly to the ground, writhing in extreme pain. Before he had a chance to even look up, she clobbered him also with the wrench, knocking him senseless. She dragged them both further in under the huge Port Jackson fig.

The two of them were now totally unconscious, and possibly would stay that way for some time, if not permanently. She frisked them both quickly, finding two hand guns and a large knife, one of the pistols having a silencer attached. She grabbed that just in case. She also retrieved four cigarette lighters. They were nothing if not prepared. She was more interested in any car keys that they may be carrying. She found a set of large keys, one a square shape, probably for a door, or a gate. She hoped that was related to some modern car or other. It was difficult in the dull light to determine exactly what sort of car it may operate.

The whole yard was covered by security cameras. These men must have neutralised them somehow as they seemed to be quite blatant in their work. Jess did not want to wait until they had set any fires at the buildings. Jess now noticed that it was definitely duller here than normal. Even in this poor light, she could see that these men were Asian, probably Chinese. She glanced around. The security lighting and the cameras had been sprayed with black paint. No wonder they were so blatant in their actions.

Jess hoped that this large single key applied to some car in the other yard. She hoped it was not an electric vehicle. As there were no strange cars in the boatshed yard, it must be in the much more easily reached, and open, restaurant car park, which would normally be nearly empty at this time of night. With this retrieved key, she walked over to the restaurant carpark and noticed immediately a car that was parked right away from the buildings, right up nearer the road. It was a late-model black Mercedes sedan, very swish. Jess clicked at the two buttons on the large end of the key and the indicator lights flashed twice. *Good* she thought. Then she walked over to it and opened the door and sat in the seat. Jess did not like automatics. She was unsure how it operated. Once it was started, she moved the lever to D. She gingerly pressed the accelerator and away it slowly went. She drove it over the dividing small barrier at the far end of the common carpark into the boatyard park and up to the shed.

It was with a little difficulty that Jess got the two unconscious men into the car, one in the back seat, one in the passenger's seat. As she was doing this, it suddenly occurred to her that this vehicle reminded her of the sort of car the mayor would drive. She noticed that it had personalised number plates. Surely, she mused, he would not allow his easily identified car to be used for such a job as this. She retrieved all the jerrycans from about the site and placed them in the back seat and the boot. Once in the car, she hunted around in the confines for any sign of something that might be the gate remote that would automatically open the electronic security gates at Mr Chung's house. Hopefully, the other item attached to the key ring was for that purpose. All her previous reconnoitring about his residence was now paying off with high dividends.

Jess had an inspiration. She suddenly thought that if she could start a fire in the open then call 000 about it, it would allude to Mr Chung that all was going according to plan. She returned to the boatyard side of the land. She re-entered the shed and tidied up to make it appear that no one had been there that night. She removed her electric bike and placed it up near the road on the steep end of the boatyard entrance. She returned to the boatyard. Near the seawall and away from all the buildings was a large pile of discarded old planking and replaced pylons. Jess poured the contents of one of the jerrycans all over it and then set it alight with one of the lighters. As she returned to the car, she dialled 000 on a phone she found in the car and reported a fire in the boat yard, trying to sound foreign, preferable Asian.

Jess then drove the beautiful, luxurious Mercedes gingerly back over to the restaurant carpark. In the adequate street lighting afforded at this point in the car park, Jess searched about in the front of the car. In the glove box and in the arm rest cavities in the centre console, she retrieved papers and documents, mostly in Chinese. Just as she hoped, there were some documents in English dealing with council matters, mostly addressed to Mr Chung himself. Jess was astounded that Mr Chung would dispatch his lackeys out in his own private vehicle. He must have had total confidence in the desired outcome of this little endeavour. Jess actually recovered two mobile phones from the console, she stashed both of those in her pocket for future use. She thought that she heard the sound of a siren in the near distance. Jess then drove the car out onto the main road above the site.

Jess knew exactly where Mr Chung lived as she had reconnoitred the place several times. It was very close by, just up the steep hill behind the main road. It was a large residence surrounded by similar properties and in a wealthy, well-to-do area. It was now about two-fifty am. Jess pulled into the narrow entrance nature-strip outside the heavy plain metal gates. She sat thinking for a moment. She thought that, if she could get the gates to open, she might just be able to slide the car into his sloping front yard and bang into things, giving him a shock and a warning that things were not as he assumed. She got out of the vehicle. She had a sudden thought. She decided to pour petrol from one of the cans all over the interior of the car and some on the car itself. She activated the gate remote. The two gates moved aside, almost silently. It pained her to potentially destroy such a beautiful machine. The sound of sirens was now quite distinct. Mr Chung would have a magnificent view of the rising smoke from his back balcony.

The lighting was quite dim just out near the gates. However, this was not the case inside the secure compound. The house was well lit up and there were several cars parked to the side of the driveway. One had a strange number plate on it. It was a pale blue colour with the initials DX and five numbers. There was one other with the Initials CC and four numbers in black on a yellow plate. They struck Jess as unusual and unfamiliar. Jess thought that these were diplomatic number plates, but was not sure. The plot thickened. Jess quickly took some photographs of the scene with one of her purloined phone cameras – it turned out to be a rather excellent quality device. There was no activity in the front yard of the house, but she could hear the dull noises occurring either at the back, or possibly now, as it was so late, upstairs in the lounges above the open garage, which was also well lit up. Stunningly, the two-car garage was wide open with the lights on inside it. Jess decided to take advantage of this unexpected offer. Mr Chung had obviously sent out this car from his own garage and keenly awaited its return to its proper home, leaving the garage doors open in preparation for its quick return and ensconcing it in its proper place, out of sight. Jess was delighted with this little proposition.

In the brightly lit garage, Jess could see the space that was probably for this lovely Merc, nearest the house steps. On the other side of the large garage was another vehicle which Jess assumed was the white mayoral council-supplied electric vehicle that she thought she had seen mentioned in the local press. The rear of the garage was lined with what Jess thought were solar batteries and some gas tanks lined the outer wall of the house. Jess exited the car. The car was still in neutral, with the hand brake on. She leaned in and disengaged the brake. At that instant, Jess hoped to drop into the car two lighters, and to drop one on the retreating roof. As the car slowly gained speed on its downhill slope, she threw in the two flicked cigarette lighters and dropped one onto the outside of the boot. She felt that she just could not refuse to take advantage of such a generously-offered opportunity.

The consequences of this action went way beyond any of the hopes of the annoyed and aggrieved Jessie. The car had gathered considerable pace as it moved on down the short slope to the garage. The flames both on, but particularly those inside the car burned ferociously and gained rapidly in intensity as the vehicle slammed into the solid brick walls of the rear of the half-empty garage. As it ploughed into the rear of the garage, it suddenly and violently exploded with one enormous detonation. In the process, it thrust upwards into the bulk of the building, sending vast amounts of building rubble violently skywards, and discharging outwards from the open garage huge plumes of acrid red and black flames and debris into the front yard and onto the few vehicles parked in the front. Jess began to click away furiously with the phone camera.

Almost instantaneously, there was a second huge explosion from within the garage itself. Jess surmised that Mr Chung must have had stored there much more petrol or maybe gas cylinders, as the second explosion was horrific, completing the dismantling of the entire front of the property. As a consequence, the front of the building began to collapse onto itself and the raining fiery debris began to ignite any and everything it contacted. The house began to further collapse and burn furiously as the flames now spread voraciously throughout the remaining building. The original site of the fire was now so intense that it began to glow with a fiery and sizzling aura of terrifying power. The fire had obviously now ignited the huge battery component of the dying EV adjacent to the incoming Merc, plus also the batteries lining the rear of the garage. The fire was now raging with an unstoppable degree of fierceness that it was not going to be quenched.

Jess stood spell-bound at the front gates watching in awe at the destruction she had wrought on this evil man and his cronies. She could hear the disintegration of the building in its death throes as it crackled wildly and the occasional screams of the occupants unfortunate enough to have been inside. Jess was enthralled at the destruction this had on the man who had caused so much trouble. It was way beyond anything she had hoped for. The fire was now so intense that it was threatening both immediate neighbours. The roof of Mr Chung's house was covered from end to end with solar panels. Once these began to ignite, there was no stopping the flames from causing total destruction. There was pandemonium as people began to run about madly with totally inadequate garden hoses that had no impact on these flames. People were beginning to assemble on the roadway to observe the conflagration.

Jess suddenly realised where she was. As the crowd grew, she decided that the deed was done. Who survived was now in the lap of the gods. Jess walked briskly back to the boatyard, securely pocketing the precious phones. The boatyard was only about a ten-minute walk away. On arrival there, she grabbed her electric bike hidden in the dark at the top of the boatyard entrance and hightailed it back to her new unit, a short ride mostly along well-used harbour-front bike tracks.

Jess disposed of her overalls on the way as well as her soft leather gloves. She had ensured all the firearms were placed back in the Mercedes at the shed, but that was now irrelevant, as that source of evidence was so totally destroyed as to be useless. All she had to do now was wait at home to see what transpired.

Jess did not want to go anywhere near the boatyard for some time. She packed her things and returned back to Auvergne. In the meantime, all hell had broken loose. It emerged, over time – a long-drawn-out time, that serious matters were afoot. Next morning, it was surmised, someone had tried to vandalise the boatyard premises and possibly the restaurant as well, as all the security gear was tampered with. There was no evidence of fuel anywhere as Jess had prevented that occurring before they had begun. More than this though, was the case of all the deaths at the residence of the controversial councillor, Mr Chung. There were at least eight deaths and two wounded, one fatally. The connection was not yet made between the two incidents, but more horrifying was the fact that not only had Mr Chung been killed in the original explosion, but, along with some known Chinese criminal connections, there were now rumours of other delicate matters involving other foreigners. More was to play out on that issue in due course, with devastating results, but not until Jess was forced to threaten to release all the details. Someone was already entailed in trying to hide the full extent of this desolation, and its full implications.

Jess let the dust settle for another two months this time, occupying herself as usual back on the sheep station. She kept abreast of matters mostly through Garth, though to her surprise, he seemed to be totally ill-informed about the whole affair. She did not enquire beyond asking about any developments in the Sydney criminal scene. Luckily, they all assumed she was at Auvergne all this time while sabotage was afoot. When Jess finally turned up at the boatyard to attend to her pet project a couple of months later, she was very circumspect and discreet. The police were unaware of her position in the hierarchy of ownership, so all dealings were with the two leaseholders and Karl Lukas, if the freehold owners were needed to be contacted. Nobody, at this stage, even contemplated that the benign and sedate little Kimberley West could possibly be involved in any way with this horrendous action of mayhem and destruction. They were all just grateful that she appeared to be absent when all this happened, she having advised them all that she had travelled home that evening by bicycle. So, there was no need to advise the police of her presence there at any stage, she counselled.

The ramifications of this momentous evening were widespread, and lingered on for some months, but Jess was only too pleased to have removed from the scene that troublesome and interfering councillor Mr Chung. Indeed, so were all the property owners along that strip of the harbour. No one had any idea whom to thank for that small mercy. It was assumed that some so-far unknown criminal-gang rivalry must be at play.

# CHAPTER SIX

n all this additional hectic activity that was extraneous to her normally sedate rural life, Jess also was mindful that she owed a considerable debt to Fiona Butler out at Wilingubra Station. Jess was not normally in any position to do much for anybody else, spending most of her life in hiding and avoiding people at all costs. But she may be in a position this time to do something for the deserving Fiona by way of, of all things, her momentous gravitas within the literary scene, a situation that she would normally avoid entirely.

She had turned her mind to this task early on. Jess was touched by the simple, naïve, rustic innocence of the output she had seen from Fiona. It possessed a certain humility and virtue redolent with the wholesomeness of her character and her existence, with the intermittent hint of far more sinister, or disturbing, activities and occurrences inevitable when living so close to nature – it was authentic and honest – at least to her mind and thinking. It also contained a mix of delicate and sharp humour, seemingly uncharacteristic of the normally taciturn and reserved Fiona. Jess would try to assist Fiona in achieving some greater recognition, something Fiona was too isolated and reluctant possibly to achieve herself, by calling on her own status within the publishing sphere, whatever that may be in actuality.

Jess really only had two extant iterations of her creative personas. Somehow, she had managed to remain undetected as the prodigious but moderately artistically gifted and creative talent known as Kimberley West. It fulfilled her waning desire to create and utilised much of her slowly diminishing time available for this time-filling activity when she was totally conscious and unable to sleep. Her tomes were long and relatively simplistic, but they were, for some reason, rather popular and very successful, earning her considerable income of which she was, up until the Doolan boatyard affair, and Graham's homestead purchase, finding difficulty in meaningfully disposing. The popularity really centred around the intriguing and absorbing storylines, as Jess still had unlimited sources of detail from her life in the Kimberley and the stories around the campfires from her old mates.

Her real and indeed significant and substantial talent she was more earnestly trying to divert into the far more prestigious and admired identity known as Catherine Holbrook Seymour. This iteration of her being was far more substantial than Kimberley West and, for her to maintain the level of merit it was known for, required her to actually apply all her literary genius to its output. Subsequently, there was far less quantity of its production and that work entailed considerable effort and thought going into its creation. She also tried to confine this output to far more meaty topics and story-lines than the more flippant Kimberley West.

So far to date, by some miracle, Jess had managed to remain inaccessible to all attempts to ascertain the real identity of these two authors. The original reasoning for keeping herself anonymous at their genesis was now really well and truly gone, but she liked the anonymity and the slight sense of intrigue associated with that fact. All her life, Jess had found the efforts in achieving her desired artistic outputs under all her guises as an author were greatly magnified by the simple act of achieving them despite enormous impediments to her possibility of so doing. She found in the challenge and the attainment of clandestinely accomplishing an output, far more contentment than the actual final product. This strange character makeup was one of the small factors in trying to remain anonymous for as long as possible. Once the ruse had been exposed, most of the attraction to the identity was lost. That probably happened in the case of George Norman Thaler. Once she was exposed as the possible creator of that persona through the medium of her traumatic trials, though that fact was never conclusively proven, she killed him off. The same applied to the flighty Jane Ransom, her very first successful attempt at clandestinely and secretly producing an output.

In the case of the crime-writing personage known as Joe Scacci, he really died a more natural death, as his *raison d'être* slowly disappeared as she attained her desired results with his withering and insightful dialogues associated with her knowledge of the criminal scenes, relevant at the time.

That left only Kimberley West and the extremely gifted, and acknowledged as such, Catherine Holbrook Seymour. Her desires in the realms of the light-weight Kimberley West were now rapidly diminishing, especially as she had latterly assumed that epithet as her own person following the last attempt on her life.

She did however, still harbour a now waning desire to produce at her utmost ability in that realm, but the output was also diminishing in quantity. Seymour was a very selective and scarce commodity, but highly sought.

Following the last two rather violent attempts on her life, both relatively recent, and both only thwarted by either fate or the hand of God, Jessie's attitude and concern about herself and her exposure was becoming more ambivalent. As her awareness of her own immanent potential death, through the constant attainment of age, was more acutely aroused, especially at the hands of others, her attitude to her anonymity was softening. She was now prepared to engage in more robust and relevant topics that might eventually lead to her identification. Her last two efforts as Catherine Holbrook Seymour contained information and directions that could lead judicious researchers to directions neared her own background. Now she was considering releasing a new tome centred entirely around the life of one of her most treasured mentors in the Kimberley, one Norman Woods.

Jess was considering this revelation for two reasons. She had all her life of knowing this man and learning his story, been desirous to tell his amazing life to the world. She always felt that such a remarkable man deserved more than just an unmarked lonely grave in the wilds of the never-never in some forgotten plot in the Kimberley. He was just too amazing to simply disappear from this world unheralded. Secondly, she felt a small obligation to fully reveal what really happened to him and his life following the efforts of others in determining his outcome. She was losing her fear of exposure now and felt that he was more than deserving of being revealed.

She was so enamoured of this man, and the source of his endless stories that she used to achieve her fame, that she had tried to honour him surreptitiously by using Norman in the middle of her clandestinely acquired early efforts at writing. She had alluded to some of his knowledge in her early works, some in Jane Ransom, but more in depth in George Norman Thaler, but she realised that she had barely scratched the surface of his background, mostly out of fear of exposure for herself, and also out of respect for her mentor. She was now preparing to cover his life in its entirety – an enormous task.

Norman Woods was not his real name. It was Norman Melville Redveres du Bois. His mother had been Catherine Bromwillis, born in 1881 and his father was Robert Charles du Bois, born in 1876, the fourteenth Earl of Bromley, of the du Bois estate, and tracing their decent all the way back to the invasion of William the Conqueror and beyond. Norman was their only child and heir to the earldom. He had been born in 1912 and his parents, particularly his mother had mapped out his entire future, including the well-connected woman he was to marry in order to ensure the line continued.

Trouble was that Norman discovered and fell for a ravishing beauty of a lesser light and, according to his mother, a totally unsuitable match. Her name was Charlotte Louise Brevis, the third daughter of Baronet Brevis, at that time, a socially unacceptable lower order. The du Bois name was connected to the Royal Family in several ways but chiefly and latterly through a lesser illegitimate son of King Edward VII. This made the stakes even higher and it was essential that the correct marriage be entered into. His mother was a severe and domineering woman and she insisted that he discontinue his relationship with Charlotte Brevis, which he overtly did. However, clandestinely he still continued to see her. His mother discovered this ruse and demanded its termination. When he was reticent to do this, she arranged for her butler, one Roderick Palmer, to sabotage Charlotte's saddle girth leather strap which resulted in a fatal fall at the hunt that next occurred.

Norman had been close behind her and watched as she tumbled and was among the first to her broken body. She was an excellent rider and he suspected foul play and on discovering the cut girth strap he raced home and confronted both his parents and the butler. A towering argument ensured in which the butler was severely struck and injured and

Norman stormed out of the castle vowing never to return. He gathered up a few precious items and walked out of their lives insisting that he would be disappearing to Canada. He arrived at the wharf but the next passenger ship departing was not for Canada but Australia. He had never considered Australia at all but on reflection decided that that would be even better than Canada. Besides, they would never think of looking there for him.

The whole thing caused an enormous scandal, not least because he was the only legitimate heir and that in itself caused considerable problems. There followed a controversial and grubby scramble concerning the claims for the vacant title. This was from various pretenders, as the earldom was a plumb title with considerable lands and much wealth and income. Because it was associated with the Royal Family, that also caused much gossip.

Norman arrived in Perth on the ship from Southampton and disembarked immediately there. The only skills he possessed were riding and classics. The latter was of little use in the colonies but horsemanship was still prized, especially in the outback. He found that there were vacancies aplenty in the north and headed that way. It was in the hotel in Derby that he had met Stuart MacIntyre. He simply changed his name from du Bois to Woods. The items he brought with him were a few books, mostly gifts from his beloved Charlotte, a ring or two with the family coat of arms and a mourning broach into which he had managed to secrete a small locket of her dark hair. One of the rings was attached to his finger and in his haste to depart, he was unable to remove it until he was well out at sea. Somehow, he could never bring himself to throw it overboard. Norm would be a major influence on the sponge-like Jessie and she listened intently to any conversation that turned to his former existence.

Over the years, and especially latterly in his waning life, a bitter and resigned Norman would unload copious and varied stories about his ancestry and his connections, which were many, to an enthralled Jessie. Norman realised that, with his departure, his entire life history would simply evaporate without trace into the ether and be lost for ever. He understood that the enthralled little attendee at his knees in the form of the delightful and reverential sponge-like mind of Jessie MacIntyre would be in no position to ever pass on any of his tales. To that end, he was totally unguarded in his tale-telling, revealing such details about himself, his ancestry, his connections and the information he knew as a cohort and associate of so much aristocracy and royalty, that Jessie was almost unable to retain it all.

Jessie's publishing life was nothing if not very complicated. Kimberley West was initially published while Jess was still domiciled on Milbark. She had used the station banking system under the guise of the notion that Kimberley West could be a new development in the west of the property. That assuaged that problem for her in those very early days. But, she wanted to arrange for these novels to be published by a Sydney publishing house, separate from her existing Melbourne publishers. The whole scenario was completely complicated by the fact that she had to use a home address that was unrelated to her other publications in order to try and avoid any connection with her other *noms de plume*. To achieve this subterfuge, Jess had nominated her old Australia Street address in Newtown as her domicile, but that she was a traveller around Australia at the time – very confusing – and that was mostly the aim. Of course, that domicile was destroyed during her trial, so she had to arrange for another clandestine address in order to keep the hounds from her door, so to speak. When she departed Milbark for the last time, she eventually had to transfer that account to her own set-up when she was finally domiciled at Auvergne, as well as tidy up her real address.

Catherine Holbrook Seymour was a different kettle of fish, however. She ended up being published with her established Melbourne publishing house through some string-pulling by herself in the guise of her other author names, so her finances with them could then be channelled through that organisation to her existing bank under a different pretext. She found the financial juggling was always a bother and a mild strain, but part of the attraction to her of all these endeavours was the clandestine atmosphere associated with their attainment.

The reason for all this complicated exposition, is two-fold. One, it does indicate the convoluted and intricate background and arena in which Jess manoeuvred her publishing activities, but it also gave an insight into the methodology that Jess was about to employ in her attempt to fulfil her again two-fold desire to assist the lovely Fiona. One, to try and keep her promise to herself almost that she would attempt to get Fiona's manuscript published, or at least thoroughly assessed. And secondly, she wished to try to improve the life of the agreeable Fiona after what she did for Jess in her hour of need by harbouring her away from threats while she sorted out her next move.

Jess spent a lot of her time recently, engrossed in the diversion of her new inspiring purchases comprising, firstly, the new unit to escape possible detection from her old previous address which seemed to be known to all and sundry, and secondly, her newly acquired waterfront premises that enthralled her enormously with its complete antithesis of activities to her normal life at Auvergne. She desperately wished to spend more time up in Sydney, but her commitments to her rural life forbad that to a large extent. There were two projects that occupied her time in Sydney, apart from the actual property interests. One was the Rolls Royce at the unit and the second was the Land Rover at the wharf.

She was now also becoming totally engrossed with her latest literary attempt; the saga that was the life-story of the late Norman Woods from Milbark. The deeper she delved into that exercise, the more she became absorbed and captivated by its possibilities and the depth of the detail she was able to recall. Her life was almost over-full right now. All this activity did remove her jangled mind from her recent traumas however. As she progressed the details of her new story, she agonised over a suitable title, a normal exercise for her. She came up with the simple one in the end of *The Marquis du Bois.*

In the throes of all this, Jess approached her Sydney agent with the manuscript she had obtained from Fiona while she was ensconced out at her property in western New South Wales. These agencies did not normally receive submissions from the budding public, as they would be inundated. But because Jess had a well-established reputation and involvement with this agency, they agreed, with some prompting from her, to peruse this item as goodwill towards her. She also indicated that she would regard it as a particular favour towards herself for there to be a fairly favourable response to the offering, Jess prepared to wear any of the detrimental outcomes from its submission. As she had never asked for any considerations before in her long association, they agreed to her request to at least check it over.

This they promptly did, considering the source of the request. The submission did have merit, they may not have quite so enthusiastically received it had it not come from the source that it did, but it was of sufficient quality for them to pursue the task if the author was agreeable. Jess was delighted for Fiona. She considered carefully her next move.

Jess was desirous to travel back out to see Fiona, but was unsure whether to go out alone or to take Thomas with her. After some thought and discussion with Thomas, it was agreed that Jess could go out there alone, as there was no need for Thomas to accompany her. Besides, apart from the gratitude of Thomas for their assistance, the whole affair was really between Jess and the Butlers. Also, Thomas was rather busy on his property and did not need unnecessary distractions. One other salient point was evident. Jess was desirous to maintain the subterfuge with Fiona of her being an Austrian tourist with interests in the rural scene.

Jess was nothing if not a genius at living a lie. She had form and decades of practice. Posing as a foreign traveller was a simple and comfortable action for the well-trained Jessie Summers. She also concocted a theory that her European publishing connections were her entry into the possibility of aiding Fiona in her attempts to get published, if Fiona so desired that route.

Jess decided to again fly out to Cobar and then hire a car at the airport and drive out to Wilingubra, avoiding the need to inconvenience the Butlers any more than necessary. She contacted Fiona and arranged for a short stay out there with her to discuss matters pertaining to her writing development.

Jess arrived by about midday at the Cobar airport and arranged to hire a car for the duration she was there. She drove herself out to Wilingubra Station and arrived late in the afternoon. Jess had not met Sid before, as he was away at his father-in-law's place when Jess was first shunted out there by Graham. Sid was an amicable and agreeable person, and held no reservations about his lonely wife being encouraged in her part-time hobby of writing about her rural life.

Sid was rather busy about the property and the boys were still attending school in town every day, so Fiona and Jess would have plenty of alone time to discuss matters. Fiona was a simple and honest person; she had no idea who Jess really was and believed her sincerely when she continued her deceit about her true self. Fiona was astute enough though to perceive that this woman was a sophisticated and worldly traveller of some note, the sort of person that she would normally never meet. She was very grateful for the encounter, and also for the trouble she had appeared to have gone to for her to even be in this position. The two women did get on very well together, a surprise to Jess, as she was usually reticent and uncomfortable with others, especially women, and especially when compulsorily confined.

As the ladies sat in the plain but spacious, simple and functional kitchen, they discussed matters pertaining to the possibility of Fiona getting her manuscript assessed and, possibly published. Jess explained all the ramifications of that achievement and all the possible impacts on her life and her time, if she so desired to go down that track. She advised that Sid should be fully informed. Fiona seemed content with that outlook. Jess presented Fiona with a common contract, one she used herself and advised that, if she thought about it over the next few days, Jess would present it to a publisher that was showing interest in the kind of literature that Fiona represented.

The two ladies decided to go for a short walk before the day got too hot. During the course of the meander, Jess was struck by the environment she found herself in. Jess was not conversant with matters botanical and biological, her talents lay elsewhere. She was struck by the difference in the ecology of life on Milbark Station in the Kimberley and the arid interior of Wilingubra Station. As the ladies chattered, Fiona asked,

'What do you spend so much time doing in the evenings on your computer?'

'I do a lot of writing, mostly scientific stuff, for journals,' she said, lying; well, lying about the content but not the process.

'How'd you meet Graham?' asked Fiona.

'Well, I was staying next door in Captains Flat when my gear was all stolen from my car back in the city. While I was staying next door to him, he helped me to arrange for all my replacements. He is a very nice man.'

'Yes, he has helped others when they got into trouble as well.'

'What do you mean?' asked Jess.

'Well, we had a similar case here a few years ago now when he helped a young woman who was being hunted by some maniac trying to kill her.'

'Do tell.' said a normally uninterested Jess.

'Yes, she was a lovely girl, real classy, and a very good horsewoman. She was another blonde, just like you. We still keep in touch with that family.' said Fiona, turning to look at Jess.

Jess suddenly propped. She stood staring off into the distance as if in a trance and deep in thought. *I wonder if that was the Faulkner girl, Sophia* she pondered.

'You okay?' asked Fiona.

'Yes, fine.' replied Jess. 'What was the name of that girl you are talking about?'

'Her name was Sophia, a truly lovely lass.'

Jess instantly assumed she meant Sophia Faulkner. Suddenly, a whole lot of things made sense to her. The camaraderie of the Faulkners towards Graham; their familiarity; their ease of association, and their seemingly mutual respect and support one for the other. It always struck Jess that that relationship was based on something much deeper, and more meaningful than just a mere acquaintance engendered from proximity of location and similarities in lifestyles and business interests. It explained the apparent respect that Graham seemed to hold for the Faulkners and the homage and almost reverence that they seemed to hold towards him, especially given the enormous disparity in their circumstances.

Jessie wished to ask more, but did not want to appear over keen on enquiring about a subject she supposedly did not know anything about. She let the desire to rest for the moment. They re-entered the house to finalise ideas about possibly publishing Fiona's manuscript.

* * *

In the meantime, things on another front were again about to explode. Jess had kept a low profile since the Chung affair. She refrained from any contact with anybody from the integrity commissions and from dealings with Garth himself. However, she had heard nothing since it all happened. Even Karl Lukas had not contacted her. She took that as a good sign, as it meant that nobody was chasing the actual land owners at all, so maybe there had been no connections made between the two events. She still found that a little strange, but, due to her hibernating lifestyle on the Monaro, deemed that as not necessarily an issue. Jess decided to contact Garth van Heiken on a single-use mobile.

After preliminary chatter, Jess asked if there were any developments of interest. Garth replied,

'Yes Kim, there has been a major development this end.'

'Why, what's happened? I have heard nothing so far.'

'Well Kim, two things have arisen in the last few weeks. I gather that you have not heard that the Police Commissioner has decided to end the work of the various Integrity Commissions.'

'No!' she exclaimed. 'I have not heard that, at all. Why would she be doing That?'

'She thinks that the work of the Commissions, or more precisely, the reasons that they were set up, has now been done and that there is no more need for this type of work to be on-going. Besides, she keeps reiterating, the officers, mostly very experienced and reliable people, would be better used in other crime-fighting areas as we are always short staffed, as you would know.'

'But Garth, there is still a lot of work to be done here. There are always more examples of corruption going on.'

'I know that Kim, and so do you. But, she is adamant. I think your incidents with the assassination attempt on the bush track and that episode with that officious little copper on the M5 did not help her profile. She blames you to some extent, and also me for the support I gave to you and your interactions.'

'So, what's going to happen to you, not to mention all the things you're still investigating?'

'Well, that's the second issue. I've been offered a posting to a regional area Kim. It is really a demotion and a way of getting rid of me out of her hair.'

'So, where are we at with regards to the Chung affair?'

'Well, that has died a natural death. I have been told in no uncertain terms not even to think of getting involved with that little number.'

'So, let me get this straight. You mean to tell me that that whole affair is now not going to be investigated?'

'That's right. I got the impression that there was some political pressure applied to her to discontinue any investigations into that matter. I was never involved with it at all, so I'm only going on hearsay.'

'You know, that wouldn't surprise me at all, considering the potential ramifications of those involved.' said Jess.

'What do you mean?' asked a confused Garth.

'Well,' said a restrained Jessie, 'considering the political and international consequences of everything about that matter, I'm not surprised that pressure was brought to bear, even from as high as from Canberra.'

'What do you mean?' asked a still confused Garth.

'Well, you know, considering that the Chinese ambassador was one of those killed.'

'Sorry, what did you just say?' demanded an even more agitated Garth.

'You know, the fact that the Chinese were involved with that creep Chung and his criminal cohorts.'

'Kim, I have no idea what you're talking about. I thought, we still all think, that that little incident was an horrific accident caused by an errant EV battery fire. What do you know about it?'

'Garth, it was no accident. What about the vandalism at the harbour boatshed and the restaurant, the fire at the waterfront and other episodes that same night at those places that that creep wanted so desperately to acquire, he and his crooked Chinese cronies.'

'What vandalism?'

'You don't seem to be aware just how serious this matter is Garth.'

'Apparently not. What do you know?'

Jess went on to explain to him that, despite not being there, (she was lying, of course), she had been able to piece together from her friends at the boatshed and those around the residence of the late Mr Chung that there was much evilness afoot that fateful night. She explained to him that the boatshed and the restaurant security systems had all been de-activated by vandalism that same evening and that, apparently, some thugs had attempted to set fire to the whole complex but were thwarted somehow, and that Mr Chung's residence was firebombed by someone who did not want him gaining access to that asset. Maybe ASIO was involved, or some other federal security agency, as they might have got wind of this adventure. But more importantly, there were several visitors at the house of Mr Chung that evening who were killed in the following inferno, and amongst them were at least two foreign Chinese diplomats, one from Canberra and one from the consulate in Sydney.

Garth van Heiken was stunned by this revelation. He had no knowledge of any of this, and apparently nor did anybody else in the police force, at least no one he knew there. He asked how she knew all this. Her simple reply was that if he asked her no questions, she would tell him no lies. Then he asked her,

'Kim, what proof have you of any of this? And we all thought that there were only two deaths that night.'

'What do you mean? There were at least eight. I have seen photos of the scene as it unfolded. Apparently, half the street was out there after midnight as the place exploded. I have seen photos clearly showing the diplomatic cars in the driveway before, during and after the fire was raging, all clearly showing the diplomatic number plates. Do you mean to tell me that someone has organised for all that evidence to be hidden?'

'I don't know what to say Kim. I'll see what I can find out. In the meantime, what do you suggest?' asked a now very agitated and mildly angry Garth.

'Right, here's the deal Garth. You go back to that miserable excuse for a Police Commissioner and tell her that if there is not a retraction of her abolition of the integrity commissions and your reinstatement to the main one by Friday afternoon, there will be released to all the press all the photos I can get my hands on showing all this evidence and all the ramifications that that will entail and a whole lot more to boot. Tell her that. By Friday.'

'I can't just threaten the Commissioner, Kim.'

'Oh yes you can. I will send you some of the copies so you can prove to her that you are not bluffing. I'll give you and all her cronies a real diplomatic incident to be going on with.'

'How can you get that to me, by Friday?'

'Leave that to me. I'll be going now. Keep your eyes peeled for this stuff. I'll try to send it from this one-off iPhone today.'

'Before you go Kim, why do you have so much interest in that particular piece of land and how do you seem to be getting hold of all this clandestine information that even I can't get hold of working in the force?'

'Let's just say, I have an association with some neighbours in Sydney that own that land, or did own it until very recently, and they have been telling me all their troubles extending over years. You know, you investigated some of it for them early on. The rumour is that Mr Chung, in connection with his Chinese Communist Party friends, wants that land for its strategic value and its position in the harbour near the navel docks. They intend to build a huge casino and hotel there and use it as a spy base, mostly using their Chinese Communist Party members disguised as punters and gamblers as the patrons. We are so silly Garth, we can't even see what's going on under our very noses.

'Mr Chung has repeatedly failed to acquire that land

despite his persecution of the previous owners over many years, and his connections to the government, and I think he was eliminated for his failings by a foreign entity, or possibly, as a final method of eliminating this continual threat to our national security, by some governmental agency in the guise of an accident. Can you begin to imagine just what corruption is going on in government circles to obtain that land? The government has to acquire it without an outcry from the public to return it to public use. That's the last thing the Chinese want.'

Jess was now letting her imagination run riot on this topic. That had two advantages. Firstly, it shifted any connection to her as far away as possible, but it also embellished the evilness and conspiratorial shenanigans of the local corruption-riddled council, at least in connection with that area anyway. She was delighted with the way this had panned out. Now all she had to do was to get copies of some of the more damaging images to Garth from her iPhone.

Jess also rang her contact at Sky News. Jess asked her to investigate what happened to the Chinese Ambassador and his posting to Canberra. Why was he suddenly recalled without proper diplomatic notifications? Her contact there was intrigued at that suggestion. Investigations were set in train.

Garth van Heiken rang the Commissioner's office that afternoon. He asked for a private meeting with the Commissioner immediately before a real disaster befell them all. The Commissioner was reluctant to engage with Garth again and avoided any meetings. Then the Sky News team released a comment about the Chinese Ambassador's sudden departure and some suspicions about the whole affair, rumours about spying cadres and Chinese triad connections. The Commissioner suddenly changed her mind. She summoned Garth to her office.

The meeting was short, terse and vitriolic. The Commissioner demanded to know who leaked the information about the Chung fire. Garth replied that it was not he, he knew nothing about it, as the Commissioner had purposely kept all in the dark. She asked,

'Where did Sky News get that lead about the Chinese connection? I did not even know about that! If I find out you have again gone behind my back, there will be serious disciplinary action. What is this disaster about to befall us you hinted at?'

'All I know is what an informant has told me.' replied Garth. 'You told the press that there were two deaths, that it was an accident and that it was caused by a faulty EV battery.'

'And that is the case Detective. There is no cover-up and nothing else to see here.'

'Well,' said Garth, slapping three photographs from his briefcase on to the Commissioner's desk with an audible slap, and peering her straight in the face, 'lies, all lies. There were at least eight deaths, it was certainly no accident, and it was not caused by a faulty EV battery.'

'What am I looking at here Detective?' she said, peering at the photographs in front of her.

'Three of many photographs taken at the home of the

disgraced and late Mr Chung clearly showing the place burning down and exploding about the occupants inside.'

'Okay, but it was totally destroyed. That would be expected.'

'Take a closer look Commissioner at those photos.'

'Yes, so what?'

'Tell me what you see.'

'Don't play games with me Detective. This meeting is about to wrap up if you don't come up with something better than that.'

Garth leaned forward towards the Commissioner over her large and untidy desk. 'I'll tell you what I see here Commissioner and the implications, for all of us.'

He then pointed to the first photograph and said,

'Look, five cars parked in the side lawn of the house. There are three photos here taken in sequence. It is clearly the Councillor's home. The critical points here Commissioner, if you did not already know this fact, are that this car here,' he said pointing at the first picture, 'belongs to the Ambassador of The People's Republic of China, that is a euphemism, Commissioner, for the Chinese Communist Party. This car here belongs to the Chinese People's Republic of China consulate office in Sydney.'

'So, what's the problem? Mr Chung is obviously Chinese, so that would not be unusual.'

'Except, Commissioner, they were there planning the destruction of the properties located on that strategic lump of land where the boatshed and restaurant are located in order to procure it for their own strategic and spying activities.'

'How could you possibly know that, Detective?'

Garth van Heiken went on to explain in minute detail the litany of council harassment that went on regarding that site. He detailed the list of sabotage events stretching back a decade and the attempts to intimidate the owners. If that were not all bad enough, there were hints of state government connivance and compliance with this travesty and federal government knowledge and acquiescence to the ambitions of the Chinese government's desires. The New South Wales Police Force was found to be also compliant and involved to a small extent in the shadowy goings-on over this land deal. The Chinese want this for its strategic location and its nearness to the harbour naval facilities. It is rumoured that Mr Chung had failed to achieve this aim and needed to be replaced. However, the assailant overstepped the mark and eliminated more than was planned for – unless that was the aim all along – or even possibly by our own security forces, attempting to protect our national security. He finished his invective with this,

'Do you begin to see the issues here Commissioner?'

The Commissioner stared open-mouthed at Garth as the story unfolded. He was unsure whether that was a genuine response or an act to disguise the true extent of her knowledge about this matter. She finally said to him,

'Detective, this is truly unbelievable. I have been told some details about this matter, but was assured that it did not need my attention. I have far more important matters to deal with than a dispute over a block of harbour-front land.'

She sat back in her huge chair, thinking. Garth was unsure how much of this was true. Then she said to him,

'Where did you get all this evidence from, and how reliable is it?'

'I'm unable to divulge that information Commissioner.' he stated rather tersely. 'But this informant has proven very reliable in the past. I'm sure you can see the seriousness of this case now Commissioner.'

She sat silently again, staring at him, deep in thought. She was obviously contemplating the ramifications for herself of this divulgence – if it were indeed accurate.

'What do you suggest here, Detective and can we keep this between us at this time?'

'There is one other factor you need to know.'

'Oh, what's that?'

Garth shifted his demeanour to a more conciliatory mode, and then said, trying not to sound threatening,

'I have been warned that all this information will be released to the press *en masse* on Friday, unless certain conditions are met.'

'Oh yes. And what are those then?'

'One condition is that you rescind the termination of the Integrity Commissions, or at least the main one and that you reinstate me to that role, with a guarantee that there will be no more interference with the running of those entities.'

'That sounds like blackmail to me Detective.' she stated rather severely.

'Yes, Commissioner, but I do assure that demand did not

originate with me. The people behind this demand feel that there is still a lot of work needs doing. This matter here right now is yet another example of shady dealings occurring in our midst. I assure you my only aim is to try to rid the force of, or at least reduce, the amount of doubtful activity to a minimal.'

'How do I know if all this information is not just a ploy to get you reinstated?' she asked.

'Are you prepared to risk it. You should see the pictures I've had access to, and the source of the information regarding that councillor. I will guarantee to resign from the police force if I have deceived you in any way or over-stated the seriousness of this matter.'

'I might just hold you to that, Detective.' she said. 'But I have already announced the winding up of the commissions. How will I handle that, if it all goes pear-shaped.'

'Just say new information has come up and you are reinstating those sections in order to look into new matters. Who cares what people say about this, as long as we are seen to be clean and doing something about this travesty perpetrated on our own people by foreign interests that have little or no concern for our welfare.

'Look, Commissioner, I know we have had our differences lately, but in this instance, I think we need to find out just who is involved here and how far up the line of command these activities are being sanctioned. I think it will take someone of your level to try to find out all this. I feel that I could persuade the people who have all this evidence and information to either suspend its immanent release or at least delay its release for the moment. I know for sure that the main informant is nothing if not a seriously patriotic Australian.'

'All right Mr van Heiken. I will do as you suggest tomorrow morning after a few enquires. In the meantime, try to prevent its release to the press while I investigate.'

'Who do you think you can get to investigate this quickly enough to prevent some sort of horror story exploding all over the press?' asked Garth.

'Heaven forbid, Mr van Heiken, but I might even contemplate you. Horror of horrors. But leave it with me until I get back to you.'

With that, Garth pushed his chair back and turned to depart the office of the Police Commissioner, a little happier than when he came in.

* * *

There was also some action on another front, this time concerning the delectable Sophia Faulkner. It appeared that Sophia was rather taken with the quietly-spoken temporary farm hand that Graham Longley had taken on board as a favour for Fiona Butler out at Wilingubra. Fiona's brother, Xavier Jennings had struck a chord with her heart now on two occasions. Firstly, with that slightly misguided encounter in the paddocks of Graham's place when she mistook him for being Graham, and then secondly, she found him most agreeable when he accompanied Graham to their small pre-Christmas gathering at the Faulkner property a few months ago.

Sophia found herself thinking about him constantly, but was rather reluctant to further their encounters given several factors. One was the traumatic experience with that scoundrel Milton B Thwaites which only terminated with his dramatic death at the hands of the New South Wales police constabulary. That episode was the catalyst for her deepening affection and eternal gratitude for the personage of Graham Longley with his asset out near Cobar. However, that experience had chastened her ardour for the opposite sex and influenced her attitude towards amorous endeavours.

Secondly, following that traumatic encounter, she also became more focused on her position in the hierarchy of Clan Faulkner. She attained more cognition of her place in the scheme of things and that her parents, particularly her father, were mindful of her eventually, if she so desired, taking on the reins of management on his demise. With this in mind, she began to think more deeply about her possible beaux. She could find no fault, so far, with her brief encounters with Xavier Jennings. His pedigree and his connections to the Faulkners through the Cobar event were issues in his favour. More importantly, she found him most agreeable. The fact that he was an associate of the highly respected Graham Longley was also a major factor in his favour. The next move would be to sound out her parents on this subject.

Sophia remained circumspect about her feelings for Xavier. Her observant father asked her for her opinion of him, but she was fairly non-committal. Xavier was rather shy and cautious about matters in his new role working in amongst so much more closely settled communities than he was used to out west. He did pass a nebulous remark to Graham that that Sophia woman was a rather classy sort of girl, and very capable. Graham was not overly alerted to anything out of the ordinary though.

Jackson Faulkner, on one of his sojourns into town, usually driving past the property where Graham now lived, he having moved permanently from the village of Captains Flat, called in one day on the pretext of a casual visitation between friends. He could see Graham in a near-by paddock and, when Graham saw him there, he came over eagerly to talk to his dear friend.

There was nothing in particular that they had to chat about, but Jackson finally said to Graham,

'And how's young Xavier going?'

'Yes, well thanks Jackson. He fits in here well, though I fear his real talents are really squandered on me in this role as a mere farmhand.'

'Is that right. We thought he was a very nice bloke. I'll keep an eye out for any other advancements for him if you like. Providing that does not interfere with any of your plans.'

'No, not at all, Jackson. I'd be pleased if something better ever came up for him. You know that is the reason he moved down here.'

'Yes, I was aware of that.'

'You know Jackson, I think he was rather taken with Sophie.'

'Is that so.' said a cautious Jackson.'

'Yes, thought I might just warn you if you have any qualms about that idea. I'd hate to be responsible for any heartbreaks here, mate, especially where Sophia is concerned.'

'Yes, thanks for the tip. We all liked him. I'll bear that in mind. Thanks for the chat, Graham. I'll see you later, mate.'

Graham returned to his paddock work and thought little more about the conversation. He was unaware of the seeds that had already been sown and that germination was imminent.

After the acrimonious and unsettling altercations between himself and the tetchy Police Commissioner, Detective Inspector Garth van Heiken had tried to make more enquiries about the sources of the information that Jessie Summers, now known to him more latterly as Kimberley West, had provided in that stormy meeting with the hierarchy of the New South Wales Government. Garth was astounded at the extent and depth of the evidence and material that she had presented in that list. He was curious as to the basis of her knowledge and how she seemed to have access to such intimate details of so many doubtful judicial characters. It was almost as if she had drained the minds of these miscreants to dredge up some of this detail.

He had several long chats to his friend and benefactor, Ian Knuckey, from whom he was gradually taking over the management of the main and original Integrity Commission, about Ian's dealings with Jessie over the many years of their association. Ian was also at a loss as to where Jessie was still gathering data regarding some of these events, particularly the more recent ones. They had no idea of the depth of the connections Jess had extracted from the hated and despised Geoffery Bales, if she had achieved that at all, by whatever means. They certainly did not ever suspect her with any involvement in his tortuous demise, but somebody must have extracted information from him before he died.

Now she was providing critical details about this Chung affair, almost as if she were somehow involved with the scandal or even closely associated with the perpetrators. Garth was a little more than intrigued about it all. It transpired that Jess was deadly accurate with her summations of the events of that evening. Once the rumours began to circulate and the press got wind of the details little by little, things really escalated into a full-blown scandal of humongous proportions, culminating in an international incident of some note, especially this end.

Garth also began to suspect that Jess had too much inside knowledge of the conditions associated with the vandalism that had been occurring along the harbour foreshore to be a mere distant observer. She may know the owners of those sites, but the depth of her detailed knowledge was greater than the offerings of some dispassionate associate of those involved. Garth thought that he might investigate who exactly were the owners of all these disparate premises that seemed to be the target of all this effort, especially following the rumours about espionage being involved.

Garth decided to go for a little drive. He firstly went to the scene of the deaths and the devastation at the ruins of the premises of the late Mr Chung. This was now still designated as a crime scene following all the revelations about the suspicious nature of the incident, and still taped off and guarded by a security presence. He managed to gain access to the site, but there was little there of interest except for the sight of so much total destruction. He did note that all the vehicles were somehow removed from the devastation. That now seemed an odd occurrence, considering what Kim had told him.

He next drove the short distance down to the harbour front where the other lengthy list of vandalism and apparent sabotage events seemed to have occurred. Garth had never been to this area before, so was a little tentative about his wanderings.

His first port of call was the restaurant, as that had the easier access from the busy road out to the heads. There he introduced himself to the head chef and main owner of that premises, Mr Ian Ellis. They had a little chat. He discussed the litany of interruptions and interferences emanating from several sources, causing him interminable angst and frustration for himself and his business. Mr Ellis did point out that that situation had changed dramatically since the arrival of the new owners. Somehow, they seemed to have been able to lessen considerably the incessant council interference and harassment, and now of course with the demise of that despicable Mr Chung, the future appeared much rosier than ever. Garth then asked Ian,

'And who is the new owner?'

'I don't actually really know.' he replied. 'I have only dealt with their local agent and their obliging solicitor.'

'And who's their local agent, and for that matter, who's their solicitor?' he asked, preparing to jot down any names forthcoming. Ian responded with,

'She's a lovely person. Her name's Kim, Kim West. Most obliging. The solicitor is a small local office not far from here, Mr Karl Lukas. Very nice man.'

Garth was momentarily dumbfounded. That cannot surely be the same Kim he knew. He smiled a small smirk, shaking his head, realising that that was one of the reasons she used that name, as it was not a unique sort of name.

'And is that a man or a woman? You called them a "she".' asked Garth.

'Yes, a woman. Charming creature. Her name's Kimberley, I believe. She actually spends quite a bit of time around here, especially at the boatyard. I think she has a separate project on over there.'

Suddenly, the smirk dissipated. Surely not.

'Describe her.' he said.

The description that followed fitter the Kimberley West he knew to a tee. He was again totally dumbfounded, and thoroughly astonished. Garth stood there in confused silence for quite some time. Ian Ellis was wondering what was the situation occurring about him. Seeing this weird sight, he asked if there was anything else, as he would like to get back to work. Garth apologised for the delay, and said that that would be all. He thanked him for his time. Garth was suddenly remembering all the secret investigations that Kim had asked for about this site so long ago now. It all began to make a little more sense; her detailed questioning, and supposedly for some elderly neighbour in her new unit block. It was all a little suspicious.

Garth wandered over to the boatyard, still a little bedazzled. He meandered about the site for some time, taking in the layout, then went into the ragged and cluttered office building, looking for the boss. He found him wheeling himself about at the land-end of the slipways of the rather large raised gantry area, looking at a large luxury motor launch. He asked if he could spare some time.

Garth went through the same exercise as over at the restaurant, only this time, he added,

'And I believe she spends some time over here with you blokes.'

'Yes, that's right. Well not a lot of time, as she isn't here all that often, though can spend all day here on her little pet project over in the other shed.'

'Oh, and what's that then?' he asked.

'She is an amazing mechanic. She discovered that we had an old wreck in the old shed. That's now been replaced by that new shed, under that big fig over there, and she is restoring the old vehicle. I think she's almost finished.'

Garth left the two operations after some time there and

thought that he just may as well visit the solicitor while he was out. He found the address and drove around to his building in a semi-commercial stretch along the main road. He thought that he would risk a chance meeting without a prior appointment. Garth was lucky in that Karl Lukas was there and when he was informed of the nature of the visitor, Karl agreed to an unscheduled meeting in his office.

Garth thanked him for seeing him immediately and apologised for coming in unprepared, as he had not known about Mr Lukas prior to venturing out to see the land in question, so he had done no homework. Garth began by asking,

'Mr Lukas, I believe you are the legal representative of the owners of the land containing the Hindmarsh shipways and boatyard and the restaurant next door. Is that right?'

'Yes, that is correct.'

'Tell me Mr Lukas. Who is the ultimate owner of those two properties?'

There was a long pause as Karl contemplated his reply. He was mindful of the discretion that was requested by Kimberley in his dealings with her, mostly, she suggested, more as a business confidence matter and that she wanted to be able to attend to all the issues associated with its problems being regarded as only the agent, hoping that would help thwart the attentions of the council persecutions, and the other authorities that seemed to have an inordinate and abiding fascination with the businesses that operated there.

'Why would you wish to know that?' he finally replied.

'There has been a considerable amount of police investigation work lately into the troubles that seemed to have been perpetrated on that site by various entities. It is now associated with the deaths at Mr Chung's place some time back now, and his interminable meddling into that site. The police have only been dealing with the lessees. I thought that they were the owners of their businesses.'

Karl Lukas was silent again for some time. That last piece of information was rather startling news to him. He was unaware that there was any connection between the two. He finally replied,

'No, you are correct, Mr van Heiken. Both those businesses are leasehold, plus the small block of units at the far eastern end of that land as well. It is all owned by another party – all of it.'

'Is that right. The units as well. I didn't know that.'

'Yes, that's right.' said a cautious Karl.

'So, who actually owns all that?'

'Why, is there a problem with that particular parcel of land? Is the owner in some suspicion over something that I am not aware of? And what has this to do with the death of Mr Chung?'

'No. there are no problems, not at this stage.' said a deliberate Garth.

'I am bound here, Mr van Heiken, by some confidentiality issues, as I'm sure you are aware.'

'Possibly, but I can just look all this up in the Australian Business Register.'

There was another long pause, as Karl scrutinised his opposite. Then he replied,

'That land was owned for many decades by a now elderly couple who are both quite ill. They are in no condition to carry on with the harassment that was being perpetrated on them by certain parties. When an advantageous offer was made by what they considered a very appropriate entity, they leaped at the opportunity to sell. It is rather a complex set-up however.'

'I'm all ears, Mr Lukas.'

'I only dealt with the actual eventual owners through a proxy that they have here in Sydney. You see, the man, I believe it is a single person we are talking about here, in whose name the title is registered, is a Mr Price. But this arrangement is rather complex in order to foil the persecution perpetrated on the owners, mostly by the council, and to some extent, by the New South Wales government, by making the trail difficult to fathom. You see, the former owner was Mrs Doolan. She inherited it all from her father, and his father before him had set up the boatyard in the 1920s. She owned it all outright by herself. They now have no children, her only child died of MS, I think it was, years ago. Mrs Doolan had a sister who had a daughter. This daughter travelled throughout Europe in her twenties during the nineteen-nineties. While there, she met an Englishman who owned and ran a tourist charter boat company in the Mediterranean, from the Island of Cyprus. That's where they met, while she was hostessing on one of his boats. Mr Price has some nautical connections here and dual citizenship with both the UK and Australia. She eventually married this Mr Price. So, you see, there is still a sort of family connection here.'

There was a long pause while Karl let all that sink in. Then he continued,

'Mr Price bought this outfit using the registered company name of Michael Price Investments. However, he then made Michael Price Investments a wholly-owned subsidiary of his European entity called Tampinyeri. I believe that is Greek, or some other local language, for boat haven.'

There was another long pause while they both sat in silence to digest all this. Then Garth asked,

'So, let me get this straight. All that land there, that is, the boatyard, the restaurant and also the small unit block on the end is all owned by this Michael Price, an Englishman living in Cyprus?'

'That's right. It is all freehold you understand. That is a critical factor here.' said Karl.

'Is that right. It must be worth a fortune.' replied Garth.

'Correct, Mr van Heiken. Being freehold, a grant going back to colonial days, no one can just resume it or acquire it without a lot of trouble. So, you can see why everyone is after it, and why the authorities have been trying to wear down the rightful owners with their doubtful tactics. They almost succeeded too, but for the timely arrival of Mr Price.' said Karl.

'And as far as you know, all is in order with all these titles?' asked Garth.

'Correct. I am their legal representative here in Australia. I am the contact address for all the company legal and business work. I was the legal contact for the Doolans for many years before.'

'There are no issues with foreign ownership then?' asked Garth.

That stymied Karl for a moment. He had never really prepared for that direct question.

'No, that was all okayed by the foreign review board as fine, I believe.' he responded, evasively muddying his elusive reply. 'Mr Price is a dual Australian citizen, with an Australian passport, and already owns property here in Sydney.'

'So, how does this guy arrange for all the works that are going on there and paying for them? And what happens to all the rents that must be coming in?'

'The real estate part of the site is managed by a local realtor and then they deal with me. That was always the way the Doolans worked it. Any other capital works are authorised by the company representative here in Sydney.'

So, if I want to talk to the owner about anything, I have to talk to you?'

'Yes.' replied Carl.

'Well, what does this agent person do? And who are they?'

After his now customary pause, Karl replied,

'Why would you need to talk to them? They just refer you back to me.'

'I see.' said Garth.

He was now wondering how he was going to introduce into

the conversation any idea of the existence of this Kim person, unless she were this agency individual – surely not! He was so sure prior to meeting with Karl Lucas that a Kim West was involved. But Mr Lukas was tight-lipped about that aspect. Besides, he seemed to have covered the ownership details in some considerable thoroughness. Maybe that was the plan all along. Maybe that was all a ruse. It certainly would be typical of the Jessie Summers he thought he knew. If it were designed to confuse, and obscure, it certainly would work. Then he asked,

'So how do you contact this agent of his?' asked Garth.

'Usually, by mail. The agent contacts me regularly by one-off prepaid sim-cards, so if anything arises, we discuss it then.' replied Karl.

'I see. You mean there is never the same mobile number used twice?' said Garth. That sounded just like the Jessie he knew.

'Correct, Mr van Heiken.'

'So, where do you send any correspondence then?'

'To a postal address here in Sydney.'

'Could I have that address?'

'It is just a post office box number. And I'd rather not divulge that information.' Karl said firmly.

Jess had certainly covered all her tracks here. It was all rather brilliant of her. Garth was now thinking that he might just have to blurt out the name of this Kim West and ascertain the reaction, if any. Mr Lucas was a seriously competent solicitor; he was not going to be easily encouraged to release that information without some encouragement. Garth did not want to engage in any form of legal threatening attitude either, as he may need to deal with this man again. Besides, he actually rather liked this Mr Lukas.

Garth was aware at this moment that, unfortunately for Jessie, the Australian Business Register required that all companies registered with them through the aegis of the Australian Securities and Investment Commission (ASIC) also required that all the correct and honest details were listed under that company title. Karl was also acutely aware of this fact, but he hoped that his diatribe about the ownership covered a multitude of sins and muddied the waters sufficiently and complicatedly enough to assuage the interests of this Detective. Besides, Karl hoped that the diversion of foreign ownership might keep investigations away from Australian sources.

That inkling for Karl Lukas, sadly, was about to implode. Garth sat thinking for a moment. Then he said,

'Okay. Thanks for all that info, and your time. May I just ask one more question then?'

'Sure.' replied Karl.

'I might just check into the ASIC files on all these companies you have mentioned. Does the name Kim, or Kimberley West mean anything to you?'

There was a long pause. Karl replied.

'Why would you ask that? Do you mean in connection with all this or in relation to another matter?'

'Either. Have you had any dealings with a Kim West?'

Karl was slightly cornered. If Garth was going to look into the ASIC database on these matters, he would eventually, and fairly simply, discover that the ultimate real legally registered director, and therefore possibly the owner, of all that land, was indeed Kimberley West, though she could be a director only and not the owner. There was yet another very long and deliberate silent pause. Finally, Karl had to reply. He began,

'Okay. Why do you keep referring back to this question? Is this person in some sort of legal trouble, or worse, involved in criminal activity?'

'Definitely not.' almost exclaimed Garth. 'Quite the opposite, in fact.'

That was of some relief to Karl. So, he began again, after a long hard look at Garth.

'The Doolans came to me many months ago now with a proposition that they had been offered by a party that they had come to know very well and had had some most satisfactory and agreeable dealing with over other monetary matters of some import to them in their state of conditions. This party was apparently a neighbour in their security building, indicating that they were of some substance in order to even be in that position. Then this party came to me with some more detailed negotiations and finally an offer regarding that particular plot. I perused this person at considerable length Mr van Heiken, as I was mindful that the Doolans were in a vulnerable position. This offer came to me from a person I deemed to appear very reputable, old money you see, not some flighty fly-by-night entity of doubtful character, considering all the implications surrounding this very valuable property. It was all very amicably agreed to and I handled all the lengthy details here. That party was fully informed about all the issues surrounding these properties, but, actually, to my surprise, they seemed to almost relish the thought of taking on these problems. The name of that party was, Kimberley West.'

'So,' said Garth, thinking as he spoke, 'you mean this Kimberley West bought out the Doolans?'

'Yes.' replied Karl.

'So,' said Garth, still thinking on his feet, 'is Kimberley West the ultimate sole owner, and was that diatribe of ownership a ruse to disguise that fact?'

There was a long delay. Finally, Karl replied,

'Yes, I must confess that that is actually the case. You understand Mr van Heiken that that information is strictly commercial-in-confidence, for several reasons.'

'Yes. I can see that now.' he replied. That response had a deeper meaning even than Karl Lukas could know. Then Garth asked,

'So, that convoluted description of the ownership you gave me was a fabrication then?'

'Not exactly. If you were to investigate the ASIC details, Mr van Heiken, you will find that indeed there is a company called Michael Price Investments listed as owning that site. You will also, find that it is a wholly-owned subsidiary of this Tampinyeri Group. These companies are not listed companies, so their provenance is not available to the casual enquirer. They do exist and they are listed on the ASIC site – all legal and above board.'

Garth sat thinking. What a set-up! Then he said,

'It must have been a tidy sum then?'

'Yes, indeed.'

'May I ask the price?'

There was a pause, then Karl replied, realising this information was available to the diligent researcher online, 'It was agreed to be exchanged for the sum of one hundred and twenty million dollars.'

'Goodness.' said Garth.

'Yes Mr van Heiken. I'll volunteer to inform you that the purchasing party actually paid cash for that sight.'

'Really!' exclaimed a surprised Garth.

'Yes. That was one of the determining factors in the agreement smoothly progressing to fruition, quite quickly. That price was a bargain-basement value, you know.'

'So, what was the explanation to you of this convoluted naming caper?'

'Kim wanted to thoroughly muddy the waters in order to make it as difficult as possible for any attempt to trace the new owner and thus simplify the improvement advances that were so long overdue.' said Karl.

There was a brief pause, during which Garth van Heiken was suddenly struck by the fact that the Kimberley West he thought he knew had spent her entire life hibernating in outback and remote rural conditions. Where would she get hold of one hundred and twenty million dollars in cold hard cash? He was deep in thought. Then he continued,

'That is one way of putting it.' said an ambiguous Garth. 'Describe this Kimberley West that you know.'

Karl went on to describe the Kim he knew so well. It was finally almost confirmed that they were all talking about the same person - the real Jessie Summers.

Karl was now becoming suspicious as to why this apparent sudden interest in these properties that he thought were just desired for their harbour location. He hoped there was nothing else about them that he did not know, and maybe needed to know. After all, his reputation was his most valuable asset. He decided to venture a question.

'May I ask, Detective, why there is police interest in these properties and in particular, in the person of Kimberley West?'

'As you probably well know, the death of Mr Chung has ignited a flurry of interest and investigations. It now transpires that that death has been accompanied by a myriad of associated activities, some bordering on criminal, some on espionage, some on corruption and some on international intrigue.'

'I was not aware of that. Does any of this involve my client, or worse, my association with this affair?'

'Definitely not. Your 'client' as you call her, is a well-respected member of the public and has most favourable dealings with the police.'

'I am relieved to hear that Mr van Heiken.'

There was complete silence in the room as the two men sized up the other and wondered where to go to next. Garth took a quick peek around the neat and tidy room that he had stumbled into without any planning. He was impressed with the demeanour of this old man, who also seemed to actually have some remote concern for the welfare of his own beleaguered friend, Jessie Summers, though Garth doubted that Karl Lukas would know half the story of that amazing woman. Garth thanked him profusely for not only seeing him without notice, but also for being so candid with his divulging of information about the whole site.

Garth was about to depart when he ventured another point or two. He asked,

'May I ask you then, whatever happened about that *Intrepid* incident?'

Karl was momentarily flummoxed. Only two or three people knew about that incident; himself, Barry Upton at the boatyard and, possibly, through her dealings with the Lukas law firm, one Kim West. He asked,

'How on earth would you even know about that, Inspector?'

'I'll tell you how, Mr Lukas. *Intrepid* was a pensioned-off old ex-police marine rescue motor launch. It was sold at auction to the new owner at quite a price. But the under-bidder was very sour that they had lost out on that sale. I learned all this from someone who became involved latterly with this episode and when we looked into it for them, we discovered who was responsible for the attempted sinking, thanks to the thorough work by the coastguard people – on another unconnected matter – but similar. There were considerable criminal overtones here.' answered Garth.

'Well, Inspector,' said Karl, 'let me tell you something. There were really only three people who knew about that crime; well, what turned out to be a crime; myself, Mr Upton, and one Kimberley West. Now, I did not tell anyone; Mr Upton did not tell anyone, so that only leaves Kimberley West. Now, the only reason she knew about it was that it appeared on the long list of outstanding issues pertaining to the sale of that property. Not even the Doolans knew about it. By this time, the Doolans were so ill that I actually kept a lot of the nastiness from them. You see, that case had hung around for three years. It was a hush-hush case, because, we were told, that the plaintiff was a significant figure in the community.'

'When the new owners of the properties sought to finalise that issue, it all came out and the plaintiff suddenly withdrew all the legal action – just like that. It was a sizable claim I might add; quite a threat to the boatyard. You have no idea what a relief it was to dispose of that issue – and so quickly. The same thing applied to several other issues that seemed to suddenly disappear on the arrival of the new ownership. Both at the boatyard, and at the restaurant site.'

There was a slight pause. Then Karl continued,

'Do we by any chance have you to thank for that set of mercies, Inspector? Through some sort of association with Kimberley West. And do you actually know this Ms Kimberley West?'

There followed a long pause of silence. As no response was forthcoming from Inspector van Heiken, Karl Lukas proffered a follow-up question,

'And if you have a seemingly intimate association with Ms West, I am wondering if she has any secrets of a criminal nature that I should be aware of, as I have gone to considerable effort on her behalf. I do not want that effort, not to mention my reputation, being potentially sullied through a lack of candour or disclosures on someone's behalf.'

'Rest assured, Mr Lukas, the Ms West we are discussing is above reproach. In fact, she is the opposite of what you alluded to here.'

'Then is it the association between the two of you that allowed for some of the rapid disappearance of so many troublesome issues that seemed to magically vanish with her acquisition of these properties? Issues that hinted at pressure brought to bear from some considerable authority.'

Garth suddenly found himself in the firing line of difficult questioning. It was becoming obvious that both these two men seemed to be very familiar with this mysterious Kimberley West. He was unsure how to answer. To Garth, Mr Lukas seemed to be a reliable and honest person where the welfare of Jessie was concerned, but he was unsure just how far to go down that road. Garth simply replied,

'Look, Mr Lukas, could I just leave this situation where we are at at this moment. I feel that you may become aware in due course of further developments as required. Rest assured; the Kimberley West I believe we are both discussing is truly a most remarkable woman. The less you know of her life, the better for all concerned, at least at this stage.'

The two men sat in silence for a few minutes. Then Garth again prepared to leave, satisfied with his enquires so far. He again thanked the co-operative Karl Lukas sincerely for his considerable assistance and let himself out of the office with a lot of confusing thoughts swirling about in his mind.

Karl Lukas also sat in a swirl of confusing and doubtful imaginings regarding this developing saga that he thought that he had basically dealt with enough to see its finalisation out of his primary concerns. Who was this mysterious Kimberley West that he thought that he knew enough about to understand her place in the scheme of things. He had a sudden thought. He reached around to his computer and typed in the name of Kimberley West.

That name pulled up multiple entries. He systematically eliminated those that appeared to him not to apply here, including, initially one lengthy entry about some Australian author going by that name. He came up with several possible candidates, but slowly, he also eliminated them one by one if there were photographs of them or they were domiciled interstate, or overseas. He returned to the entry of the author of that name, as there were no photographs of her or much detail about her personage. Surely, Kim West was not possibly also this same author? He summarily dismissed that idea. The Kim he knew must just be an ordinary person with no real profile available online. So how did she come by one hundred and twenty million dollar – cash, then? He again assuaged any lingering doubts by returning to his fall-back position of regarding her as a person of some substance, probably, as he first imagined, the results of 'old money'. These types of people usually maintained low profiles and hidden displays of any accumulated wealth.

Meanwhile, Garth van Heiken was also thinking along similar lines. He returned to his office. He decided to ring the aging Ian Knuckey. Ian Knuckey knew a little about all of Jessie's involvement in this boatyard saga, but not the full details. But Garth was more interested in the revelation that, firstly, Jess appeared to actually own this valuable plot of harbourfront land and, secondly, that she managed to get hold of one hundred and twenty million dollars, cash.

When Ian answered, Garth asked him,

'Ian, you know the trouble around that boatyard on the harbourfront here, and the Chung affair, were you aware that Jessie is more deeply involved than we first thought? Did you know for instance that she actually owns that very valuable plot? And that she paid cash – one hundred and twenty million – for that site? Where would she get hold of that sort of dough?'

Ian was momentarily astonished. No, he did not know that she owned it. That explained a few things. As for the money, he was less concerned. He replied,

'No, I didn't know she owned it outright.' There was a small silence. Then he continued,

'Garth, I'm not sure how much you really know about Jessie MacIntyre. I assume you've at least read her diary that was published years ago now, and some time after her trial?'

'No.' he replied. 'I haven't read that. Didn't know there was such a thing.'

'Well, that might be a start. I know that ceases when she is around sixteen years of age, but it would give you a sense of the mind we are dealing with here. Have you read any of the transcripts of her trial then?' asked Ian.

'No, none. I confess I haven't delved too deeply into anything like that.' said Garth.

'Okay.' said Ian, after a long pause. 'Well, one of the stunning marginal outcomes emanating from that trial was the revelation that this same Jessie MacIntyre from outback Milbark Station in the Kimberley was also a world famous – really world famous – immensely popular, *and* wealthy, concealed author using several aliases as a cover. She had a huge amount of money lying about. That was one of the main things that we had terrible trouble trying to explain initially. It finally began to come to light right near the end of that trial. But as you know, that trial was suddenly and abruptly ended sensationally when other evidence came up and before any of her writing activities could be confirmed or verified. It was only hinted at, but never proven. You would not believe the intricate and elaborate trail she devised to confuse any inquiries and to disguise her identity. It took a considerable amount of diligent investigative effort on the behalf of the intrepid Caxton Tennex, her amazing lawyer, to finally untangle her intricate web of disguised systems that she operated under. She still writes under different names to this day, but not those that were hinted at at the trial. Very famous and very secretive. You are lucky to have met such a marvel Garth. As for one hundred and twenty million, I would imagine that would be no challenge for her to muster, given her success and output. Does that answer your question?'

'Well, I never. Is that true. I had no idea. Well, Ian, I've just come away from her solicitor here in Sydney, the one who deals with this boatyard stuff, and you wouldn't believe, or maybe you would believe then, the convoluted and intricate web she's devised to hide her identity here again. It is simply mind-blowing, and almost impenetrable; the elaborate network of names and companies, all of them mostly impossible to fathom, that she has set up here. Maybe I suppose it is not that unusual for her then, if she seems to have form in this kind of thing.'

There was a small delay from Ian. Then he said,

'Garth, allow me to read you some notes from Caxton Tennex, if I can just lay my hands on them. They're here in a separate folder. Just a minute.' After a small delay, he returned to the phone and he began to read,

'Here we are. These are some of the notes that the diligent Caxton made before and during the trial. I'll only read the relevant parts. This is all about Jessie remember. *Jane Ransom wrote junk novels since 1985.* Remember, she's only eighteen years old at this time; living in the wilderness of the Kimberleys. He shouldn't really call them junk novels. They were quite good for their target audience. *Cheques were sent to a post office box that was emptied by a woman fitting Jessie's description. According to bank records, the money was either invested by Jane Ransom or withdrawn in cash. Whenever this happened it often, but not always was deposited in either an account in the name of Jessie MacIntyre or the trading account of Milbark Station.*

'This is another one of her names. This is the important one. *George Norman Thaler had his money direct-deposited into an account that was in the name of one Norman Woods, who was well and truly dead. That was okay except there was a joint signatory to that account: one Jessie MacIntyre. That money was mostly invested in term deposits also, but some was withdrawn in cash. His mail was sent to a box number in Derby in the name of Woods but emptied by a woman again matching the description of Jessie MacIntyre. Anna Delaney appeared to possibly be correct in surmising that Jessie MacIntyre was indeed also George Norman Thaler. Not only that, but also may be Jane Ransom. How could this be? This would account for all the cash that was in the name of Jessie. She would never admit it unless I can present her with incontrovertible evidence.'*

Anna Delaney was the Channel Four reporter that discovered, or at least first thought that Jessie was these authors. Here's a bit more about the station finances that Caxton wrote. *Stuart returned in a confused state of mind because he had inspected all the station's accounts and did indeed find discrepancies. These, however were in the station's favour and he was at a loss to explain how this could have happened. He was in front to the tune of many hundreds of thousands of dollars. She was paying the station bills secretly and no one would have ever found out but for the trial.*

'But, there's more.' continued Ian. 'I found out that she uses still other names, some very famous, but I never discussed any of this with her, ever, even to this day. She is no stranger to muddying the waters, Garth.'

'Well, I never. A famous author, eh? I can't say those names are familiar to me. Would I know any of her other names?' he asked.

'Possibly, try Kimberley West for a start.'

'You're joking!'

'No, I'm not. That, by the way, is confidential information Garth.'

'Yes, of course, Ian. I'm just so amazed about all that. Look, thank you for the heads-up Ian, much appreciated. We'll talk again,'

Garth sat back deep in thought. What else did he not know about this woman that he originally surmised was much simpler than he had now discovered.

As for Jessie, she was unaware that these interactions were occurring about her. She still lived in a world swirling with denial, a familiar state and sensation for her, commencing with her sojourn into authorship while still very young on Milbark Station. Her retinue of deceitfulness there always filled her with a sense of dread and guilt where her close associates were concerned. That feeling remained with her to this day – and it continued. She still had not even informed Thomas about her increasingly complicated and conflict-strewn adventures into harbour-front maritime escapades. She realised that the longer she delayed ever telling him, the harder it was going to be to explain her actions. She could, of course, just follow her well-trodden path of many years of never revealing her activities to her nearest and dearest.

* * *

The seeds of an unlikely blossoming romance between Xavier Jennings and Sophia Faulkner were given another unexpected impetus when Jackson began to consider him as a potential suitor for his daughter. Jackson could find no fault with Xavier, despite Jackson's reservations about anybody being good enough for his Sophia. Jackson was also mindful that, on his demise, or some form of incapacity, Sophia's husband could possibly or indeed, would probably take over control of the Faulkner line, a chronicle going back many generations. It was a heady responsibility to be handing over the control of this domain to the next succession, especially in this case, an outsider not carrying the Faulkner name.

Jackson thought about this topic at some length after the slight hint thrown his way at the encounter with Graham Longley. He even raised it with Edith, his wife, to gauge her reaction and her opinion of this matter. Jackson was beginning to realise that he may have to give his daughter a slight nudge in these matters as time was moving along. Xavier was a most acceptable suitor for her as he had several things in his favour. His background was sound, his pedigree was appropriate and, according to Graham, he had some rather excellent qualifications in the management and financial sphere. His connections to the Butler family and to Graham were also in his favour.

Jackson was mindful that one of his administrative and commercial managers was thinking of retiring. This man was the third he had had in this position. All three had been reluctantly appointed, and of some advanced age when selected, almost as a nominal acknowledgement to the appointee for recognition of, in some cases, decades of loyal service to the Faulkner enterprises. There was more than one person fulfilling these rolls as Jackson's management skills were learnt on-the-job and he had no formal training in any of these fields. That was not an impediment to his ability to manage and run the complex enterprise that was the Faulkner property empire, it was just that his large and diverse conglomeration was becoming more and more intricate with never-ending new requirements and reporting to be handled by someone, preferably with these skills, knowledge and ability – something Jackson dreaded doing – it was not sheep work, the thing he liked the most.

He was giving serious thought to the idea of Xavier assuming this role, possibly, if he so desired, at least initially, of taking on the role of the three people employed parttime to fulfill these roles now. The only catch that he could perceive was if Xavier were not in the least interested in a position that offered so much office work, especially if he showed a marked preference to the paddock realm, where he also had admirable skills.

Jackson was of a mind to test the waters so to speak by,

firstly, sounding out Graham, then, depending on how that panned out, touching base with Xavier himself. This initially would of course come with no mention of a connection to Sophia in any way, but as a ploy to get him on-site first and then go from there.

Two months later, Jackson again paid a visit to Graham disguised as a casual visitation by an old friend just passing by. They had their usual chat about this and that, luckily, Xavier was otherwise occupied out in the paddocks somewhere, but eventually Jackson said to Graham,

'Graham, I wonder if I might ask you how you would feel if I were to offer a job to young Xavier here. I actually have three blokes doing various admin tasks. They are all elderly and one is retiring in about three months. How do you feel about that idea?'

'Look Jackson, I'd be delighted for Xavier if he could get a foot in the door to such a huge operation as the Faulkner business. I think he would be ideal for that sort of work as I know he has some pretty good skills and knowledge in that field, he has told me about it several times concerning matters here. Not as complicated as yours of course, but he seems to be well-versed in all that stuff.'

'I don't want to tread on any toes here, Graham, but I've never actually had a trained specialist in that field before — well not one of his age anyway.'

'I'd be delighted to see him get such an opportunity.' responded Graham. 'What did you have in mind?'

'I need to discuss it further with Edith, but I'm coming

round to the idea. I need a good man in that job. If he's interested in Sophie, that may end up as a bonus. Only time will tell.' he said slightly sadly.

The two men stood momentarily deep in their own thoughts, staring out into the distant paddocks in the shimmering heat and the mild calmness of the midday sun. Graham was again mindful that he hoped there was not going to be any untoward disappointments on anybody's behalf over this potential development. There were many hearts here that could be damaged.

# CHAPTER EIGHT

t is said that we all have a novel in us. Jessie suspected, though with no real evidence to back it up, that Fiona Butler had just the one tome in her makeup. She could be wrong, but she suspected that the effort that was presented to her while out at Wilingubra Station would be the one and only story that Fiona would produce. It was rather lengthy and detailed, a superb effort all things considered. It appeared essentially to Jess as a cathartic unloading of a slightly pent-up accumulation of personal feelings and even minor disappointments surrounding the lifestyle of the author; an almost necessary product and outlet of otherwise totally hidden and even suppressed personal and emotional states. Jess had emphasised to her facilitating and accommodating publishers that she would look on their publishing this rural volume as a particular favour, if they considered it slightly substandard. Luckily, this was not the case. They might not have acquiesced to its publication so readily if it had just turned up unsolicited and from an unknown source, but, with the imprimatur of one such as Jessie, they skipped all the agonising and agreed to release it. She had, of course, not used her real identity to seek this request; she had used the medium and consequent endorsement and commendation of her alter-ego known famously as Catherine Holbrook Seymour. That did carry quite some weight.

Jess was delighted for Fiona that a major publishing house was prepared to activate her lengthy volume and to promote it as a first-time female author, with quite some potential. Jess could do no more. It was now up to the role of providence how this enterprise was to develop. Fiona for her part derived a considerable amount of self-pride and worth from the result she had achieved, albeit with significant help from Jessie, and in a roundabout way, as a result of her connections with the amazing Graham Longley, though Graham was unaware at this stage of this enterprise occurring within his domain. Jessie for her part, hoped this little escapade of Fiona's did not lead into any complications regarding her own standing within the Butler household regarding her peculiar deviousness and deceptive actions around her sojourn out there with the innocent outback family.

That was Fiona sorted, for the time being anyway. Now for Fiona's brother Xavier whom also was now in the bailiwick of the redoubtable Graham Longley. Things moved slowly at first, but Jackson finally decided to bite the bullet and ask Xavier if he would be at all interested in a primarily administrative position, with some considerable responsibility, at the main property.

Most of the employees of the Faulkner enterprises, and there were many, were located off-site in their own private accommodation, some in towns and some on other properties about the district. There were, however, several on-site cottages where the managerial staff could live, and other accommodation billets available for some of the single or temporary staff that were engaged from time to time. As the elderly man, and his wife, who were the catalyst for this eventuality, had decided to retire and move away altogether, there became available a small cottage of reasonable standard which Jackson could offer to Xavier. It was rather a grandiose proposition for a single male occupant, but Jackson deemed it admirably suitable for someone of the calibre of Xavier — an added inducement in the form of highly subsidised and comfortable lodgings for the potentially promising Xavier.

Xavier was at first nonplussed at the impressively generous offer of advancement. It was a little more progressive and prestigious than he had initially hoped for as such a new-comer to the rural arena of the Monaro, especially as he had no real power to advertise his undoubted expertise. He was eternally grateful to his most helpful and true friend, Graham Longley and realised that this offer was probably entirely from his connections to such a substantial organisation. He hoped it was not entirely desk-bound, but that was something that could sort itself out in due course.

Once the old couple had departed the scene and the initial cursory handover and accounting details were under way, Xavier had moved from Graham's place to the now vacant cottage. Luckily, the small cottage was fully furnished, as Xavier really had no possessions other than that which fitted into his ancient ute that he had owned for years now.

Jackson had his main office just inside the front entrance near the ornate double-fronted doors. There was a small room located next to it but slightly back from the hallways. It was in here that he used to dump all the paperwork that piled up from their endless works associated with running such an enterprise, then to be attended to by whom ever was so inclined, certainly and very reluctantly that was usually *not* Jackson. This small office actually had its own outside access door, so an office-holder could access this facility independently of the rest of the house and the front entrance. Jackson could bolt the door from the inside of the house, ensuring security at all times if he so deemed. This was where Jackson wished to ensconce the capable Xavier.

What Jackson envisioned for the incoming new man was a total overhaul of all the administrative processes involved with this enterprise. There were one or two now elderly gentlemen who were nominally responsible for the smooth operation of the disparate aspects of the property. They took it upon themselves to ensure that all the agricultural chemicals and additives and the veterinary medicines and products were always readily, and adequately, available and current. They were also responsible for ensuring all the fuel supplies for such a large operation were maintained and that all the machinery was kept operational. They ensured all the procedures involving sheep management were always in hand and everything was suitably co-ordinated, a complex requirement where the regular seasonal tasks associated with the sheep industry were involved.

The property owned several vehicles that were available for use to travel about the extensive holding and to drive into town for needed supplies. The two elderly men found that aspect of their day now a trifle arduous. These arrangements had sort of drifted into existence over time and evolved into the *ad hoc* measures that now existed. Jackson was of a mind to formalise and consolidate all of these procedures now that the opportunity presented itself through the medium of Xavier.

Both these honorary positions were held by men of doubtful physical capability due to their advancing years, an issue Jackson hoped to alleviate with the introduction of the young and robust Xavier. He planned on achieving this by creating a more substantial role, one now hopefully occupied by a seriously qualified person with the added ability of a rural background, a competent horseman and being conversant with all aspects of complex property management.

Jackson had always used a firm of accountants in Cooma for his taxation requirements. He now hoped to be able to present a far more professional, and comprehensive, submission to them with the advent of the arrival of Xavier.

Xavier found the office accommodation much to his

liking. He was given a free hand to wander about the place to ensure he was totally conversant with all the production requirements that he would now be responsible for. The station vehicles were also much better than his old ute for the travel to town. Xavier settled quickly into his new daunting role at the property. He found himself fully occupied learning all the ropes of so intricate and massive a conglomeration of properties, which were spread over a considerable area of the local district. The lovely Sophia was not at the forefront of his thinking right now.

In the meantime, Graham initially missed the company of the very capable Xavier. He certainly would miss the wonderful instructive abilities concerning his newly developing skills of mastering the riding of the little mare he had 'inherited' from the nasty neighbour who owned all those beautiful flats just over the ridge. All Graham could now do was to hope that his influence and impact on this new arrangement panned out with no heartache for anyone he so admired. He also congratulated himself quietly for the perceived outcome he hoped he had achieved for the deserving sister, Fiona out at Wilingubra Station.

Graham rang the Butlers out at Wilingubra just to ensure that Fiona was fully informed of this possible major advancement of her brother, as he really had very little to offer them by way of recompense for all the services they had performed for him. He felt that this went a minor way towards evening up the ledger. That was when he was informed by a rather eager and unusually excited Fiona that the lovely Austrian scientist Annika that Graham had taken out there some time ago was instrumental in getting Fiona's literary pastime activities actually published by some major publishing house in Sydney, through her connections in that industry. Graham was chuffed for Fiona with that, until then, unknown outcome. He wondered how poor Jessie was ever going to explain to the innocent Butlers her true self, and her real connections, and her real abilities, if that need ever eventuated. He was mindful at least, that Jess was used to living a lie. It sprang to his mind that, if you are going to lie, you better have a good memory. He began to envisage all sorts of complications for himself if any of her real details became evident to the Butlers, and any involvement he may have had in this subterfuge.

As it transpired, once Fiona was ensconced within the domain of the thriving authorship industry and she was firmly connected to that world through her access via the internet, that she was receiving much e-mail traffic, most of which was padding. She did, however, also receive a couple of invitations to submit her new novel to a few award programmes for new or first-time authors, mostly conducted by various universities and other spheres connected to that domain. This she eagerly did. The results were less than encouraging, but she did make the finals short-list of two of her applications and then hit the jackpot with another under the auspices of the New South Wales Literary Awards.

The issue for the Butlers became one of having to attend in person the award ceremony located in Sydney.

The Butler property of Wilingubra Station was nothing like the complexity of either Graham's or the more diverse and larger property of the Faulkners. It was basically a semi-arid holding comprising vast amounts of meagre vegetation and sparse domestic livestock. In fact, their main source of income was slowly devolving away from high-maintenance sheep and into the low-care use of the thriving wild population of feral goats that roamed that region. Things moved at a much more sedate and slower pace where everything happened at the behest of a much more benign and constrained mother-nature.

The Butlers, if they so desired, could leave the place semi-unattended for some length of time without too much potentially going wrong. So, despite this ability, Sid Butler was not a man with an over-enamoured attraction to things urban. He found the pace and the people not altogether to his liking. He was just as pleased to allow his more eager wife to partake of the magnetism and sense that pervaded the city scene – especially the giant city scene that was Sydney.

* * *

Now, another family agitation arose in the hectic and diverse life of Graham Longley. The telephone rang one evening in the hallway about seven o'clock. Not many people rang that number lately, as Graham had had to update to a more reliable and effective modern mobile, given all his increased responsibility regarding matters shearing. He assumed it would probably be his mother, Dorothea, better known to all as Dora. He was right.

Dora sounded a little agitated, not her usual confident self. She was in the throes of organising things for when the two boys returned from university up north for the semester break in a few weeks. She knew that Sally was also usually very busy and tied up lately, so wanted to give her plenty of warning if she could manage to attend a get-together.

Dora basically launched straight into a long diatribe about the weird conversation she had when she attempted to contact Sally, on Sally's own private mobile number. She stated that she rang in the evening yesterday expecting to speak to Sally. Instead, she was confronted with the voice of a strange but efficient young woman who acted more as a secretary rather than a friend. She simply claimed that Sally was occupied right now, but could she take a message? Dora asked the young woman to get Sally to ring her back. This did not happen; it still had not happened. Dora was confused and a little concerned, considering a small retinue of minor individual incidences, meaningless on their own, surrounding Sally's contactability lately.

Graham listened intently to the outpouring of his mother. He was thinking along the same lines as she spoke, that it tied in with a couple of other things which, at the time, did not mean much, but putting all these little nuances together, he was beginning to get a picture that things were not quite right where Sally was concerned. He, for instance, had not seen her for nearly two years now. That in itself was unusual.

Each time lately when he wished to go up to her little unit near the University where she had studied, he was put off with excuses such as being rather busy, or being involved with lengthy court action, or she just simply needing a bit of time alone.

After this conversation with his mother, Graham decided to give Peter Knuckey a ring at the law firm where Sally practiced her craft of legal representation, to try to ascertain any conditions pertaining to her on which he might be able to enlighten Graham. Peter was circumspect and rather evasive, assuring Graham that all was well with Sally and that she was coping admirably with the rigours of legal life, but was still finding herself in the big wide world, and sometimes required a little alone-time. What on earth was that supposed to mean?

Graham made a decision. He would go up to Sydney alone and see her to check that all was well. It was a tricky arrangement for Graham to travel to Sydney. He found the drive tiresome, the traffic at that end wearisome, and the availability of parking around her little unit was almost non-existent. It was just simply the most convenient to catch the bus from Canberra and use public transport when up there. He made some arrangements with his aging father to stay at the property to mind the dogs and feed the chickens, and he proceeded up to the city. Graham expected to stay with her as usual, so he carried very little with him, just a small knapsack that he could carry with him everywhere, plus a small shoulder bag with any personal items he needed.

Graham thought that he might just pay a fleeting visit to the office where Sally worked and see her, otherwise, if she were not there, he could talk to his friend Peter Knuckey. Graham arrived at the office of Dr Charmers about mid-afternoon. He knew that they often had extended lunch-hours, so hoped to sneak in a quick meeting. He waited in the comfortable waiting area, after talking to the pleasant receptionist. They seemed to have a high turnover of front-desk people, but they were always very pleasant. While he was waiting in the deathly quiet, a framed piece on the wall caught his eye. It was a rather decorative and artistic rendition in calligraphy. Graham wandered over to read it. It appeared to be quite old as well. Fascinatingly, it described in colourful strokes, the origin of the name Charmers. Graham did always wonder why it possessed no 'L' in it, but that mystery was solved here. It appeared that the name originated in ancient times and referred to practitioners of the art of charms, and spells. There was even a Charmers Lane hidden away in old London.

When Peter returned to the office, he graciously agreed to see him as he was a valued friend. In Peter's office, Graham asked if Sally was about, to which he replied that she was not right at this moment. Graham then asked,

'Is all okay with Sally and her work here?'

There was a long awkward delay, then Peter replied,

'Look Graham, Sally has been a little unsettled here lately. We had a couple of things happen that seemed to affect her.'

He was about to continue when there was an interruption

at Peter's door when Dr Charmers leant around the doorway and said,

'Hello Graham. I thought I saw you in here with Peter a moment ago. How's it going?'

'Fine.' said Graham. 'I just popped in to see how Sally was doing.'

Dr Charmers straitened up slightly and entered the room more fully. Then she said,

'Ah, I see. Maybe Graham, you might like to come down to my office. You may like to come too Peter if you wish.'

The two men got up and followed Dr Charmers to her more spacious office. She closed the door and returned to her chair. She stared at Graham for a moment and then began,

'Graham, Sally has been behaving a little out-of-character lately, over the last couple of years. We don't actually see that much of her just at present. I don't think it is anything to overly worry about, but it is not like her to do that. You see, we had a couple of rather nasty cases go against us, quite messy. Sally was the lead on those and I know they affected her badly. Also, about two or more years ago, we had a visit from some security people, not sure where they were from, but they were high-powered people. It involved a case that was also rather messy. Not sure what their involvement was, but they spent some time with Sally but I didn't hear much about it from her. Then there was a second visit from a different security person who took Sally out for an extended lunch break. I didn't hear much about that visit either, but she seemed to be effected by that interaction.'

'I see.' said Graham. 'She has been rather distant lately. This is the first time I have tried to see her for nearly two years. What do you think is the issue?'

'I know those cases effected her confidence, and her attitude to the system. I was somewhat surprised at her reaction. I did expect her to be a little more robust and accepting of these things, especially given her background and life experience. For some reason, the visit of those cyber security men seemed to unease her somewhat, wouldn't you agree Peter?'

Peter nodded. Then he said,

'Sally was unsettled for a while. She mumbled something about disenchantment with the whole system, not with us in particular, but the whole misguided system. I don't have to tell you about that aspect. She hinted at having some time away from it all and getting a parttime job in a café where she has a friend working there. It's in the newish Freycinet Building, down near the harbour.'

'Look, Graham,' said Dr Charmers, 'this work can be demoralising and stressful, especially when things seem to be going against us all the time. Some time away can be helpful, and of course, she is always more that welcome to return, her work here was excellent – all of it – and all of the time. She was a prodigious worker.'

'Okay.' said Graham. 'Thank you both for your time and advice. I will chase her up and let you know if I find anything of note. Thank you, Peter, thank you Lesley.'

Graham departed the office a little rattled. He was annoyed that he was unaware of any potential issues with his now seemingly neglected daughter. If she were not in the office, he thought that he might drop by her unit in case she were there.

The simplest way to her unit was to catch the train from Circular Quay on the T2 line, or any of the stations along that line, and get off near Newtown and walk to her flat which was close to the station. Graham had bought Sally a unit in a small block in Newtown because it was very close to the University of Sydney campus, and it was the least he could do for what he regarded as his neglected; no, really abandoned, daughter, following his harrying separation from his wife. As Graham approached her rather old unit block, which was set close to the street with little front yardage, he was surprised to see an elderly man apparently unlocking Sally's secured letterbox located in the low line of small boxes lining the front wall. He attempted to disguise his approach by acting casually and tourist-like, and then waited a short distance from the front entrance to see what transpired. He did not have to wait long. The man seemed to clear the box, walk inside, possibly even entering the unit itself, and then returned to the street and headed back to the train station. Graham followed him at some distance into the station and then boarded the train on its arrival heading back to the city.

The man alighted the train at the Circular Quay platform and headed up towards the nearby buildings in Phillip Street. He entered a modern tall building and disappeared into its depths. It was the Freycinet Building, as alluded to by Peter Knuckey. Graham followed him in at some distance. He entered the swanky glassed-in foyer through one of those annoying, large, fully-rotating quartered glass door arrangements into which one seemed to have to choose the appropriate moment to enter or be denied entry until the next awkward swing came around. He did despise these modern fangled contraptions. What ever happened to a plain opening door?

The foyer was bright and airy, with noticeable security personnel conspicuously visible. He thought that he had seen the old man enter the lift by the far wall and he thought that he seemed to head for the top-most floors somewhere. Graham tried to head over to the directory board by the large reception desk, but there were many vacant slots in that board that hindered his ability to ascertain the occupants located higher up. He also noticed that the security person near the lifts was eyeing him carefully. He decided to head for the café which was located over in the other far corner, with seating and views out onto the busy street. Graham wandered into the café, and up to the counter. He asked the young woman at the counter if there was a Sally Longley working there. He was met with a blank look, and finally, a decided and confused 'No.'

That was the end of that line of inquiry. Next, he ventured over to the large well-manned and busy reception counter for the main building. A pleasant young woman, well dressed and very presentable asked if she could help him. Graham asked if there was a Sally Longley working in the building. The young woman looked slightly askance at Graham, and replied efficiently,

'Of course, Sir. May I ask who's enquiring after her?' Graham responded,

'I'm her father, Graham Longley, if she is here.'

'Just a moment please Sir.' the girl said with a slight grin.

The girl buzzed a number and some interaction was conducted, most of which he could not fully hear. Then she said to him,

'Someone will be down in a moment Sir. You may take a seat over there in the waiting area if you like.'

Graham was nonplussed. What just happened? He was led to believe Sally was discontented with her environment in the high-powered atmosphere of the busy legal office, so what is she doing here in this weird place? He took a seat on the modern and comfortable seating arrangements, along with several others there. He was fascinated by the goings-on about him. There was much activity and much coming and going. A rather sombre group of very well-dressed men alighted one of the lifts, chatting in much seriousness in a guarded, but distinctly American, accent.

After a short time, he perceived a tall, very attractive and elegantly attired young woman in fashionable, and feminine, light-coloured business attire depart one of the lifts and head for the counter. She glided over to the desk in a slightly bouncy gait, arms swinging mildly exaggeratedly, exuding efficiency and poise. The girl there pointed at Graham and the new woman headed towards him.

'Mr Longley?' she enquired in a cultured pleasant accent.

'Yes.' he responded, as he proceeded to rise from the seat, grabbing his knapsack.

'My name is Rachael; Miss Longley will see you now.' she said.

The security guard eyed him suspiciously, but, as he acknowledged the young woman escorting him into the lift, he seemed satisfied with the situation. Graham was again, or was that still, non-plussed. Who was Rachael and where were they going? He just wanted to see his little girl who apparently was struggling slightly with life at the moment. What was he doing in this atmosphere?

Rachael pushed a separate button and turned to Graham.

'Here, Mr Longley, you will need this to enter the floor.' With that, she handed him a security card attached to a long dark lanyard, she smiling pleasantly and stared him confidently in the eye.

'What exactly is this place?' asked a confused Graham.

The young woman stared knowingly at Graham, smiled slightly and just turned to examine the floor indicator whipping up the floor numbers within its little gleaming metal frame on the lift wall. It rapidly rose many floors, the floor number registration in its frame suddenly ceasing, while the lift was still moving upwards, and then, with a sudden jerk, stopped and immediately the twin doors opened onto a bright, naturally-lit extensive floor. Here there were many people who all seemed to be very gainfully employed indeed. Graham was a little disturbed by all the activity and a little nervous for his daughter. There was a security barrier at the lift entrance, Graham simply followed the lead of Rachael with his own lanyard key, and then he followed her along the casually demarked access way lined with an assortment of desks and stands seemingly randomly spaced about the totally open-floor plan. Except at the far end, there was a small allotment of a few offices, almost totally of glass but each with a door if privacy was so desired.

It all briefly reminded him of his now long almost forgotten sojourn into office accommodation at the financial institution that he ditched on his resignation after the trauma of Jenny's leaving him. He was amazed at the profusion of computer hardware. Rachael headed for a large corner office and ushered Graham to enter the room. Graham hesitated for a moment, but then he saw the seemingly forlorn figure, again immaculately dressed in a business dress-suit with a dark skirt and matching jacket, standing at the far wall staring out the huge window onto the city-scape with her hands clasped behind her back, as if she were a little girl awaiting some admonition.

Graham entered the room a little tentatively, as it was a large room with a long table set on one side with eight chairs around it, set for meetings. Rachael departed, gently closing the heavy glass-panelled door behind her and the woman turned to face Graham.

'Hello Father.' she said.

'Sally!' he almost exclaimed.

'It's lovely to see you Father.' she said, a little more animated this time, and almost bounding over to greet him. She demonstratively wrapped her arms about him and gave him a serious hug. From Sally, that was a very rare acceptance of another person into her space, especially, Graham instantly recalled, as she always seemed to harbour a mild resentment and coldness towards him.

'How did you find me?' she asked, looking up at him and smiling almost excitedly.

'Sal, how are you? You look wonderful. We all thought that you were not entirely happy with life.'

'I'm fine thanks Dad. But how did you find me?'

'I followed that old man from your flat back to this building.' he said.

'Oh, that's Howard, my runaround man.'

He looked at her quizzically. <u>My</u> *runaround man* he surmised. Things were definitely not quite adding up. And what was this place anyway?

He looked discerningly at her. She seemed quite radiant to him, a picture of contentment. She wore some modest but chic gleaming jewellery, notably earrings and some rings, on her right hand, that even he could tell could be expensive. So, what was all the fuss about that she could not seem to be interacting with her family and her work colleagues?

'So, what is this place then?' he asked. 'Dr Charmers, and Peter for that matter, said that you had problems at work with some cases. They were concerned for your well-being.'

'No, Dad, I certainly did not have issues with any cases. I won't deny that I was becoming disenchanted with the whole system and the endless pointedly one-sided results that seem to be handed out. But I am still intrigued as to how you found me.'

Graham began to expand in great detail all about her

grandmother's trying to contact her, his visit to the legal office and speaking with Peter Knuckey and Lesley Charmers and all their concerns for what they deduced was some sort of disillusionment of Sally's with what was happening in her life. Sally acknowledged that she had ignored her grandmother's call and asked Graham to apologise to her for that oversight.

'So then, why are you here?' he asked her again.

'Sit down Dad.' she said, pointing to a comfortable double lounge placed along the one wall that was solid, having no glass panelling in it. Graham moved over and sat on one side. Sally joined him, grasping his hand. He was stunned; she was usually so distant, especially towards him.

'I'm so glad to see you, you know. I really appreciate the effort.'

'That's fine love. As long as you're all right, and happy.'

'I am Dad, but something *has* happened.'

'Do tell.' he said.

'Okay, this is rather complicated, but I will tell you about it if you wish. I did have a couple of bad results with cases involving difficult and controversial judgements, but that was not the problem. In some ways they were a good diversion for what really happened. You see, about two and a half years ago, a young man came into the practice seeking representation in a complex and intricate case of a relationship breakdown. He was from Canberra and said he worked in the security industry there. I asked why he wished to engage us here in Sydney. He had a long-winded explanation about the delicate nature of his work and the difficulties involved with his associations. It all seemed legitimate enough, so we proceeded, Lesley giving me the run on this case.

'The first hint that something was possibly awry with this situation occurred only a few days after his arrival. I came in one morning and I had a feeling something was not quite right with my computer. I got the sense that someone had tried, or even managed, to hack into my system.'

'No!' exclaimed Graham.

'Yes, indeed. But that was not in itself the issue, and most people would not have tweaked to that happening, but I have ways. You see, we have a double firewall security system at the office there. For someone to bypass not one but two sophisticated and advanced security protocols, means they were not your usual novice hacker. Our portal directs all in-coming traffic, and intruders, directly to our security firewall. They needed to possess advanced skills, high training and a very comprehensive understanding of computer programming and digital manipulation. They were not mugs. To access only my machine despite us having a server for that floor, indicated very advanced skills. I wondered why they would only try to hack me, and what was of interest to them about any of my cases. Or was it just someone trying their luck at random.

'I was worried and concerned about this happening, as no one else was effected. I decided to add another line of protection. I installed a new program, one that contained a sophisticated AI component that I had developed myself. What I installed was a little algorithmic device that I had been working on for years now, more as a sideline, almost a hobby.'

'But you don't know anything about computers, do you?' asked a puzzled Graham.

'Yes Father, actually I do. Don't you recall that I took computing science as an elective with my legal degree. I found it so enthralling that I majored in it as well as legal studies. It was not something I bragged about, as it was not really related to my legal course, well, not to the extent that I finally pursued it in the end. I loved it and found it totally up my alley.' she said, looking at him knowingly.

'Well, I never knew that. Good for you Sally, if you enjoyed it and loved doing it.'

'I did Dad, I thoroughly loved it, and I am very good at it.' She paused again to emphasise that fact. 'Anyway, I have been working on a different security program for computers. But I kept coming up with the same problems all the time. In the end I finally decided that I would have to actually create an entirely new computer language – totally different from all other languages, with unrelated syntax.'

'I'm not going to get lost in all this geeky jargon am I?'

'No Dad. I will keep it simple. It took me years really, but I finally began to get a system together that is unique. I call it Omicron for reasons you need not know, and it is run by my own created language called Infinity.'

'That's a nice name.'

'Yes. I call it that because this structure not only uses a near infinite number of symbols and character combinations, it also has within its program seven gene cells that also change every nine seconds. So, there is no way any computing search-engine can manipulate seven different line changes and account for them all changing variably every nine seconds.'

'That sounds awfully complicated.' said Graham.

'It is not really. Look, it's like this. Imagine you have a tourist bus full of tourists from Europe and some from Asia and even elsewhere. They all speak dozens of different languages but can communicate mostly by using English. Now imagine that bus leaves Alice Springs and heads out to Standley Chasm and Ormiston Gorge. Way out from Alice Springs, that bus meets up with an old man who only speaks Arrernte or Pitjantjara or one of the desert dialects. No one on that bus can communicate with him at all, despite having access to such a wide range of common languages. Well, I've created a unique computer language that only I speak, immediately negating all the dozens of recognised computer languages that already exist – all of them. And, at this stage, it cannot be deciphered, not by anyone.'

'What's the point of that? Don't you need to speak to other computers too?' asked Graham.

'Exactly. I can still communicate with all the world using the known languages, and they can still communicate with me and the server that controls our floor. But the instant they try to infiltrate beyond the firewalls of known security systems, and appear to be suspect, and can't talk to the computer in Infinity, they run up against the foreign language that bears no relationship to any other, and is unique. Imagine this: in English we have many words for a plate. There is dinner plate, butter plate, bowl, coup, dish, platter, saucer, and more. Well, think of a language that has an infinite number of words to describe any object – and that description alters every nine seconds. No one can interpret that language. My algorithm deciphers the meaning by the context and the instructions from overrule protocols it receives from multiple inputs aligned by the AI to navigate the instructions following a set of rules that are imbedded within the system.'

'You're losing me. What's the purpose of a computer language if it is meaningless?'

'There are many types of languages. There are high-level languages that are more abstract but easier to read and write; low-level languages that are more closely tied to the computer's hardware; procedural languages that focus on step-by-step instructions; object-oriented languages that organise code around objects; functional languages, scriptural languages and query languages for retrieving information from databases. There are also configuration languages, command languages, and transformation languages for converting data from one format to another. I combine facets from many of these systems that perform the same tasks to produce results, but use a language that optimises their strong points and is uninterpretable using any one single language that is known.

'The invading computer then tries to interrogate the foreign system, but my program confuses it entirely and it starts to disintegrate, the more it tries to delve into this obstruction the deeper is the retaliation. You see, I've installed a high-end newer AI unit in which my program is then designed to follow a double feed-back loop that begins to transmit instructions back to the interrogating or hacker's computer giving it instructions on how to interpret this new blockage. All the time, my program is slowly destroying the system from within the hacker's computer until it literally dies because of the error-loop. It is destroyed, because I have sent viruses to them using a mosquito gene. The instant they land on my patch, through the regular security systems bypass, the mosquito virus bites them and transmits viruses to the invader through my new instructions it's trying to use to break down the barrier. It will spread throughout all their server system, but not hitting their mainframe. The server then bottlenecks the modal input pipeline. Additionally, it's like a trojan horse as well, because some of it sits there awaiting activation by the invasive computer's user. It is a double whammy. They literally all go blank, or freeze *in situ*. It is unfixable because no one can interpret my new language. At least that was the theory. I had no way of ever knowing if the theory translated into fact, because no hacker is ever going to ring me up and say his computer is dead, or frozen, how can he get around my program, is he?'

'So how do you know it works?' asked Graham,

'Because, it turns out that the hackers were top-notch highly-trained experts working for a secret government security entity, I reckon it was ASIO, or a branch of that organisation and they were concerned what this client of mine might be revealing. They paid me a visit at the office, and that's when the world changed. By acknowledging their loss, it confirmed my theoretical code stream that was activated by them actually performed some task or other, just as I had hoped I had designed it to do.'

'So, what happened next?' asked Graham.

'We had a long chat. They were quite adamant and very forceful in their discussion. They insisted that I reveal all the details and explain exactly how it worked. I was threatened with all sorts of repercussions if I did not comply.'

'What did you do?'

'First, I pointed out that they had breached the law regarding unauthorised intrusion into private and personal computer domains. I assumed they knew that they were dealing with a reputable, and capable, legal office of some standing. They dismissed that argument due to their national security concerns. But, there are severe punishments for that act. Second, I pointed out that this was privately-developed intellectual property safeguarded by the Copyright Act of 1968, and other laws, and legal ownership of intellectual property by the creator. Infringement can entail severe consequences. Parts of this product are unique and have been registered under the Patents Act 1990, section 15, and third, I pointed out that this program, developed by me, and me alone, was designed specifically for this express purpose; namely: to safeguard material on the web from being accessed by unauthorised persons, to protect information and data from being stolen and by criminal actions conducted by cyber thieves.'

'That must have stymied them a trifle.' stated Graham.

'And you had to do this all alone I gather, with no input from Lesley, or anybody else.'

'Yes, Dad. But I also believed in what I was doing, and had great faith in my deductions and reasoning and I was confident that it should work all right.'

'What happened next?' asked an almost excited Graham.

'A few days later, a man come into the office and asked to speak to me about the problem his organisation had with me. He was a very nice man, elderly, and polite. He was genuinely interested in my software development and we had a long chat about its use and potential. He and I have now had a most rewarding association. I really owe where I am now to him.'

'Well done you.' said an openly impressed Graham.

'Thank you. I only hope I have not created the atomic bomb.'

'What do you mean?'

She placed her hand on Graham's leg, rubbing it lovingly, and said, staring into his eyes,

'Think about it Father. I designed this program as a defensive device to thwart cyber thieves and criminals. It is designed to filter out incoming attacks, that's all. The fact that it destroys the unauthorised interrogator is the price they pay for their intrusion. Just imagine if someone decoded the program to act as an offensive weapon and was able to unleash it onto the world in reverse. The ramifications are startling, and horrendous.'

'What's the answer then?'

'That's the next issue.' she said. 'I've spent a lot of time and thought on this product. I have installed two more coding lines into it, new algorithms written in Infinity. The first lot of security guys did not like this next bit of news, at all. One algorithm I called the Samson solution. Just like Samson, when he regains his strength, he destroys the Philistine temple, all of it and the people in there - including himself. This coding self-destructs if anyone tries to send it independently of any incoming threat, or tries to retrieve it in its entirety to move somewhere else.'

'Clever.' said Graham.

'Yeah, but there's more. As an added precaution, I added a kamikaze code. This one really threw them.'

'What's that do?'

'After three years from the date of installation, the coding begins to senesce and the random gene-changes that occur every nine seconds cease and the system reverts to a meaningless jumble of text that is just gobbledegook. I am working on that aspect of the system, mostly at their request I might add. At this point in time Dad, I am the only producer of this product, the sole world harbinger of all its capability. I don't know whether to take that secret with me to the grave, or whether to develop it further. Somebody someday will probably manage to cut into this system and manipulate it, for I don't know what purpose.'

'So, what's with this old man taking on your case? asked Graham.

He was so fascinated with this development. He saw firsthand the devastation it can cause in an organisation, and he truly wanted to advance it. He could fully see its potential, way beyond a simple little device added to some solicitor's computer.'

'Why? What has he in mind?'

'It's security potential is earth-shattering. He was impressed with the Sampson solution, as well as the kamikaze code. I also explained to him, and only him, about one other protection. I called it Clause 39b.'

'What's that one do?'

'It's another subroutine protocol I inserted. This one is for the whole overall network, possibly even including not just the server for one area, but the mainframe as well, for the whole organisation. It's a killer. It acts, and looks like an error handler, or a fault manager, but in reality, it will decouple the entire infrastructure from any central control and re-write the access permissions. It also re-assigns access privileges from everybody and anybody caught attempting to infiltrate the system. That's because you need a single digital signature assigned by the owner to regain access. And that owner of course, is me.'

'Sally, I had no Idea. You should have contacted me if you wanted to talk. I can't help you with the technical stuff, but I'm always here as a sounding board for you, you know.'

'Yes. I know. But it has all developed so quickly. I'm still coming to terms with it all. I am very grateful to you Dad for coming in today. I really appreciate being able to talk about this to someone I can really trust.'

'So, what's the situation now then?' asked Graham.

'Well, this senior officer from a secret classified security organisation in Canberra contacted me and we took it from there. He has been most obliging, and helpful. I value him being around to fend off unwanted enquiries from all over the world.'

'That is amazing. I hope I have been of some comfort to you Sal.' said Graham. He had the feeling all along that Sally was almost desperate to raise these issues with somebody, as she became more animated and almost desperate to expand on her unique creation; – but not just anybody – someone she could safely confide in. Then it occurred to him about the matter of the value of such a creation.

'It must be worth a fortune Sal.' he stated.

'Yes Dad. It's priceless. Most of those people out there in the office are not technicians, they're accountants and lawyers, and financial investment specialists.' she said almost sadly. 'I own this entire building Father, plus other stuff. You should see the technical nature of the leasing contract I devised. You have no idea just how useful that law degree has been for me in this pursuit. At this stage I only lease the whole program out, I do not sell it outright to anybody – not anybody. That is causing huge problems, but the system is so unique and valuable, if they want it, they must lease it from me – and pay a motser. I already have arrangements with many major military entities, major companies, universities, security agencies and even some smaller groups who deal in sensitive data. I point out in great detail all the condition under which I lease out this product and that it is time-limited. If I have no issues with the leasing entity, I will replace the whole program for free after the three years expires.'

Graham sat in deep puzzling thought. He was not entirely sure he fully understood all the ramifications of all he had just heard, all coming from his own little girl. He had no idea she was so amazingly cleaver and capable, and apparently, brilliant at this field that he knew almost nothing about.

'And you've told no one about this Sal?'

'No Father, not a sole. Apart from my contact in Canberra. The people working here know that I own this software product, but most are led to believe that it is just another start-up company that will probably peter out soon enough, as most of them seem to do once everybody else cottons onto the existence of the coding and it is copied easily enough, or more likely, what happens is that some major tech company buys out the product to add to their already massive productions and profit line. My main problem, apart from endless harassment from potential eager buyers, is how to handle the excessive income from the leasing program that we are operating. Most people here have no idea that I own the whole building, let alone anything else. I might have to talk to you about financial matters, Dad, as that was your forté wasn't it?'

'Well, once I had talent, not so sure now though, especially if you're talking big moolah.' he added. Then Sally said,

'I am desperate to maintain complete anonymity at all costs. I got wind of an ABC documentary that was being prepared on tax fraud and evasion when someone in the taxation office apparently leaked some financial information about one of the companies that I set up in order to hide my identity and the existence of this whole valuable coding line. I believe there was extreme pressure brought to bear on them by the security people associated with the federal government security organisation. I don't know which one, probably my man in Canberra. There seems to be many of them, most of which I have never even heard of. I believe we are talking severe jail time here.'

'Sal, I don't know what to say.' said Graham.

'Can you stay for some dinner with me tonight?'

'Sure.' said Graham.

'Can you stay with me tonight?' she asked.

'Of course. That's why I came up.'

'Excellent. Thanks Dad.' she almost exclaimed. 'Just let me see Rachael for a minute. Then we'll go.'

Sally got up out of the lounge and headed for the door. She opened it and called out to Rachael. Then she returned to her own seat behind the ornate and neat desk.

'Do you want me to leave for a minute?' asked Graham.

'No, of course not. I'll just tidy up a couple of things and then we'll go.'

Rachael entered the office and strode to stand by the desk.

'Anything of importance?' asked Sally.

'The PM's office rang again. The military chief's office also is keen to see you.'

'I bet they are.' announced Sally.

'Also, there are several American visitors lined up, plus both those universities and the medical funds have placed a deposit in the receival account.'

'Anything else?'

'Nothing that can't wait.' said Rachael.

'Good. Thank you Rachael. You can go if you like. I'm taking my dad out for the evening. I will be back in the morning.'

'Thanks Sally. See you then. Nice to have met you Mr Longley. Enjoy your evening.' said Rachael with the slightest of a pleasant smile as she exited the room.

'Do you think you can make it to the family weekend in September?' asked Graham.

'I'd love to Dad. Now you know about this thing. I will try to be there. I really don't know exactly how to explain myself.'

'Leave that to me.' said Graham. 'I will lay some ground work that will keep them from asking you too many questions.'

'Thank you Dad. That would make my visit easier. Could I stay with you out at the farm?' she asked.

'Absolutely. I'd love to have you there for a few days. And I promise not to talk about sheep at all.'

Sally smiled. 'Thanks Dad. Could I bring Rachael with me. She could keep an eye on any developments that may need attention. Besides, she could do with a break. She has never been to the country I don't think. She might like it for a change'

'Of course. She seems like a very nice girl.'

'She is. She is also very bright and efficient. I have an office manager here who can look after the office while I'm away. It would be lovely to spend some time with you at the farm.'

With that, Sally stood up, gathered a small shoulder bag and headed for the door. Graham stood up and followed her out. They headed for the floor exit and entered the lift to the ground floor. Once in the street, Graham asked Sally how she gets to her flat from here. Sally replied simply that she walked. Graham said that was a long walk. To which Sally responded, that no, it was literally just around the corner. Sally said that they would go to her place first. Then she would shout him dinner at a near-by restaurant. Graham was intrigued.

Sally was right. It was literally just around the corner. She led him to a magnificent new high-security apartment building close to the quay, and ascended to the top floor, where she entered a three-floor penthouse with stunning harbour views. She pointed out to Graham that she also owned this penthouse apartment outright. How did he like it? He was speechless. She pointed out that she still owned the old flat in Newtown, as she did not know how to explain all these new assets yet to the family.

Sally made for the enormous gleaming kitchen that had a magical view out over the harbour beyond the Opera House and the Sydney Harbour Bridge. Graham was spell-bound. She made them each a cup of coffee. Graham remarked that it was like something out of a magazine. Sally agreed, but announced that she had so little time at the moment that she rarely was able to use it fully. That is why it looked so pristine. Sally showed Graham to a third-floor bedroom and then she changed and they headed out again to a nearby swanky restaurant.

This was an experience that was foreign to the now totally countrified Graham Longley; dining out at all, let alone at some high-end ritzy establishment with a Michelin-hatted rating and some renowned chef of some considerable note. Not only that, Sally seemed to be quite comfortable in this environment and also appeared to be at least recognised as a regular of some sort. He felt a little out of place. She certainly seemed to move in more exalted circles than he ever imagined that he could himself achieve.

Sally was her usual quiet self, though she did seem a little more outwardly contented than he recalled she used to seem to be in his company. Maybe this new field and the self-worth she derived from that endeavour suited her capabilities and desires better than the straight legal work that often entailed disappointment and stress. She also seemed to be preoccupied within her own thoughts most of the time. During the evening, after a bit of meaningless chatter, Graham asked Sally if she were happy in her personal life. Did she have a man in her life for instance? Sally looked at him seriously and replied,

'No, not at the moment. I am so totally occupied with this new direction and I am perfectly happy with my lot. You can see Dad the extent to which this enterprise is so far rewarding me financially. I am awash with money and really do enjoy the work I have. I also am surrounded by some very capable and supportive people in my organisation. What about you, Dad? You happy on the farm?'

'Yes, thanks Sal. I love it immensely. Don't quite know why, but I do.'

'Have you never thought of having another woman in your life out there? It must get lonely on your own.'

'That is not on my radar Sal. You may not believe this, but I still love your mother. The woman you knew was not the woman I married. I still do love her and fondly remember our first days together. I have no desire to replace that memory with new ones. I wish to honour and respect her memory.'

Sally looked at him blankly, not sure she understood that position, especially after she discovered so much more about the disintegration of his marriage and the circumstances surrounding her father's separation.

'How long have you known Rachael?' asked Graham.'

'Oh, a long time. We met at Uni and got along really well. She's very smart. She did electives in business affairs and company management along with her law degree. I'm lucky to have her. She still lives with her parents in Elizabeth Bay. They're not short of a quid I wager. She drives a swanky European car of some sort too.'

'Well, if you want to ask her along, you're more than welcome. It's just that she struck me as a very sophisticated and glamorous woman, not the type to rough it in the backblocks of the Monaro.'

'True.' said Sally. 'I don't think she's ever been to the bush at all. She is a true cityite. I will inform her, if she's interested, what to expect.'

'Yeah, good idea. How long can you stay?' asked Graham.

'Only a few days. If it's a Sunday event, I'll try and come on the Thursday and probably have to leave on the Monday. Is that all right?' asked Sally.

'Yeah, excellent. If you change your mind and want to stay with your grandparents in town, that will be no problem either.'

'That's unlikely Dad. I don't think I can handle the endless questions for the moment. Besides, it will be nice to spend some time with you and the boys at home.'

Then Graham said, 'Sal, you really should just let Peter and Dr Charmers know that you may not be back. They were quite concerned for you and would welcome you back there, you know.'

'Yes. I feel a bit guilty about that. They were both very good to me. I don't want them to think I just used them for my own advantage. But this thing has just ballooned enormously so quickly and with so much demand, I am lost in all its workings. Besides, I am still refining aspect of it all the time.'

'Yes, I can see that. Look, I'd like to just pop back in on the way back to the farm and tell them that you are fine and happy, and maybe finding other avenues. Would that be all right?'

'Yes, okay. I will go and see them sometime, I promise. I just don't know how to tell them, or how much to tell them.'

Graham spent the next two days visiting his amazing

daughter in her new province, marvelling at what he witnessed. He got to know Rachael a little better. His first thoughts about her were proving to be accurate. He surmised that she may not thoroughly enjoy her sojourn to the wilds of the country. Time would tell. She reminded him a little of a city version of Sophia Faulkner, though her talents were a little more circumspect. He also did return to the Charmers legal office and hinted that all was well and that Sally may have inadvertently found another line of occupation involving other skills that she possessed. He did emphasise that in her new domain that she benefitted hugely from her knowledge of the law and her time with the Charmers law firm. Her new role basically evolved from her time with them. They were happy with that explanation. Sally would in due course also return to keep up relationships. She could not divulge the entirety of her creation, however.

## CHAPTER NINE

On the appointed Thursday in September, Sally and Rachael departed Sydney airport for Canberra, after stocking up on some more appropriate and hard-waring designer country apparel. Graham arranged to meet them at the airport in his father's sedan; far more suitable for the gentrified city duo than his Toyota farm ute. He then whisked them initially to his parent's place in Queanbeyan so that they could renew, or, in Rachael's case, meet, the family that was there. They had a brief luncheon and a chat before Graham headed for the ute and placed their rather bulky suitcases into the back and covered them extensively with tarps. Then they headed off to the farm, Sally sitting in the middle next to her father, on the old bench seat, as Rachael was taller and more comfortable with the added leg-room offered by the window seat. It would be a rough journey; a new experience for the urban elite.

Graham made a small detour on arrival at Captains Flat to check on the condition of the old cottage that he now rented out. When all appeared in order from across the street on the roadway, he headed off up the gravel road to the east and to his place. On arrival at the property, Sally was enthusiastic to renew acquaintances with her two brothers, Sam and Ben, and Rachael was introduced to the rigours of isolation and the two young men she would be sharing the next few days with in this totally unfamiliar atmosphere. The portents were not good at this point, as one of the very few comments the bewildered Rachael seemed to manage during the dusty and bumpy journey after leaving Captains Flat, and while Sally made the odd chatter with her father, was to proclaim,

'People don't actually live out here, do they?'

Graham could but smile inwardly and marvel at just how much he loved the whole situation where he now lived. He did recall, however, that he held similar views on his initial arrival into this wilderness, so was accommodating to her feelings.

The big event with the family was planned for the Sunday and to occupy most of the day. That left all day Friday and Saturday for the two girls to experience what to Sally was Graham's new home and for Rachael to experience some aspects of rural living. Prior to Sally's coming down to the property, Graham had contacted Jackson to see if it were possible for him to take Sally over, say for a brief Saturday afternoon gathering, to meet up again with the Faulkners and renew acquaintances with Sophia, who, along with some of her friends, had discussed with a then school-girl Sally the options and experiences of university life.

Jackson was only too pleased to accommodate that request for Graham, if Sally so desired. At that moment, Graham was not entirely sure whether Rachael would also be accompanying Sally down from the city, so he did not mention that fact. Graham did think at the time that it might be a rather good introduction for the classy Rachael to see that she at least had her equals domiciled in the rural backblocks as an added bonus.

Friday drifted by in familiarising the family with the entirety of the novel existence that was Graham's different lifestyle. Sally was keen enough to renew acquaintances with the obliging Faulkners, and assured Rachael that she would fit in admirably, as long as not too many deep searching questions were sent their way about exactly what it was that they did in the city. Graham had laid the groundwork with all and sundry that Sally was still working on legal matters and was involved as a part of that regime with some technical programming work as well. It was all rather uninteresting and tedious, as well as of course, also dealing with very confidential matters.

The Faulkners had agreed to arrange a small afternoon tea for Graham and the two women only, not the boys who would remain at the farm. It was also expected to be fairly brief, with little of note to transpire over the course of the afternoon. That was the first assumption that was to be shattered as the afternoon meandered on.

They arrived over there about one in the afternoon.

Graham was careful to ensure that Rachael in particular was able to take in the magnificent array of equine surroundings; the extensive yards, the colonial-period stables, accompanied by the double-fronted and ornate large stone building that was originally the coach house, and the high-fenced manège located prominently along the tree-lined entrance drive. Things were all progressing swimmingly at first, then after about an hour or so, things started to happen that were not entirely how the family had hoped the session would pan out. Rachael began to receive some annoying mobile phone calls. Sally had specifically requested that only the most dire of emergencies were to be sent on to the two women during their very rare absence from the office and the even rarer difficulty in, and near-lack of, contactability.

The entire party consisting of Jackson and Edith, his wife, plus Sophia and Graham and the two girls were on the spacious veranda that had an expansive view over the front part of the property that included the extensive horse facilities and the colonial-age stables and coach house, visible through the profusion of ancient exotic trees filling the manicured lawns. Also included in the party was Xavier, Fiona's brother originally from out west, because of his contacts with that sphere of Graham's holdings, plus his association with Graham. There were also a couple of other attendees associated with Graham and his contacts with the Faulkners. The two women were fascinated that these rural moguls were the possessors of the charming maid-servant that attended to their every need.

The drama began when Rachael finally had to sheepishly re-enter the confines of the pleasant veranda afternoon-tea from her conversations out on the lawns and semi-whisper something to Sally.

As everyone stopped their pleasantries and peered at Sally, she looked more concerned than annoyed and then rather apologetically announced to all that she sadly would have to attend to this troublesome call on Rachael's mobile. As she raised herself out of the chair, she enquired in a most conciliatory manner over the phone,

'Yes Admiral, what is the matter?'

There were meaningful glances cast among the gathering at that rather brief retort. As Sally descended the magnificent and ornate carved stone stairway onto the lawn, the party could hear as Sally departed their range, another almost appeasing rejoinder,

'Well Admiral, there's only two ways that can occur.'

Then the conversation went out of their hearing, but all could tell that Sally was most concerned. Poor Rachael could but sheepishly apologise for this annoying interruption. A pall of deathly silence descended on the former sedate joviality that was in evidence prior to this interruption, all sitting in total unabashed eagerness to see the next step in this exciting and unexpected little drama unfolding in their otherwise quiet, predictable and very ordinary lives. Above the deathly silence, Sally could be heard raising her voice at this Admiral, but, no one could translate the meaning of the distant conversation.

Sally returned after some time. She climbed the stone stairs and apologised profusely, looking at both the Faulkners and at Graham. She announced that she may have to depart this little affair, but would cover that eventuality as it arrived. Graham asked if all was well. Sally simply responded that there had been issues with one of her clients, a most significant entity.

Sally sighed audibly and put her head into her right hand that was leaning on the wide arm of the chair. Then she asked,

'Mr Faulkner, is there somewhere here that a helicopter can land?'

'Yes, of course.' announced a puzzled and grinning Jackson. 'Why do you ask?'

Sally looked at Graham dejectedly, then announced, turning back to Jackson, 'They may be sending one here shortly.'

Graham asked, 'Why, what's happened?'

'There's been a glitch in one of my accounts. I may have to attend to it. I've asked the Admiral, sorry, the client, if they send a helicopter for me, to ring on Rachael's phone and we will direct them to where we are.'

Shortly after, the now alert and expectant throng, listening intently for the sound of any approaching aircraft, could definitely hear the familiar sound of a heavy helicopter approaching from the north, the loud drone of its huge rotors humming distinctly through the still country air. That was indeed a very quick response to that announcement. Then the phone rang and Sally directed the pilot to land on the roadway that was the entrance to the property, and, she emphasised to them, please do not hit anything; meaning: livestock. The excited crowd leapt out of their chairs and headed hurriedly down out of the house yard and then down the roadway to a wider expanse of driveway where the large machine was already hovering high above preparatory to landing.

In a whirl of ascending debris and dust, the huge Airforce helicopter, adorned with all the official Airforce insignia, gracefully landed on the road and the large door opened allowing one occupant to alight. Sally said to Graham,

'Please don't wait for me here, I will get them to drop me off back at your farm this evening.'

She again apologised profusely to the Faulkners and turned to meet the approaching officer in his flight uniform. The machine then departed again in a cloud of dust and debris and flew off rapidly to the north.

'What's that about, Rachael?' asked Graham.

'I'm not too sure, Mr Longley.' was all she diplomatically replied.

All this formality was starting to indicate that something serious must be afoot. The remaining throng just stared at each other in total bemusement and pleasant entertainment at the unfolding excitement that they had all just witnessed. They had never seen anything like it at all before.

The afternoon faded into some mild speculation, but as both Graham and Rachael were circumspect about outcomes, the conversation drifted back to more mundane matters. Graham decided that it was time to make tracks and he and Rachael departed the bemused Faulkner estate late in the afternoon.

Meanwhile, the agitated Sally was ensconced in the noisy and vibrating helicopter headed at full speed north towards Canberra. The security director, the Rear-Admiral, once he learned that his savour was not entrenched in her usual Sydney habitat, but located only minutes away by air on the nearby Monaro, could not believe his luck, so he encouraged and pressed Sally to agree to a swift pick-up and transportation to his headquarters in Canberra. Sally was disappointingly ready to acquiesce to this request for two reasons. One was that this issue was just about unique in her experience associated with her security program, which she was still refining, but also because this particular director had been her major supporter and protector whenever nosey intrusions were encountered from any source at all; be it military, official or civilian. The helicopter made quick time to the capital and landed at the Fairbairn RAAF Base. Sally was then quickly whisked off to the nearby headquarters located a short drive from the RAAF Base and adjacent to the Russell Hill military complex and offices, still dressed in her rural clobber, albeit an upmarket variety, but nevertheless, not usual city attire.

She was then admitted to the highly-secured building by an eager Chief. Sally had asked that the room be locked down and that nobody – no one at all, be allowed to either enter or leave the room where the problem existed. She entered the room with the director and immediately looked carefully around. There were only seven people in that room, one, a woman in uniform, the rest in civilian clothes.

Sally then quickly wandered around the relatively large room but with only seven or eight computer screens in use on that Saturday afternoon. The guilty machines all stood out immediately as they were all locked in the on position, but with unresponsive screens.

Then Sally approached the group of users congregated around the near end of the room awaiting developments. She looked them up and down individually, trying to take in their personalities and appropriateness for this task. All the men were quite young to middle-aged and appeared to her to be undecipherable in that endeavour. She did pause momentarily longer at the uniformed woman, a young officer about thirty with unintelligible insignia and rank levels, at least to Sally, but she did note the name tag on her uniform. Then she said firmly and deliberately to the assembled staff, her voice exuding authority and command,

'There are only two ways this problem can have arisen. One: someone in here has tried to interrogate the software beyond their remit; and the limits of their jurisdiction.'

There was a long pause as Sally surveyed the assembled personnel. There was no reaction. Then she continued,

'Or two, someone from in here has tried to interrogate an outside entity whose machine is already installed with Omicron software, which is operated by the language known as Infinity. Omicron is the fifteenth iteration of this reality, hence the name. There are in existence some earlier versions that cannot jump forms, but, they all use the language Infinity. So, if someone in here has attempted to enter into an interrogation mode on a machine already loaded with Omicron, or a predecessor, which will also be using Infinity, that outside machine will override your machine because that is the whole point of this system. The initiated response from the attacked, or threatened machine, will then begin to transmit its expected replies.

'If, however, that outside machine realises that it has struck a fellow traveller by encountering Infinity, that outside machine will terminate its killing sequence by initiating a threat-override matrix until it is informed, *by an operator*, that the intruder is not a *bone fide* threat but hopefully a like-minded colleague; or an operator-error. Now, I can determine which of these possibilities it is quickly enough by the interrogation of each machine. The perpetrator will have been given two: that is two, warnings. The first one will have said 'error key: do you wish to proceed', with the 'yes' window in red. If you pressed 'yes', you will have been given another warning, saying, 'unauthorised directive, do you wish to proceed'. At that point, if you again pressed 'yes', the whole server set servicing those machines will set up a bottleneck mode in the input pipeline, and then it will freeze everything, but not at this stage, destroy the initiator.'

'Surely, I can safely assume that the problem is not the first case of someone attempting to investigate the operating codes of this system. I am going to assume that someone in here has encountered a machine already loaded with Omicron, or a precursor. Is that a safe assumption?'

There was initially silence and bafflement at the prologue just delivered by this obviously very advanced technical mind outlining some fundamentals about her own creation. Then the Rear-Admiral intervened, saying,

'Okay, did someone encounter these warning screens?'

Again silence. Then Sally said again. 'I can soon enough discover the culprit. But I also acknowledge that that particular someone may have been following investigations sanctioned from above and am prepared to have that scenario endorsed and rectifications can then proceed. I believe that this is a fixable issue, but I need to ensure that this glitch is a genuine Omicron reaction and not a so-far undetected malfunction.'

'Any comments?' asked the Rear-Admiral.

Finally, a young man stepped forward and asked to speak to the Chief in private. This was agreed. There was a relatively brief discussion, then both men returned to the main group. The Rear-Admiral then turned to Sally and, putting his right arm up to his chin and deep in thought, finally said,

'This man has admitted to breaching those two warning signs, but has a remit from another line of command that allowed for that possible line of interrogation to be followed. He was unaware that the object of his enquiry was also encrypted, with, what is it? Omicron? Anyway, that in some ways actually answered his question. Is that a sufficient reply for you to correct this breakdown in our work?'

'If you authorise this freezing of screens as an acceptable operator-misguided boundary overstep, I will rectify that oversight immediately, as long as you are happy with that explanation.'

'I am.' replied the Rear-Admiral.

Sally sat down at one of the screens, ensuring she was not able to be observed, and within minutes, and with a few key strokes and combinations of exchanges, unfroze all the operating computers in that room. They all flickered simultaneously into life, and rewound several key stokes.

'Is there anything else? Admiral'

'No. Thank you so much Ms….'

He was about to acknowledge her by name, but remembered just in time to refrain from that nomenclature, at least in the presence of others.

Sally stood by the activating computer and watched as the people there meandered back to their respective machines, unsure what they had just witnessed. Sally took particular note of the uniformed woman officer among them. After many minutes, allowing for there to be no more apparent interruptions, Sally looked at the Rear-Admiral and they then headed for the door.

On the way out and when they were alone, the Rear-Admiral asked Sally, 'What is this Infinity you keep talking about?'

'If you ask me no questions Admiral, I will tell you no lies.' she replied with a slight grin. Then she asked, 'Who is McCrae, Admiral?'

'Why do you ask?'

'I was taken with her. I assume she is not just there to fill in numbers. I would expect a uniformed officer to have been thoroughly vetted and assessed and have high security clearances to be working in that environment.'

'You are correct, Ms Longley. Lieutenant McCrae comes from a long line of distinguished naval people. Her grandfather was a decorated commander in the Second World War, fighting with distinction and bravery in the Pacific naval theatre, commanding several of our fighting ships in that campaign. Her father is a recently retired ship's captain from the RAN, who also served on several missions overseas during his service. She is a graduate of the Military college where she showed considerable aptitude in the line of work in which she is now involved. I might add, she was highly sort after. We were lucky to get her. I pulled strings to ensure that happened. Why, do you have an interest in her abilities?'

'Admiral, I...we, need to consider the long-term ramifications and the direction, indeed, even the continuance and survival of this development into the future. As you know, I am very sceptical about the ability of any organisation, ... *any* organisation, to be able to safeguard the existence of this creation, and ensure it is not utilised for the wrong purpose.' said a serious Sally.

'Yes.' responded the Rear-Admiral. 'I can only assure you that this present arrangement will safeguard your development. Lieutenant McCrae would be an admirable addition to any new group set up to operate that program. I am working on that issue all the time. Some of those in high places still don't fully grasp the full significance of what you have achieved here Ms Longley.'

'Well, that maybe all to the good Admiral.' she responded.

'They just might be getting a hint in the next little while I might add.' he continued.

'Why, what's going on?' she asked.

'There's been talk in the industry of a serious and major total blackout in some foreign group now caught trying to hack into some secret American devices. Caused terrible trouble for all involved. Especially as no one can explain the outcome, or the source of the blackouts – not yet anyway. I'll keep you informed – and them away from you.' he said. 'You recall, we agreed to some initial distribution to the Americans on a trial basis and have leased this product to someone in the US.'

'Yes, I well recall. Thank you, Admiral.'

They reached the waiting security vehicle. Sally bade farewell to the Rear-Admiral and climbed into the car to be sent hurriedly on the short drive back to the awaiting helicopter at the RAAF base.

It was now quite late in the afternoon, but there was still a little available daylight. The pilot took off immediately and headed south towards the new destination of the farm of Graham Longley.

By the time they arrived at the farm following some difficult directions passed on over Rachael's mobile, it was well and truly dark. Graham managed to light up an area in the paddock near the house using a couple of farm vehicles with spot-lights. Sally was now rather exhausted from this whole harrying experience, so was not in the mood to discuss it at the moment. She was also aware that Rachael was not usually privy to quite so much intimate detail about exactly it was that Sally did.

Sunday was a pleasant day all round. Graham had persuaded his parents that Sally was involved with several different assignments, all of which were of course confidential, and that she was highly sort after and consequently, very busy. She was also quite content with her lot and very happy in her roles. The two boys were impressed with the apparent success of their older sister of whom they were both proud and fond, remembering all she had done to keep the family together and then united with their father. All they were now, they owed to her. Early Monday morning, Graham ran the two women to the Canberra airport, and they returned to their preferred habitat in the city.

Sometime after the screen-freezing incident, the Rear-Admiral wandered out of his office located in the shadows of Russell Hill and glanced around the floor. It was approaching evening and the floor was attended by a minimum of scrutineers and programmers. Lieutenant McCrae was still at her desk alternating between looking at her screen and gazing at some text at her side. The Rear-Admiral stood looking at her for some time, then he strolled a little towards her. She looked up, acknowledging him with the slightest of nods, maintaining her stare in case more than a nod was the required response. The Rear-Admiral then said to her,

'Lieutenant, would you have a moment?'

'Yes Sir.' was her crisp reply.

'Step into my office please.'

Lieutenant McCrae stood up and headed for the office of the Rear-Admiral. He asked her to have a seat. That was often a little unusual. She hoped it was not a portent of something sinister or even wrong. There was a long pause as the Rear-Admiral stared at her. Then he said,

'What did you think of that episode the other day, Lieutenant?'

'I'm sorry sir, I must admit I did not follow that story in full. It was a bit out of my league.'

'What about that woman that came here?'

There was another slight pause, then she replied,

'She appeared totally out of place at first. She was dressed like she had just come off the farm. Nice designer gear though; expensive, you know. I bet those diamond stud earrings were real too, Sir' she added in parenthesis. 'Then she launched into this geek-speak that I had no real idea what she talking about, Sir.'

The Rear-Admiral smiled at that comment,

'Don't know about the designer gear, as you put it, or those diamonds, but you were correct. We had just flown her up from a sheep station down in the mountains. Very lucky to get her at all. Anyway, what are your plans for the future, Lieutenant?'

'I hope to continue on in this field Sir. I like what I do, and, I hope I am satisfactory at what I do, Sir.'

'Yes indeed, Lieutenant. No plans to move on at all as yet?'

'No Sir. Have I not been performing adequately, Sir?'

'Definitely not, Lieutenant.' The Rear-Admiral reached over to a folder on his right and picked it up. He passed it over the desk, saying,

'Lieutenant, would you mind reading this document for me?'

'No Sir, glad to.'

'Read the first page to begin with; aloud if you please.'

Lieutenant McCrae grabbed the folder and opened the cover. She glanced at the first page in confusion, looked up at the Rear-Admiral, then back down at the folder, and began to read, slowly and deliberately,

'This is the leasing agreement between Sentinel (the supplier) and NAVSEC (the leasee) for the supply and maintenance of the supplier's product known as Omicron.

'This product is supplied under stringent conditions as detailed herein. This product is governed by strict intellectual ownership laws and several patents, and patents-pending.

'Please read all the conditions before signing this agreement. Dated this day blah blah blah.'

Lieutenant McCrae looked puzzled and bemused. She looked up at the Rear-Admiral awaiting clarification as to what she was just reading aloud, and why. The Rear-Admiral looked at her with a slight smile.

'Lieutenant McCrae, could I ask you to read that document, in full, carefully, and then we can discuss it.'

'Yes Sir.'

'You can read it here Lieutenant. And please read it very carefully, and please take your time.'

'Yes, Sir.' she replied meekly, glancing down at the thin folder.

She began to read the document. The Rear-Admiral turned to face his screen and resumed his work that he had abandoned to seek out the lieutenant.

She read the document over a couple of times, the contents not entirely making sense to her at this stage. But she knew a serious legal agreement when she saw one. When she satisfied herself that she understood the contents to a level commensurate with her lack of background, she closed the folder and glanced up at the expectant Rear-Admiral looking at her.

'Do you have a driver's licence, Lieutenant?'

'Yes, Sir.'

'Good. Fancy a trip to Sydney?'

'Yes, Sir, if that is appropriate.'

'Indeed, Lieutenant. Now any questions about that document?'

'Yes Sir. This seems to be some form of contract between someone called Sentinel and NAVSEC, which I assume is us, though I thought that we were…. "under the radar" so to speak, Sir.'

'Correct, Lieutenant. On both accounts.

'So, who is Sentinel? And what is this Omicron I keep hearing about?'

'You remember that woman - in the designer bush gear – that came here that Saturday afternoon?'

'Yes Sir.'

'Well, she is Sentinel, and she owns Omicron, outright and in its entirety. I assume you fully understood the conditions detailed in that document?'

'Yes. I think so, Sir. They are rather harsh and specific when it comes to conditions and withdrawal or cancellation of the …. whatever it is.'

'Precisely, Lieutenant. You witnessed yourself the power of that system the other day. And may I say you are among the privileged few ever to do so. This is all highly confidential you understand, Lieutenant. I know you have the highest clearance level. Well, this goes above that, even.'

'I see, Sir.'

'I am trying to create a new cadre of extremely restricted-clearance personnel to install and maintain this Omicron development. Needless to say, this one will not only "fly under the radar" as you put it, it will not even be known at all to even exist. You have no idea of its power and potential. I want to ensure it is safeguarded for our future and for this nation. You would not believe what havoc this program can wreak on the world, and our enemies if we can control it. I want you to possibly be a part of that team. More importantly, I believe that the Omicron creator may also accept that offer.'

'I don't know what to say, Sir.'

'Say absolutely nothing, Lieutenant. You will possibly not even exist if we go down this road.'

'I see, Sir.' she replied, suddenly a little nervous and alarmed at developments.

'I am trying to arrange a meeting with Sentinel, owner of

Omicron, in Sydney. I may need you to accompany me there, at short notice, if I can set up things that end. I'll keep you informed. Thank you for your time, Lieutenant.'

The Rear-Admiral was conducting discussions with the over-arching Director of his particular security division, but also with much higher-level officials as well as a minister or two. The problem he had, was to try to get across to people the significance of this development without disclosing too much confidential and classified information to people who would probably have no idea of the significance of this product, with possibly the exception of its monetary value. That was an issue of absolutely no importance at all to his acquaintance that created this marvel. It was a delicate path he was treading trying to navigate the nuances of her desire to protect the integrity of her creation and safeguarding its appropriate application. Money was of no concern to her.

Finally, Rear-Admiral James Walker (AO Mil Div) (Retd) managed to procure an assurance that, if he successfully pursued, and acquired access to, or preferably the rights to, what he called Omicron, the minister would establish a separate functional body to oversee its implementation and appropriate distribution, within the topmost military security circles. It was now up to the Rear-Admiral to liaise with the owner of the intellectual property; one Sally Longley. He finally arranged a meeting with her in her offices in Phillip Street, Sydney. He was planning on taking with him Lieutenant McCrae.

Sally had a lot of meetings and discussions with many

entities and government authorities, mostly military or security bureaux. Many were brief and cursory; many were just tyre-kickers, unable to sustain the required assurances, or have the requisite justification for this product, let alone often, the required financial backing to acquire it.

She was not surprised when Rachael announced that Rear-Admiral Walker was attending a scheduled meeting for the morning of the eleventh, two days away. She wondered at that occurrence, so soon after the abortive free-time with her father down on the Faulkner property. He was listed as coming from the well-known Australian Security Organisation, though she knew full well that that was just a ruse to disguise his real location, that very few people really knew about.

When the team from Canberra arrived, they were met in the foyer by Rachael and escorted up to the floor where Sally's office was located. Sally was very surprised to see the familiar face of Rear-Admiral Walker, but also accompanying him was Lieutenant McCrae. That was unusual, he normally came alone, on the rare occasions she had met him here. Once in her office, Sally sat bemused at her desk scrutinising the pair, but not entirely reluctant to renew acquaintances with the uniformed Lieutenant. Then the Rear-Admiral said,

'Morning, Ms Longley. May I formally introduce you to Lieutenant McCrae, whom you encountered recently. Thank you for welcoming us here. You may be wondering why I have brought Lieutenant McCrae with me.'

'Yes, I was wondering that. I assume you have a good reason.'

The Rear-Admiral then went on in great detail to explain

that he was in the process of finally gaining permission to negotiate with Sentinel on some form of long-term agreement or arrangement, or even an outright purchase of Omicron from the legal owner. If that ever came to fruition, Lieutenant McCrae would be one of the few foundation members of that highly-classified team. They were here to begin initiating talks around that goal, among other matters.

Sally was ambivalent about this topic. The Rear-Admiral was aware of that fact, and fully understood her position, and her apprehensions about its existence outside her control. She was going to need time to consider this development, and time to discuss it with others. In her case that meant initially, with her father, though, no one else knew that fact. This was all going to need to be handled with considerable delicacy and caution. Sally did not indicate that she was in any way opposed to that idea, at least at this point in time.

That discussion was relatively brief, but a lot of groundwork was laid for things to move from there, or not as the case may be. There was one other matter that the Rear-Admirable wished to raise with Sally. It involved a confusing incident relating to a property located on the foreshore of the harbour in Sydney Cove, close to the naval dockyards. He said to her,

'You may have heard in the news some time ago about the death of the now notorious mayor of the council that operated in the vicinity of a facility known as the Hindmarsh Boatyard.'

Sally did not respond, she actually never heard about that incident. The Rear-Admiral then went on,

'At first, it was nothing, just an incident involving local

criminal associates, apparently. Then, sometime after the event, someone somewhere accused the local mayor and some of his cronies of being Chinese spies. When we tried to find out about it from the police, we struck a web of denials, deceit and obstructions on a grand scale. One of our operatives was authorised to determine the extent of any threats, as that shipyard is almost adjacent to the naval dockyards, so there were concerns raised. When he finally thought that he had located the actual owner of the site, and that was a veritable web of tangled associations, and any shenanigans going on there, he apparently tried to read into their contacts, and guess what! He lost his computer, and also the server for that group. It just went stone-cold blank; then froze. It could not be reactivated. None of their so-called experts could revive any of them. They were totally confused. I thought to myself, when news of this spread around the traps, that sounds awfully like the curse of Omicron. Tell me you don't lease out Omicron to individuals, do you?'

Sally was shocked. She remained silent for a minute. Then she uttered,

'No, I haven't leased it out to any individual person.' she said, evasively. This was technically true, in that she had not *leased* it out to an individual. She had actually given it to one – and only one. Surely, this episode did not occur to the one and only individual to whom she had donated Omicron.

Graham had alerted her to the fact that the person to whom he had requested this product be availed upon was a very remarkable and outstanding individual whom, she was assured, was even more secretive than Sally herself; and for very good reasons. That person moved in the most rarefied and exclusive arena of society and was a most reliable candidate. That person was none other than – Jessie Summers.

Sally sat momentarily in total and obvious dismay. Her mind was racing madly as she tried to quickly recall all the relevant matters that surrounded the operation of loaning out Omicron to her father's friend, Jessie Summers.

Sally recalled that her father had enquired if it were possible to provide an individual person with this software. Sally said to him that she had never contemplated that scenario, but that it was possible, because she herself had installed it onto her own machine in the office of Dr Charmers, though that used a server for her floor. Sally was aware through her grandmother that Graham was somehow extremely indebted for some reason to Jessie Summers for some service he had provided for her. She in return had somehow become involved with Graham's acquisition of the farmhouse next door to his original property that only possessed a shearing shed, no house. None of the family understood just what had transpired between the pair, but they were mutually very supportive. That was all they knew.

Sally had also learnt through her associations with Peter Knuckey and his uncle, the retired Inspector Ian Knuckey, that Jessie Summers was responsible for some sort of total resurrection of the retired detective through some means or other to do with her background and inside-knowledge of criminal activity. It was all becoming a bit messy, and worrisome to her.

Sally was very reluctant to endorse this request. Graham started to tell her a long, complicated story involving corruption, fraud, malpractice, misconduct and dereliction of duty and abuse of power within the judiciary and the police force that Jessie Summers was associated with in bringing into the open and revealing some of the perpetrators. She had been the recipient of that kind of treatment, he assured her, not a perpetrator. Her knowledge of these kinds of events placed her in mortal danger permanently. Her life had always been lived on the edge as she was a hunted and sort-after exposer of some nasty people. There were many that wanted her dead.

She recently had two serious attempts on her life that were only foiled by timely interventions by fortuitously-placed saviours and good luck. Her husband had been shot and seriously wounded and she had been attacked several times by the supposedly law-enforcing agencies in more than one state. He believed that she was living on borrowed time. She suspected that her mobile phone and her computers were being monitored and possibly hacked. She did not ask for this service, Graham was merely enquiring if it were possible and available.

Sally was influenced by the persuasive arguments presented by her father. She knew that he would not enquire frivolously, especially for a stranger. She was also slightly influence by the opportunity offered to test the software system on a trustworthy private individual in an outside position. She gave it serious thought.

She cast her mind back to the one and only time she ever met this woman she knew as Jessie Summers. It was almost by accident. She was accompanying Peter Knuckey during a trial early in her days as a full-time lawyer with the firm, as he went to meet up with his uncle, Ian Knuckey for a lunch break. Sally never forgot the impression this Jessie had on her. Her appearance, her manner, her whole persona were a revelation to her. She had never seen such a piercing and deep stare. Sally was slightly intimidated by her mere presence. Even then, she had asked Sally how her father was, so their relationship extended way back. But her background remained deeply hidden and mysterious.

Sally finally acquiesced to that suggestion if Jessie could arrange to bring her computer up to the Sydney office. No one knew that Jessie owned an apartment in Rushcutters Bay, so for her, it was not such an imposition.

Jessie teed it all up with Graham and Sally for an afternoon appointment several weeks later. Sally asked if Graham could attend, as she recalled that Jessie seemed to be an awkward customer to socialise with as she recollected how her last interaction with her went. They arrived on time, and entered Sally's office. Sally looked at the strange woman before her, she certainly was an enigma to Sally; aloof, remote and almost imperious, quite intimidating to a gentle, reserved type of person that sally generally was. Finally, Sally said,

'Mrs Summers, I am prepared to offer you this product

on certain condition. I will give you a copy of my leasing contract, more for information rather than for any monetary transactions. But you need to understand a few details, and repercussions or impacts that this installation will entail.'

Sally went on to explain in great detail what installing this creation onto her private computer would entail. It became quite technical, and daunting. She was warned what happened if anybody tried to access her computer remotely without authority, and that she would never know if anybody attempted that, unless in the unlikely event that they ever actually contacted her to inform her what had happened to their machine.

Jessie was grateful to Graham for initiating this action, and for Sally for agreeing to install this marvellous software. She was mindful of the potential repercussions and agreed to advise Sally of any kind of interaction emanating from this arrangement that she ever became aware of.

The first Sally had any hint of a problem then arose only with the advent of the visit of Rear-Admiral Walker. Sally did not need any kind of action calling attention to either herself or her valuable product. She was a little annoyed at this occurrence. She was also concerned that her creation had possibly been lent out under some form of false pretences. She would contact her father to discuss matters.

Meantime, Sally finally returned to a more normal reality of her present circumstances. After an indeterminate delay to the Rear-Admiral's revelation, Sally said to the expectant pair,

'Okay, we may have an issue here, Admiral. You tell me

all you know about this waterfront problem and I will confide in you some more details about the possible recipient of Omicron.'

'Well,' said the Rear-Admiral. 'We had terrible difficulty in determining the actual owner of the property in Question. It was hidden in a multitude of cleverly-orchestrated legal constructions and organisations. We ended up dealing only with their legal representative here in Australia. When we went to the police, the Police Commissioner knew almost nothing about it, but we were put onto a Detective who seemed to know a lot more about it than he was prepared to reveal. We obtained a name and when we followed that up, we ended up with a totally different person. But we are confident we know who it is.'

'How do you know?' asked Sally.

'Because we were able to place a tracker on her vehicle.'

'And what is the name of this person?'

'That's confidential, Sally.'

'Not if you want to know where my software is going.' she stated firmly.

'This is all very confidential, and sensitive, Sally.' he reiterated.

'Excellent! Now tell me her name.'

'How do you know it's a woman?'

'Because, you said "her".'

'Okay.' said the Rear-Admiral, stalling. 'The ultimate ownership of the property is actually in the name of a Kimberley West. Now, we finally located her, and when we tracked her vehicle, it led to a rural property where she seems to really live.'

'And…...what is her name?'

'We believe that this Kimberley West is actually a Mrs Jessie Summers.'

Sally was dumbfounded. She stared, thinking for a minute, at the two people in front of her. Then she mumbled, almost to herself,

'Jessie Summers, eh? Who'd 'a thunk it.'

The two visitors looked at her, their faces expressing considerable perplexity.

'Do you know either of these people?' asked the Rear-Admiral.

Sally did not answer that question. Instead, she launched into a rapid response by asking,

'Tell me what you know about this Jessie Summers?'

'Well, according to the police officer, she was the one who warned them of the espionage threats. Turns out she was more than just right, but she informed them of the depths of the problem; and it is a deep one. Once we started investigating, we found all sorts of potential issues. We would dearly like to talk to this Jessie Summers, but have basically been warned off.'

'By whom?'

'By the police. Or more strictly, by this detective we spoke to. Apparently, she is not to be messed with, and holds a lot of very valuable information that they do not want compromised or threatened.'

Sally just sat there in amazement, astonished at these revelations. She just kept mumbling through her slight smile, *Jessie Summers, eh?* Rear-Admiral Walker began to formulate the thought that somehow Jessie Summers was known to Sally Longley. But the connection alluded him at present. Sally asked the visitors to expand on their knowledge of the circumstances surrounding this apparent security threat to our military establishments and just exactly how Jessie Summers, who apparently lived on a remote farm, was not only involved, but, also seemingly way ahead of the game as far as the surveillance of our military assets was concerned.

Rear-Admiral Walker explained the little detail that the detective was prepared to divulge. He also did point out that so far, there is no real definitive proof that these allegations were genuine, only that their suspicions were now alerted by these revelations. They did discover, through this detective, and, he emphasised, sourced from this mysterious Kimberley West, that the Chinese ambassador was suspiciously 'recalled' immediately after this 'accident', an apparent euphemism for his death, along with a fellow Sydney consular official whom apparently suffered the same fatal fate. How Kimberley West, aka Jessie Summers, knew all this was not divulged.

'Is Jessie Summers also this Kimberley West?' asked Sally.

'Almost certainly. But we have been asked to steer clear of her.' answered the Rear-Admiral.

'Is Jessie Summers some kind of crook?'

'Definitely not.' responded the Rear-Admiral. 'Apparently, she is some kind of a paragon of virtue that has been so beneficial to the police over some time that they will go to extraordinary lengths to protect her. I can certainly vouch for that fact. That's all I know. Do you by any chance know either of these women, Sally?'

'I certainly do not know a Kimberley West. Let me do a little investigating, Admiral, into this issue. I promise I will get back to you fairly soon.'

'Okay. Excellent. How 'bout I suspend all our investigations into this event momentarily then?'

'No, by all means, continue on investigating any foreign interference in our affairs. Just leave Jessie Summers out of this while I check up on a few things. I desperately hope none of my work has gone to anybody suspect.' said Sally. She was now very mindful that her father was the instigator of Jessie Summers obtaining access to her top-secret, military-grade security software. She wanted to discover his involvement, if any, in this controversial matter, before she was prepared to reveal anything further.

The Rear-Admiral was satisfied with the progress so far with this visit. It had laid the groundwork for the advancement of negotiations into the future of this valuable product. It had opened discussions on the mystery of the Hindmarsh Shipyard, and it had introduced the name of Jessie Summers into the conversation. He was convinced that Sally knew this Jessie Summers, and therefore probably also this Kimberley West. Either one of those two he was desperate to talk to about the espionage potential, and how she knew about it when no one else seemed to. The carnage that occurred back at his headquarters building seemed to emanate from Jessie Summers' machine, so Sally must be the source of that supply. It was all very intriguing. He and Lieutenant McCrae departed for now happy enough with the encounter.

Sally, for her part, was keen to contact her father to discuss this matter. How to do it without using equipment that could be bugged? She would dearly love to see him again. When Sally contacted her father and hinted that she would like to see him in person for a short while, he jumped at the offer, considering the coolness that had always seemed apparent from her towards him in the past.

Graham travelled up to her apartment this time. He chose to drive himself up as her penthouse apartment had ample parking for several vehicles. She had prepared quite a feast for her father, so they dined inhouse, so to speak. It was during the evening, when they were basically recovering from the lavish fare, that Sally got down to the business for which she had really summonsed him to herself. She was not entirely sure how to broach this subject, as she was aware that her father and Jessie Summers were serious friends. Following her conversation with the Rear-Admiral, she was also aware that there may be delicate topics involved with this subject.

On his arrival, Graham had asked Sally if all was well. She simply replied by saying that the situation was as usual, but that she did have one point she would like to discuss with him, maybe later in the evening. It was left at that at the time. After dinner, they adjourned to the spacious lounge that also had a rather magnificent view out over the harbour and across the northern parts of the city. Sally finally began,

'Father, I have got one topic I wish to raise with you. It may be a little delicate. I had a visit from that Admiral that interrupted our visit to the Faulkners some time back.'

'I see.' he replied.

'He was here on a couple of matters, but the one I want to talk to you about concerns my software that I gave to Jessie Summers. You see, as you hinted, somebody did try to hack into Jessie's computer.'

'I thought you said that you would not be able to tell unless they contacted you themselves?' interrupted Graham.

'Well spotted, Dad.' she said.

'The trouble is, that somebody did not contact Jessie, or me. You see, that somebody was actually a branch of one of the Australian security services, I don't know which one, but the Admiral got wind of it and, as he is one of the very few people that knows this fact, that it will freeze up the hacker's computer, it occurred to him that it sounded awfully like what happened to him, and for the same reason. So, why would the security people be wanting to delve into the life of Jessie Summers, who, as far as I thought, lived in the sticks?'

There was a long pause. Graham was not stalling in order to prevaricate; he genuinely believed that Jessie's only potential interrogators would be the police, or some criminal organisations. He was momentarily bamboozled why any national security agency would be interested in her. He was deep in thought. As he did not immediately reply. Sally then asked,

'Do you by the way know a Kimberley West?'

After a small pause, he replied,

'No, I don't know anybody by that name. Why do you ask? And what's it with Jessie being hacked into?'

'Well, does Jessie own a boatshed, or a boatyard or whatever it is here in Sydney on the harbour right next door to the naval docks?'

'I have no idea. I doubt it very much. If you knew her story, you would not think that very likely at all.' he said. 'And who's this Kimberley West you're asking about?'

'The Admiral believes that this Kimberley West, who appears to own this very valuable, and strategic, boatyard thing is actually Jessie Summers. He has pretty convincing evidence that this is so. He desperately wants to speak to her, but he has been warned off by some high-ranking detective who strongly advised him to let her alone. I think the expression he used was "she was not to be messed with."'

Now, that made more sense to Graham. Her issues were with the judiciary and the police, and for that matter, with the criminal fraternity, not the security agencies, as far as he knew anyway.

'Look,' said Graham, 'what Jessie does not know about the criminal world is not worth knowing, at least that was the case years ago. She and Ian Knuckey, Peter Knuckey's uncle, go way back, years. As I told you, she has had serious attempts on her life and it is still happening. She is on a top-ranking police officer's hit list. Ian knows all about it. I thought your thing would be a help in preventing them from finding her and following her movements. I'm not aware that she owns anything in Sydney, though.'

'Well, could I ask you in the first instance to check with her and see if there is any reason for the security services to be looking into her affairs, for me?' Graham agreed, and to get back to her soon. It was left at that for the time being.

Then sally broached another related topic. She began to discuss in an ambling and almost bewildered manner the other option that the Rear-Admiral had raised; the topic of selling the rights of her development to an Australian security agency, and all the implications that entailed. Graham let her ramble, as he deduced that she was not only sounding him out, but also collecting her thoughts out aloud on somebody who would listen dispassionately.

The follow up to the first question of Sally's to Graham eventually came, and it entailed some complex interactions. About two months later, Rachael interrupted Sally in her office to say that a Jessie Summers was down in the foyer waiting-area wishing to see her. It was pointed out to Sally that she did not have an appointment. Sally was a little stunned, she already had several meetings and appointments in her busy schedule, but she dearly wished to see Jessie, not only to discuss restricted matters, but to try to gauge this enigma with which her father seemed so intimately associated. Unbeknownst to Jessie, was that also waiting in the wings was none other than Rear-Admiral Walker and his now permanent associate, Lieutenant McCrae.

Sally asked Rachael if she would mind asking the Admiral to wait a little longer and then to bring Jessie Summers up to her office. Jessie had spent her waiting time closely monitoring and observing her surroundings, her permanent state of alertness, she being constantly vigilant to her spatial circumstances after years of needing that caution. She had noticed, among others, the air of a military bearing of the dapper elderly gentleman seated some seats away from her, accompanied she assumed, by the uniformed officer beside him.

She watched as a tall, elegantly-dressed woman in high-heeled pointed-toe shoes that clocked on the hard marble floor exited the lift and strode meaningfully over to the reception counter. Her light-brown hair was neatly gathered behind her head with a large coloured clip. She was then pointed in the direction of herself. Jess was momentarily conscious of the fact that she was attired in country apparel, albeit high quality, compared to the potentially approaching modelesque figure and attire on display. The stylish and graceful person then headed directly to the military-type man who was dressed in a business suit seated next to the uniformed woman. After a brief encounter, she turned and headed for Jessie.

Jess noticed that several people in that area were closely observing her departure, including the military pair. Jess kept her darkened glasses on in the brightly-lit lift. She noticed that this picture of sartorial splendour also possessed particularly well-manicured nails and a modest adornment of jewellery as she pressed on the lift-floor button. Jess was momentarily conscious of her rather weather-beaten hands and chipped finger nails.

On arrival on the desired floor, Jess finally removed her darkened glasses and slipped them in to the top of her pale blue blouse and left them hanging exposed down her front. Once in the office of Sally Longley, again very elegantly attired, not quite how Jess had remembered her from her very first original encounter, and seated opposite her at her spacious desk, Jessie stared at poor Sally, taking in her surroundings, and using that devastating, almost death-like stare; the look that only arose when the bearer felt particularly ill-at-ease or wary of her setting. Sally was unsure how to begin, and she was momentarily mesmerised again by the fascinating set of cobalt-blue eyes just staring unblinking at her. She had originally forgotten that aspect of Jessie's appearance from her earliest encounter, as it was darker on that occasion. Finally, Jess offered, in her usual soft mellifluous way,

'Sally, I believe that you have concerns around some aspects of your installation on my computer at the Cooma property.'

Sally paused, she felt a little intimidated by her opposite. After a considered thought, she replied,

'I am not sure exactly what you know about the concerns arising with regard to yourself, but it turns out that my father was right to suspect you were under possible threat of intrusion on your device. However, he believed, and I was also led to believe, that that threat came from the criminal fraternity. It has come to my notice that attempts were indeed made to access your data, but may I say, from a completely different source.'

'Oh.' said Jessie, after a small pause. 'And what source was that then?'

'You have no idea?' asked an incredulous Sally.

'No. I was informed only that there had been a breach and that you, Sally, were concerned about the fact that not only had it happened, but also from whom that breach had originated. That was all I was told. I decided to visit you out of respect for your kindness and to alleviate any concerns you may have.'

'Well, I appreciate that, but let's not beat about the bush here Mrs Summers. Do you know a Kimberley West?'

Jessie was momentarily stunned. Where did that question come from? And how would Sally Longley even know of her existence. There was a very long silent pause, with both women gazing at each other. Finally, Jess asked, in her soft measured way,

'What do you know of any Kimberley West?'

'Let's save time here Mrs Summers.' said a now more confident and assertive Sally, dealing as it were with her own speciality. 'Someone from a secret Australian security organisation was looking into the tangled mess that is apparently known as the Hindmarsh Boatyard affair. The eventual real owner of that piece of harbour-front property has been traced to you. Any comments?'

'How could that possibly be?' asked Jess, meaning, how did they trace it to her, as Kimberley West, let alone how could it be her as Jessie Summers.

'Look Jess. May I call you Jessie.' she asked, giving Jess a determined gaze.

'Of course.'

Sally continued,

'The man who can explain all this to you is actually sitting downstairs right now. It seems my creation has worked here, too well. This man, who dearly wants to speak to you is awaiting his scheduled meeting, and you are eating into his time. I do not want to pry into your private or business life other than any effect it has on me personally. Would you be prepared to meet with this man to clear up matters. He desperately wishes to know how you knew about this thing and what else you may know. I really know little about the details myself, only that it happened on my watch.'

Jess thought hurriedly. Then she said,

'All right. That may be helpful, because I also want to know how he located me, and maybe why they were unaware of so blatantly an obvious security breach that was happening right under their noses; if he is from some national security organisation.'

That comment staggered Sally. It indicated to her that there must be some truth to the allegations that Jessie Summer was involved, or at least of her knowledge of this incident.

Sally asked Rachael to fetch the Admiral from the foyer. He entered the room along with Lieutenant McCrae, who was now travelling about not wearing her name tag on her uniform. The now familiar person to Jess from the foyer was in front of her. The Rear-Admiral was momentarily immovable as he gazed almost unashamedly at the stunning countenance presented in front of him now. Those penetrating eyes were the eyes of a serious hunting creature. He knew a superior character when he saw one so closely presented, yet she looked and spoke in a deceptively soft and unassuming manner. Jess was deeply aware of this constant surprise gaze at her. Her permanent fear was that the person was staring at her not because of her stunning appearance, but because they recognised her from her past, especially somebody older.

They introduced each other and took up chairs alongside Jessie, the Rear-Admiral trying to take in as much as he could of this woman now sitting beside him that the little time he had would allow. Jessie moved her chair away from the new pair and nearer to Sally and the end of the desk. Then he said,

'Thank you very much for agreeing to meet with us. Can we first establish exactly with whom we are dealing.' stated the Rear-Admiral.

'Whom do *you* think you're dealing with? And more importantly, how did you discover me?' asked Jess.

The Rear-Admiral realised that, after his discussions with Detective Inspector Garth van Heiken, and his warnings about the nature of this person with which the Rear-Admiral was seeking to speak, that he would have to tread carefully here and approach this issue with some diplomacy and delicacy. He also was recalling that this Kimberley West appeared not to exist. She had no passport, no licence that was investigable, no Medicare card, she was not enrolled on any electoral roles, no traceable Tax File Number and no car registration on record. Yet here she was supposedly sitting next to him. Jessie Summers was also of a similar ilk, seemingly possessing none of these attributes either. He was unable to locate any marriage certificate for this Jessie Summers. Who was she? He hesitated for some time, deep in thought. He had at least been able to establish that she wore absolutely no jewellery at all, anywhere – including a wedding ring. Her persona reignited that expression the Detective had used that 'she was not to be messed with'. He initially interpreted it as meaning she was a protected species. He was beginning to believe that it actually meant she was a dangerous individual capable of any act. He could believe either of her now that she was in front of him. Finally, he said to Jess,

'Mrs Summers, with great difficulty and some access to very private and secure resources, we traced you, firstly through a very circumspect, almost may I say, unhelpful beyond the obvious, a Mr Karl Lukas. He turned out to be the legal frontman for the complex commercial arrangements for that plot of land, part of which is the Hindmarsh boatyard. We finally went to the police about the waterfront vandalism and the mayor's death on that evening, and the Chinese Ambassador's disappearance, or "recall". We approached the Police Commissioner's office. She was again unhelpful and almost unfamiliar with this issue, but she put us onto the man who seemed to know an awful lot about it. He was not forthcoming at all either. But, he did give us, or rather, confirmed our results, that this Kimberley West was the full and sole owner of this property. We ascertained the registered legal business address of the owner, away from that legal office of Mr Lukas, bugged what we thought was her vehicle and tracked it to you; all legal, and defensible, I can assure you. I will emphasise here Mrs Summers, that you are *not* in any way in any trouble at all, but rather, seem to be the holder of an amazing amount of information that had illuded those who should have been aware of it themselves. I am curious as to how it was that you were able to discover this potential breach, and, what else you really know about this.'

Jess found that preamble rather conciliatory. She was warming to this man. He seemed to be diplomatically assuaging any reservations she held about this unexpected encounter. She would accommodate his enquiries to the extent that she could safely do without revealing anything about herself as far as possible. Jess surmised that, if this pair were from a secret Australian security source, that at least anything she reported to them should go no further.

'Mr Walker, it is not I you should be interested in at all, but the people behind this travesty.' Jess retorted.

There was a long pause. Jess peered at the assembled attendees in the office with a deep scrutinising stare. It was a little unsettling, especially for the women. Then she continued, in a slow, determined tone but still softly,

'The former owners of that property, and the tenants, endured years, and I mean years, of torment and persecution from the local council, mainly the former mayor, but there were others. Sadly, that harassment was aided and abetted by certain people in both the New South Wales Government, and, also from some people in Canberra. There was also collusion from parts of the New South Wales Police Force. Somebody in authority wanted that parcel of land desperately. It was rumoured to be desired for community use, or bike path continuation, or greenspace or whatever reason, any excuse to resume it. It was secretly desired by some entity that wanted it for its security potential. I believe that entity was a foreign power. Trouble is, that block is all fully freehold, very rare in that location.

'The Doolans were on the brink of caving in to these endless attacks. When I became associated with them, I had access to much more superior, high-powered and determined investigative and enforcement liaisons that began to analyse this issue and uncovered all sorts of nonsense occurring at that site. The harassments were ceased, under some threats I might add, and things settled down for a while. But I know for a fact that the mayor was livid that this opportunity, the results of years of persecution, was lost for the moment. I gathered that his puppet-masters were also very unsatisfied with his efforts. I also know for a fact that the Chinese Ambassador from Canberra and the Sydney Consular-General from China were both at the property when it was fire-bombed.'

'I thought that was an accident.' interrupted the Rear-Admiral. 'And that there were only a few minor injuries.'

'Accident, my foot!' exclaimed Jessie. 'I have seen all the

proofs you ever need to show just who was there and just what happened to all present. The police have all the evidence you could ever desire. Somebody wants this all covered up.'

'What have you seen, and how do you know all this?' asked the Rear-Admiral.

'Never mind all that.' said a stern Jess. 'The issue here is; who covered up all this activity and who covered up those deaths. It can only be one of three sources, mate. It was either the criminals who were annoyed at the continual failings of the mayor; the Chinese agents here in Australia who were also very annoyed with this failure; or, it was some Australian security agency that took this opportunity to eliminate this frontman, and to send a warning, for all the espionage going on about that site so near the naval docks.'

There was another long pause. In the silence that followed, Jess finally interpolated a small comment,

'I feel that whomever carried out this attempt, if it were one of the first two that I mentioned, accidently went too far, way beyond their remit. I believe of course they did not intend for those diplomats to die. This makes me think because it was so thorough, that some Australian authority carried it out. It was just too professional – and complete, to be a coincidence.'

Jess was also mindful that she had somewhat embellished her original story, but now was trying to ensure that all the ducks lined up after her first enthusiastically imaginative runaway comments. She also wanted to ensure that there was no way any suspicion could ever be forwarded her way.

The room was filled with a deathly silence as each of the

recipients of this cavalcade of amazing information that tumbled out of the enigmatic and mysterious Mrs Jessie Summers, digested and analysed her revelations. This was a more complete picture of the conditions that appeared to operate at that site than the reluctant Detective Inspector was prepared to divulge to them, let alone the taciturn Karl Lukas.

Suddenly, the silence was disturbed by the soft buzz of an intercom system on Sally's desk. She quickly picked up the receiver, in silence, then replaced it. She then glanced at the collected group and said,

'Something urgent has just arisen. Could I adjourn this meeting for, say fifteen minutes while I attend to this matter. There is a coffee shop downstairs if anyone would like a quick break.'

There was general agreement. The Rear-Admiral looked at the Lieutenant and they both nodded in acquiescence to avail themselves of that offer. They looked at Jess, but she declined that opportunity; time to be alone for her. They all departed the office as Sally quickly strode out and down the floor. The naval officers wandered down to the lift and out of that floor, while Jess meandered along the level to look out the windows among some suspicious-looking gazes. She found a quiet seat in the far corner not far from the desk of the pleasant Rachael, who acknowledged her with a smile, and she availed herself of the offering and sat there to contemplate. And, she had plenty to contemplate on.

She sat a little dejectedly deep in thought. Jessie was now trying to navigate a sensitive and delicate path; one she had trodden before, in the dark past. She had form. But not since Milbark Station days had she encountered so much devious nuances in the people with whom she was engaged. She did not ever envisage her life would again become so entwined, requiring constant vigilance to avoid exposing things to one party that she did not want exposed to others. In her mind, she laid out all the entanglements. There was Garth van Heiken. He knew her as Kimberley West, but also as Jessie MacIntyre. Karl Lukas only knew her as Kimberley West, so far. Graham Longley knew her as Jessie MacIntyre, but not as Kimberley West. Now Sally Longley knew her as Jessie Summers and possibly as Kimberley West, but not as Jessie MacIntyre. She hoped that Graham could keep his secrets from his daughter. Now Rear-Admiral Walker knew of her as Jessie Summers and possibly as Kimberley West, but definitely not as Jessie MacIntyre. To totally complicate matters, Jess had still not told her husband Thomas about her escapade into the maritime industry in Sydney as Kimberley West. Talk about *déjà vu*.

It all came flooding back. She cast her mind back in time; how she had deceived her mates and her mentor, Stuart MacIntyre about her age; with her publishing antics; and intercessions with the constabulary of several jurisdictions, back on Milbark Station, and the heartache that eventually led to for all concerned. She seemed to be inexorably drawn down the same path again. The longer she delayed clarifying the air, especially to Thomas, the worse it was becoming and the deeper she seemed to sink into this quagmire. She dreaded the potential consequences, and the startled attitudes of any of those that discovered any of her secrets that they were unaware of at present. Deep down, she had a mild sort of exhilaration reliving all those clandestine manoeuvres she engaged in to keep her activities secret. It did slightly dismay her, the elation that she derived from designing and scheming activities that she initiated but did not disclose to her associates around her.

Jess was so deep in her own thoughts that she was momentarily absent from her present surroundings. She was suddenly and shockingly returned to the present by a commotion occurring outside the building. Jess jumped at the sudden intrusion into her drifting sojourn back in time. Someone at the other side of the floor had uttered a load yell of horror at something occurring at that side of the building. Jess, after jumping up in fright, gazed around to see what had happened. People were rushing over to the window. Rachael leapt up and ran over to the window as did the man at the desk near her. Jess was not that interested in the unfolding events. She could see clearly enough what was transpiring, but it held little interest for her. There was a two-man gantry platform outside the building and two men were cleaning the windows. She could see that one cable holding the platform level had sagged considerably and the platform hung at a precarious angle, but not at this stage death-causing. Jess nevertheless decided to slowly wander over to observe the activity as the inside crowd were very animated and disturbed.

As Jess passed the desk of the man close to Rachael, she

could clearly hear the sound of faint voices emanating from the pair of ear-buds that he had abandoned in his haste to observe the drama outside. Initially, she assumed that it was just a radio broadcast he was listening to as he worked. But, as Jess passed, she was struck by the fact that it clearly sounded as if it were the voice of Sally now returned to her room and still on the office telephone, the cause of their temporary interruption.

Jess was startled. She leaned down as if adjusting her boots and, yes that was definitely the voice of Sally, and it was live. Jess glanced in the direction of Sally's office and she was still on the phone. Then she looked at the exposed screen which the man, in his haste, had not blanked and she was doubly startled. There in clear view to anybody able to read the text was a screen in what Jess knew as old Gothic or Fraktur-font German. This was an older style of German writing that had fallen out of favour because of its difficulty in being read. But luckily, she had been exposed to it early in her life from both Werner in Australia Street Newtown as a child and especially from George, the Austrian mechanic on Milbark Station.

More startling however, was the fact that, in the short time she felt able to read the notes, because she did not want to be observed reading his screen, were the words in a neat list: *die Sommer; die Spatz; der Geher* and numerals with the word *Uhr.* Jess was staggered. *die Sommer* was the German for summer, but in German it is a masculine noun. Here it was deliberately denoted in an incorrect feminine form. She deduced that it referred to herself. This was followed by *die Spatz*, which is

German for sparrow. Again, sparrow is a masculine noun in German, but here it was also deliberately misspelt with the feminine *die*, she assuming it referred to Sally. She could pass as a sparrow in code work. Finally, there was the word, *der Geher*, which is the correct delineation in the masculine gender for a walker; or a hiker. It obviously referred to Rear-Admiral James Walker. Finally, there was a simple line that read *Sie heißt McCrae*.

Jess moved away from the machine and back to the desk of Rachael to think. The man, realising that he had hastily departed his site, turned and headed back to his desk. Jess hoped he had not seen her glancing at his screen. He quickly re-attached his buds and began to work on the keyboard. Jess was momentarily stunned. She was also now quickly becoming very angry, not a good portent for such a case as the volatile Jessie. She gathered herself together and contemplated what to do.

Jess knew that Sally was involved here with something rather remarkable. The extent of that achievement was unclear to her. Graham had told her very little, only that it should totally prevent unauthorised access to her equipment. She was grateful for that protection. She really had no idea of its significance. The fact that this Rear-Admiral and some navy personnel were here talking to her through Sally was an indication of the potential significance of this idea. Jess would normally just deal with this intrusion herself, in her own way. But in this case, she was hampered by the fact that it was not her realm and not her domain. But she was not going to let it get out that she was here or that some of her aliases may be spread further than they already were known. What to do?

The man continued on as before, so she hoped he had not observed her scrutinising his screen. Shortly after, the Rear-Admiral and Lieutenant McRae returned and headed for the office of Sally. Jess followed them in, still deep in shock and thought. Sally's office was obviously bugged, by a professional, but who, and from where. As it was all in old German, and going on the little she had read, Jess began to suspect a European source.

The Rear-Admiral turned to Jess in order to continue clarifying more details of what she knew about any foreign threats at the naval docks in the harbour. He was about to speak, when Jess said to the assembled company,

'It's stuffy in here, could we just step outside for a minute or two?'

Sally looked at the group, then at Jess. She appeared a little annoyed. Had not they all just had the chance to do just that for the last fifteen-twenty minutes? Jess got up and headed for the door, and the others reluctantly followed for the moment. Jess headed back down towards the lift area and past the desk of Rachael, who was busily occupied on the phones. Once out in the lift area, outside the security barriers, in a reasonably large congregational space, Jess turned to face the three of them. She had a cold, hard deep-staring countenance; her jaw was set firmly and she exuded extreme annoyance, even the others could now see this.

'Is everything all right?' asked Sally.

'No, indeed not.' stated a determined Jess. 'Do you people realise that our entire conversation has been bugged, and listened into – live – and information passed on directly – live – as we spoke, over a computer contact right under our noses?'

There was stunned silence. No one knew what to say, or even whether to believe such a thing. In the hushed startling silence, Jess went on in full detail exactly what she had heard and exactly what she had seen. She explained about the names and the method of disseminating, or forwarding on the information, and she emphasised, about the revelation of herself to whom she knew not where; a serious breach of her safety.

There followed a deep discussion about how to attack this issue. Finally, it was agreed on a plan of action that would safeguard access to the computer before he had time to remove any evidence that they wanted to peruse. The offender was approached and restrained quickly enough to prevent any tampering, then Lieutenant McCrae and Jess carefully scrutinised the screen while Jess tried to decipher the awkward older style gothic script. Rachael was asked to summon one of the security people from the foyer area and the man was led away and taken into custody for further interrogation, initially to an Australian Security Agency site.

Needless to say, that was the end of any more discussions on matters relating to the harbourfront or the Doolans. Jess was livid, demanding to be fully informed of all the details that at least pertained to herself. Sally was horrified that such an occurrence could be perpetrated upon her, let alone witnessed by two of her closest working allies. Her apparent naivety in matters pertaining to top-secret security was fully exposed. She assumed that all the security checks she had conducted on her associates in her building were professionally and competently done. The significance of this breach was not missed on her.

Jessie went back to her Rushcutters Bay apartment. She stayed only a day or so, then headed back to Auvergne Station. She was disturbed and concerned, so much so that she may have to confide in Thomas as this was now getting out of hand. Jess also wished to discuss matters with Karl Lukas and DI Garth van Heiken.

There were many repercussions from this small sojourn into the wilds of the espionage game. Jess was not fully informed of all the nuances, but Sally certainly was. With the aid of the deciphering of the old-style German script that Jess and Lieutenant McCrae studied together before Jess left them there, Rear-Admiral Walker was able to get enough of a picture to begin investigations. He prudently decided to include DI Garth van Heiken in his interrogations, aware that the safety of Jessie Summers was a side-line to this event. It was she that uncovered all this anyway, and he wanted to ensure that, not only did he have the imprimatur of a senior police official with him to emphasize the significance of this breach, but to also ensure that Jessie had an agent inside all the searches in order to be informed of anything detrimental to herself.

The trail eventually led, as Jess hinted, to a European source. It finally came to light that it was a clandestine EEAS operative, from the official diplomatic representative of the European Union located in their building in Canberra. It was a very sensitive development. There were no official NATO people here in Australia, but the EU had an ambassador-type representative in their legation. There was some very high-level Governmental toing and froing under way, as it was not the actions of an ally to be spying on a friend. It turned out that the Europeans had heard whispers from their American allies that someone had developed this program. At first, it was not believed that Australia could possibly devise this, let alone achieve it, but when it was more or less confirmed, NATO wanted to know about it, as it appeared at this stage, they were having trouble obtaining information and access to this development themselves.

Initially, Sally was involved at the periphery, but she bequeathed the responsibility for navigating the sensitive inter-governmental negotiations and fall-out to her trusted and experienced, proxy, Rear-Admiral Walker. He proved to be an admirable choice for piloting all aspects of this sensitive international intercourse whereby it reached ministerial level. This also had the unexpected benefit of alerting the totally uncomprehending ministerial and governmental advisors that were advised of this whole affair, just what it was that they were dealing with here with this advanced product. The penny finally dropped to them that it had international consequences, significance and applications.

It also had the undesirable side-effect of troubling Sally Longley, who all along held fears and reservations about the creation of her pet little sideline that had eventually developed into something very impressive. Her father was the recipient of much heart-felt discussions and concerns from her. She even found herself thinking along the lines that she dreaded and feared the most; that of being able to send off her creation to seek out and destroy threats that she encountered independently of being attacked herself.

In her dismay at the way things had transpired, she even raised that thought with her father. She said to him that she could devise a method of achieving this, but it was difficult to arrange without very precise coding. He strangely confided in her that the best way to achieve that outcome would simply be to get someone inside the desired target to try to hack into her own system and then her normal line of attack would be initiated. She was stunned at the simplicity of that concept. It would take a highly trained operative to manage that feat, but wholly feasible. She gave it much thought.

# CHAPTER TEN

One of the matters of interest to Graham when he took Sally and Rachael over for the afternoon gathering at the Faulkners, and before they were all interrupted by the helicopter caper, was to enquire of Xavier how he was faring in his new position at the Faulkner station. Xavier confided in Graham that he was coping well, but that it was a challenging position, given the magnitude of the requirements and the range of management areas involved with the position. Graham also surreptitiously probed Xavier whether he had advanced any form of devotion towards Sophia, given their now close proximity.

Xavier was circumspect, but did advise that it was early days, and that he did find her particularly attractive. He was slightly daunted by the fact that not only was she a superior type of woman; accomplished, talented and admired all round by others, but that her family was also rather intimidating given their acknowledged gravitas, wealth and standing in the industry compared to his lowly station in life and that he was not from a local family of any note.

Graham also managed to ask the same sort of theme from Sophia herself. She was rather more forthcoming to her friend Graham, more so than Xavier was. She found Xavier an attractive prospect and, compared to the other experiences in her life with assorted beaux, she regarded him as a thorough gentleman and very unassuming. She had actually discussed her feelings with her parents and found no obstructions where they were concerned. She also confided in Graham that, if things advance any further, that she was already contemplating what sort of wedding she would like to have for such an occasion.

Graham was rather chuffed at that revelation. If that ever eventuated into something truly lasting, it would be a momentous achievement, one with which he would feel quite proud within himself of being, in his eyes, considerably responsible for the attaining. His feelings of any satisfaction at this stage were always tempered by the dark thoughts that accompanied his own early blissful state of matrimony, only to have that disintegrate into total and complete disaster and annihilation of that union. He always carried this latent sense of dread where human relationships were concerned. He would try and furtively monitor this situation. Afterall, he had both parties to be mindful of, not to mention the Faulkner association. There was a lot at stake and a lot more to play out on this topic over the next little while.

On the other topic concerning the Cobar connection, the case of Fiona and her sojourn into the publishing game, there had been developments. Because of the input and encouragement of the reclusive Catherine Holbrook Seymour, not in person of course, but from the shadows, the publishing company had expedited the advancement of Fiona's manuscript and had also heavily promoted her output, not only because of the imprimatur of their most famous client, but also because Fiona's output did have some intrinsic merit, plus it was the product of a new female author.

Fiona, as warned by Jessie if all went really well, was invited to some launches and promotional signings while the demand was so keen in the initial stages. It was while she was with her publishers and the bookshops promoting her effort in Sydney that Fiona was confronted with some sources of confusion for herself.

Fiona was almost overwhelmed, and slightly embarrassed, by the attendance bestowed on her by the accommodating publication people and the sales outlets, she found the attention made her almost uncomfortable. She was naturally unassuming and shy around strangers, considering her isolated rural existence. When she pointed out these matters, she was met with a small account of the support she had obtained from a very successful source, and that she had some extremely influential backers behind her. Fiona was non-plussed. She pointed out that she thought that she only had some guidance from a visiting Austrian author named

Annika. That name meant nothing to her new publishing house. It only left Fiona even more confused. She was wondering who these influential supporters of hers were supposed to be. She would have to discuss this with her new friend Annika if she caught up with her again. She could always ask her other benefactor, Graham Longley.

Fiona was quietly excited about her diversion into this encounter from the humdrum of her isolation that she could not hide the fact from her good friend Graham. She rang him to tell him of her impending visitation to the big smoke and what was involved with that effort. Graham was also duly pleased for her, and in no small way felt a tinge of self-accomplishment in her achievement via the role he played through the introduction of Jessie to her scene.

Graham took note of all the timelines Fiona mentioned and offered to try to see her in the city at her odd appearances. Graham asked Sally if she would mind if he stayed with her again over this short duration. He was also keen for Sally to meet Fiona from his Cobar connection if she got the chance, she never having even been out to that property, let alone met any of the Butlers. Fiona was also keen to follow up with Graham the name that the publishing house had mentioned in reply to Fiona's question that, if Annika were not the source of her patronage, then who was, and who then exactly was this Catherine Holbrook Seymour that they accredited to her for her support.

On the first allotted morning, set for ten am, Graham wandered up to the enormous bookshop that was offering this opportunity to Fiona at about nine am. He found her busily sorting out copies and preparing for a hopefully mild rush from the eager public to meet this new author. There was actually a very short queue already, but it was still quite early. Fiona was pleased to see the familiar face and have the support of her dear friend Graham on hand for such a momentous occasion.

In her nervousness, Fiona was pre-occupied with all the organisation, but she did manage to ask Graham the one point that was puzzling her over her rise to notoriety. She again openly acknowledged the help and guidance provided by Annika, but the publishing people had never heard of any Annika. They let slip in some mild confusion when Fiona admitted that she was grateful for Annika's words, that it was mostly the well-known Australian author Catherine Holbrook Seymour that had put in the good word. Fiona was puzzled, as she admitted that she had never heard of anybody called Catherine Holbrook Seymour.

Graham was also puzzled, as he had never heard of her either. On enquiring of the publishing people there in support of Fiona, they proudly preached the marvels of one of their most prized associations, that of Catherine Holbrook Seymour. They even had on hand a copy or two of her last monumental tome that she had published, originally to show to Fiona on her admitting that she had never heard of her. Graham duly took careful note of the name and tried to scrutinise the book in order to ascertain who this author was. He was so intrigued by the short biography of the reclusive author, that he decided to buy a copy, as she sounded awfully similar to the kind of scenario that the Jessie MacIntyre he knew would exhibit. Graham was aware from her trial and through Ian Knuckey, but mostly through his late Captains Flat neighbour, Tony, Antoine, from Jessie's Australia Street days, that Jessie MacIntyre was originally thought to possibly be some famous reclusive authors even way back then. This did prove to be true, but not officially. Though it was never proven, it was highly likely that she was indeed so. He considered it highly likely that she was possibly now still so. Could this be one of her later incarnations?

After some thought, Graham decided that he would indulge Fiona with a little subterfuge of his own. He hoped he was not becoming infected with the Jessie MacIntyre affliction of deceit and shady dealings when it came to all their associates. He gently advised Fiona that Annika was actually a well-known foreign author among her peers. Perhaps Annika knew Catherine and asked her to intervene for Fiona as that would have more impact than an overseas person. Graham was pleased with that little stratagem; it gave him a slight tingle. He could see how Jessie would get a high from harmless successful falseness.

He momentarily contemplated raising this issue with Jessie herself when he next contacted her. Then, after some deeper consideration, he decided to drop the whole topic where she was concerned. Maybe the less he knew about her the better. He spent some time supporting Fiona and got a mild sense of satisfaction in seeing her so enthralled in her sideline. He saw her several times when he could, but spent most of his time with Sally, and returning to the farm which required much laborious input. It all gave him much to ponder.

On that theme, it was a on a lazy, sunny, warm Sunday afternoon that he grew pensive. Sunday was not a particularly different day to Graham, it was not an official day of rest, there was always plenty to do on his farm. But he tended to operate at a more leisurely pace than on other days, a sort of nod to his near-dormant childhood recollections of that once holy day. But his mind kept drifting back to the topic that had been occupying his thinking a lot lately; that of his beloved daughter Sally. He marvelled at her entire being. He thought about her amazing mind that conjured up this thing she called Omicron, and that she was able to confide in him alone about its creation, its development and its connection and distribution on a huge scale; all by herself – unaided. He knew for a fact that she was entirely responsible alone for his reunited family. He contemplated the conundrum about her. From where did her ability and inspiration originate? Where on earth was she ever going to find a man of her equal, let alone a better, or a partner. He feared for her future. Maybe she was already fulfilled with her lot. But when she lay on her death bed thinking, will she look back with regret or contentment? Then he thought about the other women marvels that had been thrust upon him here in this isolation. Jessie Summers, Sophia Faulkner and even his late wife Jenny.

He thought back to his grandmother's age, and his late aunt Alice, she whom had gifted him this life. This would simply not have been possible for a woman to achieve this level of independence and achievement in those bygone ages. There was no chance for a Jessie MacIntyre to arise in those dim distant days gone by; to achieve what she had achieved. He contemplated the marvel that was Jane Austin. He had seen a little about her. She was almost unique, an enigma from her days. How she achieved what she did then was a miracle.

He thought about Sophia Faulkner. She was an exceptional horse-woman, a champion rider. That was almost impossible in her grandmother's day. Where were these types of successful women going to find an equal in a man. He hoped Xavier was up to the task of being considered a suitable consort for the over-achieving Sophia.

The answer to that question came rather unexpectedly and also rather quicker than he was planning on. Xavier had only been there for a little over eight months when he and Sophia drove over to Graham's farm to announce to him that they were preparing to become engaged and that they were planning a celebration of the event at the Faulkner property in a few weeks. There followed a long conversation in which Graham established what the plan was and how much was involved in this planning. The engagement party was to be a little smaller than the planned wedding event. Graham would get an invitation in due course.

Four weeks later, said invitation arrived by hand from a beaming Sophia accompanied by a sedate Xavier. To Graham, Xavier appeared slightly bemused at the enormity of the coming event. It was to be a sizable affair. Graham was alerted to the fact that most of the family would be there for this engagement, including two of Jackson's sisters and sadly, for Graham, Ophelia. Sophia looked Graham in the eyes and said pointedly that Ophelia was coming, and she hoped to meet up with him again. He was very wary.

Graham was advised that he could bring whomever he wished to the day. He gave it some thought, as nobody in his family really knew the Faulkners to the depth that he did, if at all. There was really no reason to invite any of his own family, with the possible exception of Sally. He might ask her if she were interested. He thought that Sally might find this enterprise of interest at her age. Besides, Sally carried quite some gravitas within the Faulkner clan following her helicopter caper; they thought very highly of her, and understood that she obviously was engaged in some high-level associations. In addition, she might just also be a counter to any desires the clingy, prowling Ophelia might display.

The big event, and it was a big event, was planned for the end of next month. Graham was offered an invitation with an open-ended number to accompany him, but to reply with that number by the due date. Again he was in a quandary as to whom to ask to attend with him, as, quite frankly, none of his family were really acquainted with the sprawling Faulkner conglomerate, again, with the exception of sally.

Graham gave the issue some thought. He contacted Sally one evening and offered her the opportunity to accompany him to this important social event at which there would be some considerable array of highly-esteemed local identities.

Sally might find the attendees of quite some interest, besides, she could get a feel for a serious high-class gathering as conducted in the far reaches of the distant rural countryside. He advised her that he would not be asking any other members of his family, as none of them really knew the Faulkners. Otherwise, he would be going alone.

Sally rather willingly decided that this event would be something that would be of interest to her, not so much the venue, as attractive as that appeared to her to be, but more so for the type and class of the people that Graham had intimated would be attending; a real variety of high-achievers and socially distinct members of a totally different class of society. Graham began to realise that the daughter that he had so callously abandoned those many years ago, was now used to mixing in with some very powerful connections, but of a totally different societal hierarchy. She would find this mixture a brand new experience, but still being more than capable of successfully integrating. She could again stay with Graham and avoid too much time with the rest of the inquisitive family who were constantly and sneakily trying to pry from her her real activities.

On the big day; it was a Saturday affair occupying most of the day and into the evening, Graham borrowed his father's much more comfortable and elegant sedan in order to accommodate Sally's misgivings regarding Graham's rather inadequate mode of transport as far as she was concerned, especially if she were going to go to some effort for this occasion.

On the way there, Graham had a few words to Sally

about certain matters. He tried to point out who some of the people were that she would be meeting there, especially other members of the Faulkner family. Then he broached the sensitive subject of Ophelia. Graham warned Sally that he thought that the Faulkners were subtly trying to arrange for Ophelia, Edith Faulkner's single sister, and quite an achiever in the equestrian world, to latch onto Graham. He said to Sally that he might have to try to keep her at bay by relying on being able to spend a little time with Sally if that ploy were deemed desirable. Sally just nodded non-committedly.

On the morning after the extravagant affair, Graham was up fairly early, but not so Sally. She was used to late nights and long hours, but, Graham discovered, she had turned more into a night-owl rather than a greeter of the rising sun; a product of both her genes and her demanding life-work situation. He had managed to navigate the whole day without too much of an interaction with the mobile and circulating Ophelia. He felt that his openly-displayed ambivalence shown towards her was finally beginning to make her realise that he had no desire to further their relationship at all. He would prefer, however, to avoid any contact with her, not entirely out of ambivalence, as she was quite an attractive woman. He always consoled himself with the thought that their worlds were really very different.

Graham spent most of his time getting to know the extended family members of the Faulkner clan, many of whom were not of a rural bent. He spoke at length with both Sophia and Xavier and was able to mostly avoid Ophelia, who was definitely enjoying the copiously freely-accessible alcoholic beverages that were generously laid about the lavish affair.

Graham also spent some time monitoring his daughter. He was concerned that she might feel out-of-place in such a gathering. He need not have worried. Not only did she seem to be quite at home amongst the divergent throng, but, possibly following some alerting from Jackson that she just might be far more interesting than she appeared, she seemed to have been slightly even sought out as a person worth a chat. He was both delighted to see her so at ease, but also rather impressed with her obviously polished demeaner in such a different crowd.

Later in the day, Graham enquired after her condition and how she faired at the party. She seemed to have enjoyed herself and had some fascinating conversations. Graham left it at that, satisfied it had all gone better than he had hoped. In a quiet moment after such a big day at the engagement party, while Sally and Graham were sipping coffee at his kitchen table, Sally said to Graham,

'Father, I was thinking. I'm sorry that you have to keep borrowing Grandfather's old car just to pick me up every time I come down. Why don't you buy yourself a more suitable car for this kind of occasion, as I might try to come down more often now.'

Graham put his mug down and looked at her. Then he said, 'I'm not really in a position to buy what I would regard as adequate for you Sal. Besides, it would need to be a four-wheel-drive for the times the roads are knocked about. You've seen their condition; and in the wet, they deteriorate quickly out here.'

'No Dad, I didn't mean for you to buy it. I would gladly give you the money for that.'

'I couldn't take that from you Sally.' he almost exclaimed.

'Why not. I'd love to repay you for all you've done for the family. Besides, Dad, you've seen what money I have. I could buy it for you through one of my companies, give you an account with plenty in it so it costs you nothing. I am at quite a quandary what to do with all my income at the moment; and there is a lot of it; a real lot.'

Graham was momentarily speechless. He suddenly felt quite a turn of emotion at those words from his daughter. He was very touched that she would even consider such an idea, or even harbour such feelings about the family outcome.

'But, Sal….' was all he could muster.

'I don't know anything about cars, Dad. I'd have to leave all that up to you to decide.' she said.

'Let me think about it Sal.' was again all he could say.

'There's nothing to think about. I'd love to do that for you. I am investing as much as I can while this lasts, Dad. It could all end abruptly any moment, you know.'

'I see. Well you do that. Very wise. What are you investing in?' he asked

'I've got a couple of buildings, and my unit. But, you know Dad, I got some advice from a friend I knew at uni who's with an investment house. You know what he suggested that I do if I have some spare cash? He said to invest in rare earth minerals. I'd never heard of them, but he advised me about how rare they are and how essential they are for the future and that Australia has loads of them but it is not yet developed here. I thought that might be a long-term gamble that might just pay off. What do you think?'

Graham was deep in thought. Then he replied,

'I've totally lost touch with all matters relating to finances. I am really not the man to ask about such matters now. But that sounds like a solid idea to me. Any other ideas for your future?'

Sally responded, after a little pause, and looking slightly sheepishly at him,

'You know what else I've been doing? You might think it a little silly.'

'Don't be ridiculous. Nothing you do is silly.' he responded.

'I've been buying up a few shares in famous Australian brand names that are still manufactured here but are foreign owned. You know, like food brands and some industrial companies.'

'That's not a silly idea. I think that's a wonderful idea.' said Graham.

Sally, a little encouraged by his enthusiasm, decided to elaborate some more, as she knew that he did once work in finance himself. She continued,

'What I've done, is to buy up shares using five different companies that I set up to spread about my income and also spread the risk. Then I set up a holding company as the owner of all the others. Some of my own companies that now own shares, quite a lot in some cases, are mentioned on the stock exchange now by law, but the holding company is not. I am trying to get to fifty-one percent ownership through the different companies so I can have a say in the running of the places that sometimes don't always have the Australian interests as their top priority. It's been some fun at times. I have a couple of blokes supervising that aspect for me.'

Graham was deep in thought. He did not reply, so Sally continued,

'You know, I don't regard that expenditure on shares as an investment but rather as losable amounts. I have written it off. But I do regard my buildings as a serious investment. I bought my office building when I was offered the chance so I could set up all the security in the way I wanted. I value those office buildings as a true investment for my future, whatever that holds.'

'Good for you Sally. I am proud of your efforts and proud of your planning. I hope you remain happy in your lot.'

Graham sat in deep thought. He was totally contented with the way his daughter had turned out. He felt a tinge of real pride in knowing she was his.

* * *

Jessie Summers was touched by the musings of John Summers. She found in them, reminiscences of the thoughts and utterances of the classically-trained mind of her first really great influence, the absconding Earl of the estate of du Bois out in the wilds of the Kimberley. There was a marked contrast however, in the sense and depth of the delivery of the message. Norman Woods, aka the Earl of the du Bois estate, delivered his reminiscences with a bitterness and resignation that was not missed by Jessie. John Summers on the other hand, espoused his beliefs with a sincere degree of self-worth, genuine belief and true satisfaction with his lot in life.

Jessie was not necessarily moved by the messages *per se*, but rather the eloquence and literary delight in the presentation, and the impact the poetic language had on her pleasure in the lyrical hearing.

Jessie MacIntyre lived in a fantasy world divorced as much as possible from reality; had done so for decades. Her world was made up of make-believe characters and imaginary scenes which helped to navigate her through the unwelcome humdrum and dangerous real world in which she really existed since first being hunted from her haven at Australia Street. In this imaginary world there dwelt a myriad of exotic characters and situations that kept her so occupied that she often had several scenarios occurring at the same time. If she struck a rich vein of inspiration, she would dwell on it for long periods and develop her stories from there, often then incorporating actual events from her vast store of accumulated incidents and strange characters that peopled her so varied a past existence.

But, unlike John Summers, who thought of others often in his existence, and even sacrificed, or donated much of his time and money to the aid of others over his long life, Jessie

Summers was typically very self-orientated and loathe to interact with others. This was the result of several colliding circumstances. Her character make-up determined her attitude in this subject, but also her dramatic life experiences reinforced her natural inclinations to emphasise this trait even further. Her offerings to her life-saving friend Graham Longley of the property next door to his original farm was about the very first time she had ever done anything like this for someone else. To compound her deviation from the norm, she indulged herself again in a similar fashion with the Doolans over the Rolls Royce, but particularly with the acquisition of the waterfront property on the harbour. Admittedly, these latter two interactions carried considerable benefit to herself in that they opened up gainful employment and a diversion from her troubles. Nevertheless, she did contribute to the benefit of others, a rare occurrence for her.

Jessie Summers had accumulated a vast amount of wealth over her long literary career. She was mindful of the fact that she was not in a position to help many people herself and on her demise, the lot would just dissipate into the hands of others of no consequence to herself. She was unable to enjoy it that much herself, but she certainly was contented with her lifestyle, especially of late with the acquisition of the Doolan properties.

Jessie also now realised that her unintended benefactor in the guise of John Summers was decidedly succumbing to the rigours of advancing old age. She began to occasionally attend the semi-compulsory family gatherings and meetings normally conducted on every Sunday. The actual meeting was for the shareholders only in the private family company, but the spouses and others would avail themselves of the opportunity to congregate and socialise away from the business side while it was under way.

One concession John did make, and it was supported by all the family shareholders, was to re-arrange the original weekly meetings to occur now only once a month. This made it easier for Jess to attend, as they were now much less frequent and regarded as more serious as they were so much more intermittent. John seemed to deliberately seek her out and ensure that they touched base with each other, as he really did value her conversation and he also realised that she was a serious wonder in the known acquaintances that he had accumulated in his long life. Her life experiences were truly unique. It was at some of these semi-private conversations that Jess began to get a deeper feel for not only John's understanding of matters on the meaning of life, but it also awakened in her the serious stirrings of contemplating the topic herself. She found his company very reassuring.

For his part, John now spent much time in contemplation. John Summers would sit on his unadorned familiar veranda, soaking in the warm afternoon air. He was comforted by the serenity and the accustomed sounds of his rural habitat. He was definitely feeling the effects of his advancing old age. He had lived a long life; he acknowledged that fact to himself openly; and a blesséd one. He thought often of his late beloved wife Livinia and all the blessings that had accompanied her inclusion into his existence. She also brought a deep spiritual dimension to his life; an appreciation of the divine mysteries associated with being human. It gave him much food for thought as he advanced through time. With the luxury bestowed by the gift of unfettered leisure, and the wit to still contemplate logically, he approached the inevitable with a peaceful soul.

She had been a devout person with deep beliefs. He was not quite so inclined. He carried within his heart the ever-present accompaniment of the realisation that he had achieved all this wonderment, and apparent blessings, only through the sinful and errant act of his relieving the disingenuous adoptive Merritts of their apparently also ill-gotten gains when he was a very young man. It was a constant niggling companion to his conscious at all times. He had managed to navigate through life thus far carrying that burden totally undiscovered by others, at least that was how he perceived it all. He was mindful that both Jessie and Graham had access to information that was sailing close to the wind, but so far, no acknowledgment of any revelations had been notified to him. He lived in hope that that would be the case on his death.

That constant thought brought to mind several statements uttered by various religious mentors that had accompanied their sojourn through this brief interlude known as life, or verses he had encountered in his rare ventures into the holy book of instructions that came his way via his wonderful wife. A couple stuck in his mind. He contemplated them often when really alone and in deep commune with his spirit in such tranquillity that pervaded his admired environment.

He mulled over a couple again. *Fear of the Lord is the beginning of wisdom*, said the psalmist. John feared very little in life. But he did indeed fear the Lord. Whether that gave him 'wisdom' was another matter. Livinia had often espoused the gospel to him whenever a serious family tragedy or crisis rose. He marvelled at that revelation. He was not always totally convinced that it was actually that simple. John did really believe that Jesus died on the cross, that he was buried and that he rose again on the third day. The reason that he did believe that thought was that he understood enough about humans to realise that they would not give up centuries of tradition and deep ingrained beliefs just to follow any old myth, or fairytale that proffered a new message, especially if that new myth was attended by death. No, in the end thousand actually saw the risen Lord, according to the Bible. People died for that vision; people were martyred for that image. They did not give up life for a mirage.

It also made sense to him when Livinia explained that Jesus was a Jew. The Jews acknowledged that they were corrupt sinners, but, once a year, they could gain atonement for their sins and transgressions on their holiest day of the year, Yom Kippur; the Day of Atonement. God demanded sacrifices – blood sacrifices – to achieve that end. That usually most often meant a lamb. Now he understood just why Jesus had to die as a permanent replacement for the yearly sacrifice. It was now done once and for ever, by the gift of the Holy Lamb.

Then Saint Paul explained: *for by grace are ye saved through faith; and that not of yourselves: it is the gift of God: Not of works, lest any man should boast.* It all seemed too simple. Truly and sincerely confess your sins, believe in your heart in the gospel and you are saved. John did believe these truths, but the lingering doubts persisted within his heart. Sometimes John thought that rejecting that gift of God in his own ambivalence, was actually an insult, an affront and disrespectful to God. Saint Paul had actually written: *so your minds should be corrupted from the simplicity that is in Christ.* because even then, at the very beginning, the easiness of the gospel was an issue and that people were trying to upgrade that simple method constantly by adding works to the already done event.

John could work himself into quite a muddle contemplating this mystery. He would console himself by leaving it in the hands of eternity, he would find out soon enough the truth of these matters, but he was in no hurry to cross that line, whenever it arrived. He satisfied himself over the accumulation of endless blessings, seemingly gifted to him through application, and sacrifice, that a man would live and die by the saying: *for whatsoever a man soweth, that shall he also reap.* He also consoled himself with the homily that *to whom much is given, much is expected.* He certainly prided himself on his material possessions, his frugality and firmly believed that he had achieved far greater response with his provided 'talents' than the spendthrift and improvident Merritts, from whom he had relieved their share of 'talents'. Would God judge him as deserving of his master's praise?

In his tranquillity he slowly dozed in and out of contentment. Within his calmness and satisfaction and fulfilment, his soul would often slowly drift towards its recall to its eternal home. The acceptance of his fulfilling sojourn was evident on his calm smiling face. One day soon, one of these heavenly risings would terminate in permanent departure, but not just yet.

John smiled to himself. He had an amusing thought, well it was amusing to him. It had a touch of unaccustomed elegance and a deeper philosophical bent, a little unusual for the pragmatic John Summers. He looked back at his life; the lowly and deprived beginning; the loss of his parents at three months of age, apparently murdered; the denial of siblings; the deprivation and torment during his youth; then the imposition of a rural life, not the glamour of his father's trade. This led to the temptation of the huge cache in his grandmother's safe. Was that a kind of test? – did he fail that test, or did he pass? Then he thought about his rise – his day in the sun – the resurrection of the Summers' name – one summers – him. One summers' day! That sounded almost like a full recompense.